THE
BITTER
TRUTH

Books by Shanora Williams

The Perfect Ruin
The Wife Before
The Other Mistress
The Bitter Truth

SHANORA WILLIAMS

THE
BITTER
TRUTH

www.kensingtonbooks.com

Dear Reader,

I'm so excited that I get to share my fourth thriller novel, *The Bitter Truth*, with you! It was truly an experience sinking my claws into these characters and seeing how it all ended, and now I get to share that experience with all of you.

Despite my bubbling excitement, I would like to mention that there are moments in this novel that may be triggering for some to read. There is a heartbreaking situation of rape/date rape and the misuse of prescription drugs, domestic violence, mental health disorders, food and eating disorders, and body shaming.

Though this is a work of fiction, I always like to provide a gentle warning about the traumatic events that take place in my books because something I can handle and process, others may not be able to, and your mental health is top priority.

I believe reading my books should spark juicy conversations during book club discussions, or even with your reading buddy, but many of us in this world are still healing and we owe it to ourselves to protect our peace.

With love,

Shanora

To my grandma Gwen

THE
BITTER
TRUTH

PROLOGUE

He stood in front of the cabin, drawing in a breath as he dug his nails into his palm. His backpack was heavy on his back, loaded with several textbooks and twelve dollars he'd gotten for helping Chris Moran with an essay. He licked his lips, then swallowed. All he wanted was to go into the cabin, fill a cup up with ice water, and guzzle it all down, but something was making him wary.

Pointing his gaze down, he focused on the black and white Chucks on his feet. They were dirty, and there was a hole on the side of them. Fortunately, everyone at school thought it was cool and were making it a trend. The truth is, there was a hole because they were the only pair of shoes he had left. His mom hadn't bought him any in months, though he'd been begging her to.

His mom wasn't the same person anymore. She'd changed, even more so when she was released from the detention center. His uncle kept telling him to stick it out, to be there for her, that she would get better, but he was absolutely positive she was getting worse.

The branch of a tree above the cabin croaked and he shifted on his feet. He spotted the faded burgundy Buick parked to the left. She was home. It was now or never. He moved ahead and didn't stop until he was at the front door. When he twisted the doorknob, it was locked, as expected, so he pulled out the key from his pocket, unlocked it, and walked right in.

As he shut the door behind him, he noticed how eerily quietly the cabin was. He was used to quiet, but this was a different type of quiet. It was *too* still. The faucet in the kitchen, which usually dripped at a steady pace no matter how hard you twisted the knobs to shut it off, wasn't dripping. The house didn't creak either, not until he slid the straps of his backpack off and it thudded on the ground. He was tempted to call for his mother, but instead went to the kitchen and filled a cup with water. When it was at the brim, he gulped it down in four swallows then set the cup on the counter.

A creaking noise came from the back of the house, and he made his way toward the hallway. The hallway light was on, but the two bedroom doors were closed. He checked his room first, because sometimes she liked to curl up in his closet with a bat. She didn't like being in her closet because that's where all the personal items were, the important documents and information, and his mom didn't want the "people" looking for her to find them and steal her identity. When he saw the closet was empty, he ventured across the hallway.

A slow breath slipped between his parted lips as he gripped the doorknob. "Momma?" he called. He swallowed, waiting for a response. The only response was the heavy creaking coming from her room. He peered down the hallway, where he could see the plaid furniture. *Maybe I should just go study, or take a nap*, he thought to himself. His mom would come out sooner or later. Sometimes she acted like nothing was wrong, and she'd cook dinner and ask him to set the table. But during the other times . . . oh. The other times were bad. He didn't want this to lead to the bad times. But studying and napping wouldn't lead to the good.

If he wanted to get a hold on the situation, he needed to face her now. Maybe he could give her some pills to make her sleep the rest of the night so he could have the whole house to himself. He could use his twelve bucks to run to the store, buy some waffles and Cap'n Crunch, and eat as much as he wanted while watching cartoons. His mom never let him have that kind of food. Excitement took hold of him.

With that idea in the back of his mind, he twisted the doorknob to his mom's room and pushed it open. But he shouldn't have, because as soon as he saw her, he felt the urge to vomit.

She hung from a cord wrapped around a frail beam in the ceiling, feet dangling, her face a dangerous blue purple. The end of the cord was wrapped tightly around her neck and her eyes were wide open, looking right at him.

He wanted to scream.

Wanted to cry.

He wanted to call his uncle and tell him to come and get him right away.

He didn't do any of those things though.

Instead, he sighed with relief as his mother's lifeless body dangled from the ceiling.

PART ONE

ONE

DOMINIC

Many things can change the course of someone's life.

A new job.

An eviction notice.

Being diagnosed with a terminal disease.

Life is never as simple as humans believe. We coast along, adapting to new environments, clinging to hope, but we all have our faults that trigger those changes. Our flaws are, ultimately, our downfall, and they are what weigh heavily on Dominic Baker's mind as he sits in his office.

He listens to his wife Jolene move about in the kitchen, causing dishes to clink and pots to clatter. Prior to him entering his office, the kitchen had been vacant, which meant Jolene must've gone for a jog. He should've gone with her, but with the campaign for his second term as governor going and elections fast approaching, he was drowning in stress.

They're due in uptown Raleigh so he can speak to a collective in the park. According to Jim Pilton, his campaign manager, over six hundred people will be attending today. Everyone is anticipating his presence—the well-known, forty-year-old candidate with the brown skin and perfect smile. Everyone has high hopes for Dominic Baker, the man uplifting North Carolina. That's his slogan, anyway. *Uplift North Carolina.*

Now, he wishes the campaign wasn't happening at all. He wishes that four years ago, he hadn't been selfish and taken the role as governor. He'd have more privacy and much less to lose.

Dominic has always wanted to be in politics, though. It was his dream since high school, and he wasn't going to let a minor mishap mess that up. He'd gone to college, run for school boards, the Raleigh city council, and was even lieutenant governor of the state prior to becoming official governor. He'd worked hard to build his status, networked with professionals, and the hard work had paid off. But, as with any successful career, there are mistakes that shape us and secrets we long to bury, and Dominic realizes this as he studies the letter on top of his desk.

Written in permanent marker that bleeds through the thin sheet of notebook paper are the words: **I KNOW WHAT U DID. WHERE'S BRYNN?**

Reading them again causes his heart to slam repeatedly against his ribcage, but not as hard as it had when he'd found the letter wedged between the stack of mail in his mailbox. He'd gone out to check the mail, sifted through the junk and bills, until the folded sheet of paper fluttered to the ground. He picked it up and as he'd read the words, all the loose envelopes scattered from his hands. He felt his chest cave in on itself, his throat coated with something thick and heavy.

He turned rapidly, taking a sweep of the neighborhood, but nothing was out of the ordinary. Suburban houses were off in the distance, fir and elm trees providing privacy . . . and places for anyone to hide. The only car parked on the street was the police cruiser on the other side. One of the officers started to get out of the cruiser and help him with the scattered mail but with a wave, Dominic told him he was fine and proceeded to collect the papers whilst hiding the note.

With shaking hands, he made his way toward the house, gripped the doorknob, and clicked it shut behind him. He waited by the door a moment, out of Jolene's view, and took several breaths before stuffing the letter into his front pocket. He dropped the rest of the mail on the coffee table and bustled toward his office. That was nearly ten minutes ago, and still, he can't stop his hands from shaking.

Who sent this? Who would *do* this? And how the hell do they know about Brynn? His eyes flicker up, and he listens harder for his wife who is still in the kitchen rummaging around and oblivious to his fear.

He snatches open the bottom drawer of his desk, pushing loose papers, packets of gum, mints, and loose cords out of the way until he collects a clunky Nokia flip phone. The phone is dead, so he snatches one of the cords out and plugs it into the nearest outlet. When there is one notch of battery and it powers to life, he calls the only number stored in the contacts, but not before closing his office door as quietly as he can. The last thing he wants is Jolene hearing his conversation.

Dominic clings to the phone, his ear flush against the receiver as it rings and rings until finally, an answer.

"Boaz," a gravelly voice answers.

"Someone knows," Dominic whispers.

"Knows what?" Boaz snaps.

"About that night. The girl. The *rug*." He tries speaking vaguely—no names, no locations.

"How would someone know?" Boaz counters.

"I got a letter in my mailbox. Handwritten. They know where I *live*, Boaz. You said you took care of it! Why the hell am I getting anonymous letters?"

"Look, just calm down."

"Don't tell me to calm down!" Dominic snaps. "The only people who know about this are you, me, and that cleaner. I know you aren't stupid enough to tamper with this, and you said you've worked with that cleaner for years. Why would he be doing this?"

"It isn't us, boy. Are you crazy? Look, it's probably just someone trying to mess with you."

"You said no one saw us that night."

"They didn't." Boaz pauses. "They couldn't have."

"So how . . ." Dominic trails off, drawing in a long breath. He isn't sure what to say. There are so many questions running through his head, and none of what's going on right now makes any sense.

"Look, no one can know a thing. I was careful," Boaz goes on. "I wouldn't put my life at risk by leaving loose ends."

Dominic wants to find relief in that, but he can't. Boaz is meticulous and safe, but that doesn't mean someone wasn't *watching*. The house he was in with Brynn was on a private property and there were so many trees and places for someone to hide. But who could it have been? No one knew where he would be except John, the owner of the house, and he damn sure wasn't behind this. John had his own secrets that Dominic knew all about, and if he wanted to keep them contained, he was guaranteed to keep his mouth shut.

"I have to go," Boaz grumbles. "Don't call this phone again unless it's life threatening." With that, Boaz hangs up, and Dominic lowers the phone, hunching against the door.

A lump forms in his throat as he racks his mind for possibilities. Only Dominic and Boaz were there that night. No one else. Not even Jolene knows. He told her he was staying at the Ritz Carlton. He thought he was careful, but clearly, someone was watching. He doesn't know who, or when, or how. But they were.

I KNOW WHAT U DID. WHERE'S BRYNN?

The words taunt him and suddenly he can't breathe. He clutches his chest, stumbling toward his chair and slumping in it. He drags in breath after breath, stomach coiling into knots.

In this moment, as the burner phone slips into his lap, Dominic is certain of one thing: the life he built is over if he doesn't find out who's doing this.

TWO

JOLENE

Red juice spills on the cutting board as I slice the grapefruit with a hum. Turkey sausage sizzles in the pan, and four eggs are boiling. I slice again, locked on the glint of the knife, the handle stiff in my grasp. I relax my grip and sigh.

I have no idea why I'm preparing a meal for my husband. He likely won't sit down and share it with me. I suppose it has come to this—a loveless marriage where our actions are only a performance. I never wanted it to be this way, and it should show considering I've devoted the last eleven years of my life to him. I give him stability. I give him drive. I give him every single part of me, some of which he doesn't even deserve.

I hear the door of his office click shut and know he's hiding something. *Again.* I stop humming and start listening. I hear the murmurs, the mumbling. He has secrets. We all do.

I dump the flesh of the grapefruit into the juicer and watch it blend into a beautiful, pink-red concoction. It isn't until I've poured the juice into two slim glasses that I hear his office door open and Dominic's footsteps drifting down the hallway. He enters the kitchen, impeccably dressed in a navy-blue suit with an American flag pendant attached to the lapel. The suit is creaseless and clean, courtesy of our local dry cleaner, and the suit is tailored to perfection, molding to his body perfectly.

It was always my father who said for anyone to take you seriously, you must dress the part. When I met Dominic, he wandered around in plain T-shirts, jeans, and sneakers. Once he was mine, I invested in his style. I started slowly, with button-down shirts and jeans. I allowed him to keep the sneakers but only to show him that the people we surrounded ourselves with do not wear sneakers every single day, and if there's one thing I know about my husband, he does *not* like to be the outcast. Together, we've progressed to full suits and designer dress shoes.

I almost sigh. Look at him. So handsome. Sometimes I miss the old us. His hair is cut army short and wavy at the top, his tie neat, as if he's recently adjusted it. His skin is golden-brown and satiny smooth. In the light of the kitchen, his skin glows and the sun reflects off his light-brown eyes.

There was a time when he'd greet me in the kitchen with that full, perfect smile. He doesn't smile anymore. Instead, he steps toward the counter to pick up one of the glasses of juice along with three sausage links.

"Rally is today. Will you be there?" he asks after guzzling down some of the juice.

"Of course I will," I say. "Appearances are everything to you, right?"

He gives me a look, one mixed with confusion and aggravation. He gulps down the remainder of juice then collects his keys from the hook attached to the wall, as well as the folder he'd left on the counter last night containing his speech. I'd written the speech for him several weeks ago. Does he thank me? No.

"Don't be late, Jo," he says, leaving the kitchen. When he's out the front door, I watch him through the kitchen window above the sink. If things are going well today, I know that state troopers are parked at the curb of our house, waiting for the governor's departure. In the driveway is a running black Tahoe. Dominic climbs in the backseat of the Tahoe and it pulls out of the driveway. Our driveway is built at an arch, so from the kitchen, I can't see the main road. At the end of the driveway, the land is lined with a knee-height brick wall, green hedges, and a gate that closes us in.

When I can no longer see the truck, I rush out of the kitchen and into Dominic's office. My husband is hiding something. I don't know what it is, but it *has* to be here.

I check the desk for anything new, but it's all the same. Printed speeches and loose papers. Paperclips, pens, a stapler. I grip the handle of the top right drawer, and nothing is inside but loose stationary. On the top left drawer, it's crammed with chewing gum and sunflower seeds, his vice when he wants to avoid drinking. When he has events, he aims not to drink liquor the night before.

I check the bottom drawers and it's no surprise they're locked. Ever since we moved into this house, he's kept them locked. I thought nothing of it at first. After all, we all need our privacy. I have a secret treat stash that I keep in a chest on my side of the closet. I keep the chest locked too, so Dominic can never see exactly what I'm stashing there. I sit for a moment, trying to think of where he'd have the key.

Normally, I don't pry in my husband's things, but ever since his campaign has started, he's been more on edge, more secretive. He leaves early and comes home late. He's not the Dominic Baker I married all those years ago. He's someone else—a stranger residing in his body. Or perhaps this is the real him, tried and true.

A chiming noise blares in the room, causing me to gasp. I relax when I realize it's my phone ringing in my pants pocket. I snatch it out to see the reminder alarm: **Coffee @ Daphne's.**

I can't be late, and as badly as I want to find the keys to those drawers, I let it be for now and tuck the chair beneath the desk.

I hurry to the kitchen to drink some of the juice, collect my purse and keys, and leave the house. On the way to my best friend's house, I find my mind sinking deeper into a bad place and all I can think are the same words: *He's hiding something. He's lying. Figure it out.*

THREE

BRYNN

Four years ago—New Orleans

I hated everything about New Orleans. Of course, it wasn't always like that. I'd moved to New Orleans when I started college, but that was nearly ten years ago. After being cheer captain in high school *and* being the most popular girl, might I add, I was offered only one scholarship to college, at Loyola University of New Orleans.

At first, I was ecstatic because I'd never been outside of North Carolina, and it was better that I had *some* interest from a college than none at all. I'd seen many girls in my cheer squad graduate high school with nothing in their back pockets. In a way, my scholarship was owed to me. I kept the team in tip-top shape. I made sure practice ran as scheduled, and it gave me escape from the awful reality I faced at home. Growing up poor with a verbally abusive father and a spineless mother was for the birds.

When I'd taken a bus to get to New Orleans with two suitcases and one duffel bag full of my belongings, I was pleased to see the live oak trees swarming the land and eccentric people on the streets. We passed marshes and bayous with trees that hung with Spanish moss, colorful houses, and restaurants on the water. It was all so new, so refreshing. It was a fresh start, a new beginning, and I was ready to tackle the opportunity headfirst.

I wish I could go back and slap that happy, naïve version of myself. In the movies, you get a glimpse of New Orleans and the nightlife, the Mardi Gras parades, a bachelorette party celebrating a bride-to-be, or a collection of men looking for a good time at bars or strip clubs. But the low-down dirty truth is New Orleans was filthy and chaotic. I didn't mind chaos, so long as it was the controlled sort, but New Orleans wasn't controlled by any means. People ran rampant, women with their breasts out and some men even slinging their dicks around, just to get a reaction. Vomit on every corner of the street, homeless people demanding money, and tourists crowding the areas, making it hard for cars to pass.

I was a victim of the latter, sitting behind the wheel of my car, groaning as a line of elderly people walked along the crosswalk in matching neon pink shirts. Summertime in NOLA was ground zero for tourists, and I couldn't stand it. As soon as I'd saved up enough money, I would leave this place and find somewhere quieter, a suburban area where I could hear more crickets chirping than car horns beeping.

I glanced at the clock on the dashboard of my dingy silver Volkswagen Beetle, tapping my fingers on the wheel. I had six minutes to get to work and my job was twelve minutes away. Once the elderly people moved, I floored it and was glad there weren't any more red lights or pedestrians to stop me.

When I pulled up to Franco's Italian Restaurant, I collected my purse and hurried through the back door of the building, apologizing to my manager Trent for being late for the third time this week.

"One mo' strike, Brynn! I mean 'nat!'" Trent boomed in his Creole accent. I ignored him, throwing on my apron and rushing through the double doors that led out of the kitchen.

It was hard being on time when I worked part time at Nulli's Mini Mart. As soon as my shift was over at Nulli's, I would rush to the bathrooms, change, and hustle to Franco's.

Franco's was an upscale lakefront restaurant, a hidden gem according to online reviews. It was also the only other job I could get until I found one more suitable. Truth is, I hated my life. What was the point of spending all those years in college learning and studying, just to come out of it with a mountain of debt and *still* having to work a bare minimum job to pay the bills? I'd majored in Business, yet I didn't have the time or resources to start my own. I'd dreamed of opening my own restaurant one day, or perhaps something quieter and quainter, like a bed and breakfast. I had dreams of this bed and breakfast existing in New Hampshire, where people would come during the spring and summer, sleep in, then wake up to delicious food from my kitchen. Because that was another thing I was good at, cooking.

The last time I was late on my rent, my roommate fussed for a bit, then told me things would get better, but I couldn't trust Shavonne's advice because she was up to her neck in debt too. Both of us struggled monthly to pay our $1250 rent, and I was almost positive Shavonne was selling ass or something on the side because she never came up short.

I let the idea and internal rant go, collecting a notepad from the hostess stand as said hostess informed me which tables I'd be serving. There weren't many people in yet, but within a few hours, once the sun dipped and the golden light spread over the tables, it would be packed. That's what the couples loved about Franco's. It allowed a romantic night by the water as they drowned themselves in hot Italian food, wine, and love.

I stopped at my first table where a middle-aged woman was scanning the menu with rectangular glasses low on the bridge of her nose. She requested a water with lemon to start and after I prepared it and set it down on her table, I gave her a few more minutes to peruse the menu. I made my way to the next table. Two men sat there, one of whom had his back to me.

"Hello. Welcome to Franco's," I said, focusing on the man I could see. He was older with pasty, greasy-looking skin. He was balding at the crown of his head, and his nose was bulbous and red at the tip as he sniffled a bit. Definitely wasn't a looker, but it was clear he had money by the way he was dressed in his crisp suit and the gleaming watch on his wrist. I didn't want to get my hopes up too soon about him leaving a generous tip, though. It was always the rich people who stiffed me on gratuity. "I'm Brynn and I'll be your server tonight. Can I start you off with some drinks?" My eyes turned to the other man to level the attention and I instantly hitched a breath when familiar light-brown eyes locked with mine.

Oh, God.

I couldn't believe it.

It was *him.*

Dominic Baker, my high school sweetheart. We'd dated when I was a sophomore, and he was a senior. He took me to prom, and shockingly, we won as prom king and queen. We were so young, so popular. Life felt unreal back then, like we were a famous couple. My chin was practically on the floor and my heart pumped twice as hard as I gawked at him.

Dominic appeared equally surprised to see me and I cursed internally for not putting on more makeup and at least *attempting* to look prettier that day.

"Brynn Wallace," Dominic said, and his voice was like brown-sugared honey. It stuck to my insides, hot and sticky, as I got lost in his eyes. "Wow. Look at you. I never thought I'd see your beautiful face again."

Beautiful face? He still found me beautiful? I'd put on a few pounds since high school—who hadn't—and my skin was worse, thanks to the terrible fast food I ate. My hair was pulled into a low ponytail and needed a relaxer badly. But that was beside the point. Dominic Baker was sitting *in front of me,* and I'd never really gotten over this man. I'd tried, even after we drifted apart when he went to college. He'd stayed in North Carolina and attended Duke University with a full-ride academic scholarship, and though it was only a few hours away, the distance was unbearable. It was silly of us to think it would work—that our relationship would last despite it. Our relationship ended because of a slow pull away. Sometimes Dominic would go days without texting or calling me back, then other days we'd be on the phone at night for hours catching up. Eventually, that tapered off too. I can still remember the conversation we had that tore my heart to pieces.

"This isn't working, is it?" he'd asked with a voice full of sorrow.

"No, it isn't," I answered.

I regretted those words, even more so now. I should've made it work. I should've gotten a damn car sooner than my junior year so I could drive to Duke and visit him. I was so proud to know he was going to that college. He was always so damn smart, so wise beyond his years. And sexy. God, was he sexy. We kept in touch every few weeks after the breakup, but that only lasted a few months.

Now, he looked good, dressed in an expensive gray suit, shiny shoes, with an expensive watch on his right wrist. The man sitting across from him looked between us with a critical eye, waiting for an explanation, or an introduction at the least.

Dominic, realizing his impoliteness, pulled his eyes away from mine and provided one. "John, this is my good friend from high school, Brynn. She was top cheerleader of her class. Went to Loyola University with a full-ride scholarship because she was so good."

I blushed, and also wanted to throw up a bit. How could he brag about me when I looked like *this*? Dressed in pants too tight, a white button-down shirt with a monogrammed F on the chest, and a freaking waist apron over it stuffed with straws, loose papers, and pens. I was *nothing* now—a meager waitress in comparison to . . . *whatever* he was doing with his life. How could he not see that?

"Nice to meet you, Brynn," John said. John's eyes scanned me from head to toe. His tongue ran over his dry lips and there was something about him that made me feel gross beneath his stare. I let the thought go when his head dipped, and he focused on the menu. "Can I get a whiskey, neat? And I'll start with the crawfish," John said.

Oh. Right. I was meant to be *working*, not ogling my exboyfriend. I cut my eyes to Dominic, who gave me a sympathetic smile. And there it was. His pity. I was simply the waitress, and he was some bigshot. I scribbled down their orders then rushed toward the kitchen to put them in.

I didn't bother speaking casually to Dominic or asking him how he'd been after that—not that I could anyway. He and John were heavily in conversation each time I stopped by. John would pin his eyes on me every time I attempted to approach, like he didn't want to be interrupted, so I backed off when necessary. Whatever they were discussing was clearly *not* to be heard by anyone. I suppose I didn't need to speak to Dominic too much anyway. I noticed the wedding band on his finger as he ate. It shined as sunset rays made their appearance through the restaurant and practically blinded me as I topped off their waters.

Dominic and John paid for their food, then they left.

I thought I'd never see my ex-boyfriend again until I spotted the signed receipt from their table. On it was a phone number and beneath that number were the words, **CALL ME**.

FOUR

JOLENE

One thing I love about my best friend Daphne's house is how normal and lived-in it is. As I pull into her driveway, I can't help staring at the ranch home. It seems so simple from the outside, with the golden oak shutters and white exterior. The hedges are trimmed, the lawn perfectly manicured, and bushes with white roses cling to the house. Every detail of Daphne's house from the exterior to the interior was created by her and her husband. They had this home built from scratch. They are a duo, who do everything together with passion and love. And that's why I'm happy to be visiting them today.

I step out with my purse, shutting the door behind me and walking to the porch. As I knock, I hear a whirring noise and peer up at the camera built in above the door. My eyes shift to the left, and another camera hides in an artificial plant.

The door swings open and my best friend Daphne Bailey-Juarez stands on the other side, a goddess in all her beauty. Her makeup is simple, but perfect on her light brown skin. Her natural hair has clearly been braided out to support the sleek crinkles. She wears gold eyeshadow and highlighter that makes her skin pop.

She spreads her arms in the poofy-sleeved sienna maxi dress, enveloping me in a hug. She smells of expensive vanilla and amber perfume as I hug her back. I forget how I can wrap one arm all the way around her. Daphne is so thin. It's natural to her, and I always feel a pang of envy about it.

"JoJo," she croons over my shoulder. "Thank you for letting me see your pretty face today. I've missed you."

"I've missed you too." I sigh, holding her a few seconds longer. It's been several weeks since I last saw her. Work has kept me busy, as well as Dominic's campaign.

Daphne steps back, gesturing inside the house. "Come in, come in." I step inside, immediately coming out of my heels and placing them against the wall.

"So, I know you said only coffee this morning, but I couldn't help popping over to Mirren's for chocolate croissants." She grins as she rounds a corner and enters a spacious kitchen. The kitchen is all marble and chrome, with orange dahlias in a crystal vase on the island countertop to add a burst of color. The table is already set up with two coffee mugs turned upside down on small dessert plates, as well as cream and sugar.

"You know I shouldn't, Daph," I say as she saunters to the kitchen to collect a brown box. **MIRREN'S** is stamped on the side of it.

I place my purse down on the counter then pull a chair out, sitting as Daphne approaches. She removes the mug from my dessert plate and sets a croissant in front of me. It's golden and flaky, the chocolate oozing out of the ends. A drizzle of white and dark chocolate is on top. My heart thumps a bit and my mouth fills with drool. I shouldn't eat it. No, I *can't* eat it. Hopefully she won't notice if I only drink the coffee.

"Thank you," I murmur as she sits and places one on her plate as well.

"Of course. So how is everything, girl? Fill me in. Do-

minic still blazing through that campaign?" She pours the coffee and when my mug is filled, I grab the cream.

"Everything is okay," I tell her. A white lie. "He has a
rally today. I'm supposed to meet him in a bit. How's Ricardo?"

Daphne straightens in her seat at the mention of her husband, providing a small smile. "He's upstairs right now, actually."

"Not away for work?"

"Not this time," she chimes. Her eyes drop to my left
wrist, locking on my bangles. Or I think she's looking at my
bangles.

"Well, that's a first." I huff a laugh, adjusting one of the
bracelets to cover the bruise. "But who am I to even say that,
right? Dominic's *always* away." And distant. So very distant.
Mentally and physically.

"I get it, trust me." Daphne looks me up and down, watching as I sip my coffee. Neither of us have touched the croissant. I have my reasons, but I wonder what Daphne's are.

For me, I have a massive sweet tooth and, during college,
I was fifty pounds heavier than I am today and could hardly
walk up the stairs on campus without breaking a sweat. Sweets
had become my enemy, plus it wasn't until I'd lost the weight
that Dominic noticed me. Daphne was always my friend
though. We were roommates at Duke University actually, indulging in sweets at the local bakery, oblivious (or uncaring)
to the calories we consumed.

I woke up one day and had had enough of eating myself
into a coma, waking up with headaches, and feeling like crap.
I was tired of being made fun of and crying myself to sleep
about it. I began working out at the campus gym twice a day
between my studies. I'd changed my life and swore to never
go back to being that sad, fat girl. I was worth more. Daddy
always said so. Mom too, in her own cold way.

I take my mind off of my weight and focus on Daphne with a bright smile. I really am happy to see her.

"We'll be taking a trip soon," she says. "Ricardo and me."

"Really? When? Where to?"

She hesitates. "I . . . can't say. But it'll be next month, and I'll take pictures and show them to you when I'm back."

"That would be nice."

Daphne sips her coffee, the slurping filling the silence. "So have you found out what's *really* going on with Dominic?"

There it is. That monstrous elephant in the room. I'm glad she's asked. The last time I spoke to her, two days ago, I'd called her crying like a teenage girl. I found an email on his laptop while reviewing his speech. An email from a woman named Nia Hall. Nia hadn't said anything important in the email really, just that she enjoyed one of his interviews and couldn't wait to see him at the next rally. Dominic had responded—a little too flirtatiously in my opinion—and told Nia he would be looking for her. Sure, it could've been a genuine response, but I know my husband, and deep in my gut there is more to it.

"I haven't yet." I run a finger along the handle of the porcelain white mug. "But I know he's hiding something, Daph. He's been weird lately. Sort of pulling away. For a while, I was blaming myself for it, thinking maybe I was pushing him too hard, but all I want is for him to succeed, you know? Well, it *was* what I wanted."

She nods, her eyes rounding.

"He came from nothing. Literally *nothing*. I've done so much for him."

"He should be grateful he found you," Daphne says.

"He should, right?"

Daphne nods, then twists her lips. "If he's having an affair . . ." Her voice trails, and my heart wrenches tight in my chest. "You can't just pull away, can you? Imagine what the press will be like? All those people wondering why the governor and his wife are splitting up in the middle of a campaign. Not that I think you should stay with the asshole, but timing is important, and you deserve to walk away unscathed."

I work to swallow the bitter taste of coffee lingering in my mouth, then rub the tip of my nose. "You're right, girl. I'm just so tired of dealing with him. I want this marriage to be over."

"Aw, Jo." She reaches across the glass table, taking my hand. "I'm so sorry. You deserve far better. I know how it is in marriage, though. And I won't blame you if you decide to make it work. As badly as we want to be done, we manage to stick. Because, regardless of the shitty aspects, working it out is much easier than ending it all." I know she's talking about herself too.

I sigh, picking up my coffee with the other hand. Footsteps venture our way and I glance over my shoulder as Daphne's husband, Ricardo, enters the kitchen.

Ricardo Juarez is what women would call tall, dark, and handsome. His dark hair is cut into a low buzz cut, and he wears jeans and a solid black shirt. His skin, usually a light yellow brown, is tanned like he's traveled somewhere sunny recently. It's now a golden color. It looks good on him.

"Oh, hey, Jo!" he calls when he spots me. He collects an apple from the tray on the counter. "Don't you have a rally thing today?"

"Yep." I flip my wrist to check the time. "I should get going, actually. I want to get there early before parking gets too crazy."

"Oh, no. Did I ruin it?" Ricardo glances at Daphne guiltily. "I can leave. I'm headed out right now. Have to make a run anyway."

Daphne and I both laugh. "No, it's okay, Ricardo. I really do need to go," I tell him. "Thank you for caring, though." At least *someone's* husband does.

Ricardo gives me a nod and I collect my purse. I eye the croissant, and Daphne walks around the table, picking it up and sliding it into the box it was originally in. She hands the box to me, and I carry my gaze to hers.

"Don't let it control you," she murmurs.

I press my lips, and with her words lingering, I take the box and leave the kitchen.

FIVE

DAPHNE

My smile collapses when Jolene pulls out of my driveway. I close the door and make my way back to the kitchen, finding my husband next to the table with my half-bitten croissant in hand.

"She asked me to talk to you," I say, clearing the teacups from the table.

I glance at Ricardo, who inclines a brow. "About what?" he asks, mouth half full.

"Things with her husband are not okay. Did you see the bruise on her wrist? She needs our help, Ric."

Ricardo chews a bit more before placing the remainder of the croissant back down on the plate. His brows pucker as he dusts crumbs off his shirt. "This is why you never should've told her," he grumbles.

"I know. But she's my best friend, Ric, and it just slipped, I swear. She won't tell anyone."

"I hope she doesn't, and I'm not saying that for our sake. I'm saying it for *hers*." He approaches me as I lower the cups into the sink. My husband, though devilishly handsome, can be intimidating. Perhaps that's because I know what he does for a living. To many, his career would be frowned upon. It's not your traditional job, but it makes him a *ton* of money.

"Is that a threat, babe?" I ask as he closes a hand around my waist. He reels me forward so our bodies merge and bows his head so our lips touch. I can't help smiling. As daunting as he is, I still get turned on. Those hands of his have done unspeakable things, yet they're so tender on me.

"No, it's not a threat. More like a promise. I know she's your friend, but we can't jeopardize what we have just because her life isn't smooth sailing. Make sure she stays wise with the information she has about us because at the end of the day, it's us before everyone else."

He plants a warm kiss on my lips, tasting of chocolate and buttery bread and I sigh behind it, lacing my arms around the back of his neck. I drop my hands to his waist, feeling something hard beneath his shirt. His pistol. He never leaves home without it. I give him one last kiss before he takes off.

When I'm finished cleaning the kitchen, I shoot Jolene a text: **He's not refusing to help but you have to be sure and you have to keep it quiet.**

SIX

DOMINIC

It's a surprisingly warm day for it to be the end of October in the Carolinas. Dominic is sweating through his suit. It doesn't help that he's had two cups of coffee this morning during his meeting with the team. His nerves are shot, and the paranoia has stolen his peace.

He points his gaze to Jolene to see if she's sweating too, but of course Jolene is in pristine condition. Not a bead of sweat on her as she stares at the screen of her phone. She wears cream pants and a white blouse that makes her appear angelic, though he knows she's anything but. Her singlet braids are pulled into a neat bun with a handful swooped into a side bang. Her pearl earrings dangle from her tiny earlobes, and though she has a good bit of makeup on her dark bronze skin, none of it runs.

Perhaps he's hotter than usual because of the call with Boaz this morning. Stress drives the body wild, and he's been crammed with it in less than five hours.

"Do you want some water?" Jolene asks, eyeing him. Why is she looking at him like that? What does she know?

He finds relief when his wife shifts her attention to his assistant, Melissa, who stands beneath the shade of the tent, her brunette hair pulled into a bun so tight it seems she's gotten Botox. She offers waters to the attendees, and Jolene waltzes over to grab one. When she returns with it, Dominic guzzles the water down rapidly.

"Two minutes," Jim's voice booms, startling him. Jim, the campaign manager.

Dominic nods. "Right. Got it."

"Dom, you look sick." Jolene's voice is in his ear. "If you're not feeling well, we can reschedule this event for another day."

She'd like that, wouldn't she? So she can bitch to him more about how he's not doing enough, not striving for more, not working hard or sticking it to the man. Then again, she'll never let that happen. She'll let him work to the bone before he ever quits and destroys her reputation.

"No," he responds abruptly. There's no way he's rescheduling, despite the letter in his mailbox this morning. Like Boaz said, there's no proof. He made sure. Paula Howell, the main competitor running for his governor's seat, is higher in the projection polls than he is right now. If he reschedules today, he has a feeling she'll go even higher, and that woman doesn't deserve them. He's met her once, during a dinner. She was snarky, crass, and ignorant.

"I have to do this," Dominic says.

"Okay." Jolene rubs circles on his upper back, all for show of course. It's good. People need to believe they're in love. It makes you look better as a candidate when you have a strong marriage.

"Let's go, boss," Jim says, gesturing to the small stage ahead. The stage contains a stand with a microphone and a podium, though Dominic hardly ever uses the podium. The podium restrains him. He likes moving across the stage, connecting with the people. He can't do that if he's stuck in one place, plus the people like that about him, how he shifts from left to right, taking in all his supporters, looking deeply into their eyes.

He turns his eyes to Jolene as a woman named Heather, dressed in a sky-blue blazer and matching pants, stands on stage to introduce him. He gives his wife a kiss as all eyes turn to him. Jolene smiles, revealing dimples, and for a split second he thinks it's a genuine smile, one fueled with love and desire. As he walks up the steps to reach the stage, he's surrounded by cheers and is facing supporters in blue Baker 2023 T-shirts. On the front of their shirts are the words **Uplifting North Carolina**. On the back is **Baker 2023**. All proceeds from shirt sales fund their campaign. As he stands a moment, collecting the microphone in his grasp and allowing his supporters to settle, someone in the crowd catches his eye.

A woman stands in the front row, her hair streaked with silvery gray—but not the sort of gray you get from aging or stress. Her hair has been dyed that color, the rest black, thick, and falling into crinkly waves. An emerald scarf is wrapped around the edges of her hair and her clothes aren't like the others of the crowd. Everyone is casual, but she appears more witchy bohemian, in a burgundy camisole beneath a deep V-neck T-shirt, khaki palazzo pants, and weathered sandals. A nose piercing is in her left nostril, copper bangles on both wrists, and a layer of necklaces around her neck, one of them made of little skulls. Her outfit stands out boldly, but her eyes are what he notices most. Dark and intense, surrounded by lashes caked in mascara, her eyelids heavy with shimmery purple eyeshadow. She seems to be in her early thirties. As others cheer, smile, and gawk, she simply stares. She doesn't frown, nor does she smile. Just stares with hardly a blink. For a second, Dominic assumes she isn't real—that she's a figment of his imagination. He blinks but she's still there.

She isn't his usual supporter, but he's seen people from all walks of life show up to his rallies. There is something about this woman, though. Something hauntingly familiar, yet he can't put his finger on it. Or perhaps it's nothing at all, and it's simply the way she glares at him so intensely that makes him uncomfortable and more aware of her presence.

He begins his speech with a bang, thanking his supporters for turning up. He moves across the stage with his microphone gripped in hand, focusing on another member of the crowd. He figures if he focuses on others, he won't be so distracted by the witchy woman.

It works for a while, until the little voice in his ear tells him to switch to the other side of the stage again and level the attention. The little voice is Jim, the eagle-eyed manager. As badly as he wants to ignore the voice and stay on the right side, he has to move. He has to sell it if he wants that position, so he saunters to the left, expecting to see the witchy young woman with the intense eyes, but she's no longer standing there. He surfs the crowd, mouth still working out that speech, realizing there is no sign of her anymore.

She's disappeared, and a bad feeling sinks into his gut like a block of lead. He isn't sure if he's simply paranoid from this morning, or if this woman is someone to watch out for. Could she be the one who put the letter in his mailbox? Is she trying to blackmail him? Impossible. How could she know a thing?

He's definitely paranoid. The body can't be found. Only he and Boaz know where it is, and it'll stay that way. He should be relieved the witchy woman is gone, but something about her disappearance causes him worry instead.

SEVEN

BRYNN

It was stupid on my part to even bother entertaining Dominic. I had the receipt with his number on it clutched in my hand and sat behind the wheel of my Beetle. The radio poured out a mixture of static and Alicia Keys while I chewed on my bottom lip.

I couldn't believe I was contemplating it. Everything in me was screaming *not* to do it, especially when I saw that wedding band on his finger. He had a wife now. A new life. He'd moved on from me and that should've settled it. Things like this happened and I just had to accept it.

But I saw the look in his eyes, that spark he'd always reserved for me. Something between us still lingered, and though I shouldn't have, I did. I called the number he provided, and he answered on the second ring.

"Hello?" his voice was still sticking to me—that sweet, tempting, gold honey.

"Hi. Dom?" I asked, gripping the phone tighter.

"Oh, Brynn. Is that you?"

I huffed a laugh. "It's me. I think you accidentally left your number behind."

He chuckled then said, "Nah. It was no accident."

That familiar feeling struck me, the one I had when I would see Dominic in the school hallways first thing in the morning. Or when he'd show up at my house with a stolen pack of Hershey Kisses when my momma wasn't around. Butterflies in the belly, a quickening heartbeat, a slight clench between my thighs. There were guys I'd been with during college, of course, but I had a bad habit of comparing them all to my high school love. In fact, I'd made a habit of checking to see what Dominic was up to after our breakup, but he had no social media presence. Of course, back then there was only Facebook and Twitter. He'd never liked social media. He was always more private, and I think that's why our relationship had lasted so long then. What happened between us, stayed between us.

"Listen, I'd love to see you outside of work. Do you think you can meet me for a drink?" he asked.

"Yes." I responded much faster than I should've. This man was married!

But divorces happen every day.

I swallowed that intrusive thought. I was getting ahead of myself now. "I mean, yes," I said again, more calmly. "I'll be happy to meet you."

"Great. I'll be hanging out at the Ritz Carlton. Why don't you meet me in the Galveston Lounge."

"Sure. But I just got off work. Can I meet you there in an hour?"

"Of course. Just text me when you arrive. I'll be waiting."

My heart swelled, but I played it cool. "Okay. See you then."

I drove home right away, and Shavonne was sitting on the sofa, reading a book when I barged into the apartment.

"What the hell, Brynn?" she snapped, a hand clinging to her chest.

"Sorry, sorry!" I ran straight to the bathroom, starting up the shower and jumping in after stripping out of my clothes. I gave my ass a thorough wash, shaved, then got out to sift through my closet.

As I plucked out a red bodycon dress with a draped collar—one that I knew would bring Dominic to his knees—Shavonne knocked on my door then cracked it open.

"What's the rush?" she asked, as I dropped the towel and applied lotion. She never minded my nakedness. It sort of became that way for us since we had to share a bathroom. She'd be showering and I'd be brushing my teeth or styling my hair. Perks of being roommates with one bathroom, I suppose.

"I have a date," I told her, smiling over my shoulder.

"A date? With who?" she asked, folding her arms over her chest.

"This guy I met at Franco's." I wasn't about to tell her it was Dominic. I may or may not have mentioned him to her a time or two . . . or twenty.

Shavonne asked, "What's his name?"

"I can't remember," I lied as I slipped into the dress.

"Brynn, are you out of your mind?" she snapped. "Going out with a man whose name you don't know? There are all kinds of predators out here."

"He's not a predator." I found my strappy black heels in the back of the closet. "He has money."

"Okay? Predators can *also* be rich," she countered, sticking her neck out. "Should I drop you off?"

"No, Vonne, I'm good. Okay?" I told her, breathless. I was struggling to breathe while bent over to strap the shoes.

She huffed. "Alright. Whatever."

I rolled my eyes as I put on the other heel.

Shavonne was paranoid in all ways. I suppose I couldn't blame her. She'd lost both her parents during this crazy cruise accident. She had to live with her aunt and uncle who were these hippie potheads—good people with great intentions, but completely blitzed all the time and forgetful as hell.

I watched Shavonne walk away before going to the bathroom to apply a little makeup. I checked my phone and was losing time. It would take me twenty minutes just to get to the Ritz Carlton from my apartment and I'd spent a good twenty of it showering, plucking, shaving, and applying makeup, so I went for my purse and popped a mint instead of brushing my teeth (what? I brushed them that morning) and headed to the door.

"Text me!" Shavonne yelled before I could escape.

I would text her, but I wasn't sure how much information I would feed her. This was likely going to be a one-time thing. One night with the grown and sexy Dominic Baker and it'd never happen again. As much as I loved Shavonne and felt like I could tell her everything, some secrets were best kept to myself. Dominic had always been a sore subject for me, and now that he was back, I wanted to make him mine again . . . quietly.

EIGHT

DOMINIC

The crowd is eager to meet Dominic after his speech. These moments are what give him drive and the will to continue. He'd done everything he needed to do and traveled all over the state of North Carolina to try and win the people over. He'd had his share of bad luck with some people throwing eggs at his car and even fruit at his suits, but it came with the territory. Not everyone was going to like him, and he was aware of that *way* before running.

He was a middle-aged Black man and if he had to be honest, North Carolina wasn't the friendliest place in the world for a Black man to be. Not to mention his competition, Paula, had a lot of connections in the state—way more than he did— but that wasn't going to stop him. All he had to do was push through, keep his head up, stay out of trouble, and remain positive, but that was much easier said than done. He lacked sleep and he was becoming so stressed that he had to start dyeing the grays in his hair.

He hadn't slept properly in months—*years*, actually—and he couldn't blame it on his campaign. It'd started long before that, but he tried not to think of that terrible secret as he shook his future voters' hands and smiled, took selfies with some of them, and handed kids stickers that Jolene insisted was a good way to engage the kids and warm the hearts of the mothers.

At the thought, Dominic's eyes swiveled to his wife, and he did his best not to frown as he spotted her talking to the Lieutenant Governor, Samuel Sanchez. She was laughing about something, while Samuel leaned in with that stupidly charming smile.

"Hey, Mel, can you tell Jo to come over and greet the people with me," Dom requests and Melissa turns and makes her way to Jo. As Dominic shakes an older man's hand who is talking about his situation in a retirement community, Dominic cuts his eyes to Jo again. She places a caring hand on Sanchez's upper arm, smiles at him, then follows Mel toward the waiting crowd.

Instantly, Jo is smiling and interacting with a middle-aged woman who has a toddler on her hip. He hates how she does that—just flips a switch and pretends she didn't make a mistake. The toddler, a chubby-faced girl with sepia skin and pig tails with pink bows, is sucking her thumb and blinking slowly, as if she needs a nap, and the mother is very animated as she blabs about women's rights and how empowered she feels seeing Jolene being such a force as a wife and working woman.

That pleases Dominic to hear in more ways than even Jo realizes. His wife, though infuriating at times, *is* a force, and her skill in marketing and even with his speeches has proved that. She doesn't do all his speeches, but she definitely assists him with many. She knows exactly how to pull at the heartstrings of the crowd with her words, while also making them sound like his. She knows his voice more than anyone and without her, Dominic wouldn't be doing nearly as well as he is now. That, plus her A-plus marketing has truly skyrocketed Dominic's campaign. There isn't a corner you can turn in this city without seeing a Baker 2023 poster, and she and Melissa have set up many local interviews for him, so his face is consistently on local news channels, and even a few national news channels. They pencil him in for the best events to attend to further boost his image and he's grateful for that.

Jolene wraps up with the giddy mother and Dominic takes her hand. When her attention is on his, he squeezes her hand tightly, and she works her jaw. He wants her to know he's angry about Sanchez, but they'll discuss it later. Right now, they need to keep up appearances.

Dominic uses his other hand to shake, smiles, and does his bidding. But then his heart drops to his belly, and he can suddenly hear his pulse in his ears. In front of him is the witchy lady who was in the crowd. She stares at him—*through* him, really—her brown eyes near black and a barely-there smile on her mouth. She stares at him like she knows things, like he's made of glass. He studies the security detail officers on the other side of the gate with relief. He can't guarantee this woman won't jump forward and slice his throat or something else crazy.

"Oh, wow!" Jo's voice snaps him out of his daze as she moves in closer and focuses on the witchy woman's chest. "I love your necklace! Where did you get it?"

"Thank you. I made it myself," the witchy lady says, a brief smile to Jolene before cutting her eyes to Dominic again. *What the hell? Why is she staring at me like that?*

"That's incredible, and so creative." The necklace isn't Jo's style, but Dominic figures his wife is just being nice because that's another thing about Jo. She always tries to find something to compliment someone about. She's trained herself to be that way and never to look for the negatives. Dominic, however, can only see the negatives of this witchy woman as she stands before him. There's something ominous about her that makes his mouth feel dry and his hands shake.

"Mr. Baker, your speech today was really touching," the witch says, smiling at him. She reveals teeth that aren't exactly straight. Her upper right canine protrudes a little further out than her other teeth.

"Thank you." Dominic shifts on his feet, glancing at security again. "I appreciate that and thank you for attending."

"Of course. I wouldn't have missed it."

Dominic wraps his arm around Jo, reeling her into his side. He wants some kind of comfort—*any*, really. "I work on the speeches with my wife."

"Hmm," is all the witch says. She isn't completely abhorrent of the idea, but not delighted either.

Dominic stands taller. "I'm sorry—I didn't catch your name."

"I never provided one." The witchy woman stretches her arm to offer him a hand. Dominic glances down at it. Silver and copper rings are on her fingers, and henna art is on the back of her hand. There's ink on her palm of an open eye. "Eden," she announces, awaiting his hand.

Dominic's heartrate picks up a notch, but he keeps calm on the outside and takes her hand in his, just like he would anyone else's, and gives it a shake. Her hand is clammy and slightly cold, despite it being rather warm outside, and as he looks into her eyes, he can't help noticing them narrow and darken. A jolt rocks through his body, one he can't quite wrap his head around. Or perhaps the jolt is all in his head. Eden holds his hand tighter while he resists the urge to pull away. Pulling away in front of an enthusiastic crowd will be seen as rude, and it's like Eden knows this.

Too many eyes.

Too many cameras.

Can't jeopardize the reputation.

"I think you'll win," Eden tells him.

"What?" Dominic mumbles.

"You think so?" Jo asks, her eyes brightening.

"I think so. But he'll have to fight very hard to do so and reveal a lot of truths."

Dominic swallows hard, relieved when Eden releases his hand.

"Good thing our Dom's a fighter," Jo says, patting him on the chest. "And he's always honest. *Right*, babe?"

"Absolutely." Dominic puts on a tight smile for his wife. *What is she getting at? She's lucky we're in public.*

"Nice meeting you, Eden." Jo shakes her hand, then turns to her husband. "Shall we meet the next person?"

"Sure," says Dom, keeping his voice level.

"Oh, before you take off." Eden's voice stops them in their tracks, and she digs into the burlap bag strapped over her shoulder, withdrawing a black box. She starts to give it to Jolene, but one of the security officers stops her by lifting a hand to intercept.

"It's fine, Frank," Jolene snaps at him, and he steps away. Jolene is tripping. She knows they don't take things from the public. Not that Dominic assumes everyone is out to get him, but you can never be too careful these days. He could place a confident bet that there is someone out there who wants to kill him simply for breathing.

Eden glances at Frank before focusing on Jolene again. "I can only imagine how stressful campaigns are on the body. I just started a tea collection that's holistic, organic, and I have a certain tea called Purple Sky that works wonders. It helps to relax your body and open your mind." She offers the box to Jo. "Hopefully you'll give it a try and let me know what you think? I know that you run a tea shop and if you love it, I'd be more than happy to collaborate. I'm on Instagram under the name mysticcgoddess. Two c's. There's a card in the box in case you need my info."

"Wow. That is so nice of you, Eden! Thank you!" Jolene says, accepting the box. "I love tea! I'll be sure to give it a try and look you up."

"Thanks, Eden," Dominic forces himself to say. What he

really wants to do is knock the box out of his wife's hand and bolt.

Eden nods, her eyes shifting to Dominic's again. "Good luck with the rest of your campaign, Mr. Baker."

"Thanks." Dominic turns away with Jo, no longer interested in shaking hands with anyone else. He nods as Melissa, who takes the gesture and approaches the remaining crowd to let them know the governor has other matters to tend to. Some people moan, others suck their teeth, but for the most part they disperse.

Fortunately, thunder rattles the sky, taking the attention away from him. He walks past Jim and Heather, his hand pressed to the small of Jo's back, but not without looking back at Eden. She's standing a few feet away from the crowd, looking right at him the same way she was during his speech.

Not blinking.

Not smiling.

Just *staring*, only at him.

Regardless of the heat, or the humidity that's well on its way from the moisture accumulating in the air, a chill slides down Dominic's spine.

He snatches his eyes away, giving himself a mental reminder to get that box from Jo when she's not looking and toss that shit.

NINE

JOLENE

I sit at a table of the Fox Trot, a glass of wine in hand and my focus on Dominic as he makes his rounds, thanking his team for their persistence and dedication. Jim has somehow swindled us into attending an after-rally party in a private bar.

I *should* be up with my husband, but I'm tired and partially ashamed. After the rally, I shoveled the croissant from Daphne into my mouth and can still feel it sitting in my gut like a brick. I don't know what I was thinking. It was like a beast had taken over me, or perhaps I was angry at my husband because I saw him flirting with a woman in the crowd after everyone left.

Look, I get it. My husband is state governor—and one of the youngest to boot—so the need to charm and make a person smile comes with his position. He must sway the crowd, make them smile, get them on his side so he can count on their vote. But there's a difference between being professionally charming and downright flirtatious. This woman in the crowd, she was beautiful with coiled hair and umber skin. A journalist. She was Nia Hall. After she'd asked him a few questions, he leaned into her too closely and she giggled. It was disgusting and I watched it all from a distance. Melissa cut her eyes at me at one point as she stood behind Dominic, and I had to look away. No way did I want our assistant's pity. I searched for Samuel Sanchez, the state's lieutenant governor, hoping to get another laugh or two with him, but he'd taken off. He never stayed at the rallies for long.

So, what did I do while my husband was flirting? I stormed to my BMW and sat in the driver's seat. I tossed the box of tea from that woman in the crowd onto the car floor, breathing hard through my nostrils. I smelled the chocolate wafting in the air and though I tried ignoring it, it was suddenly all I could think about. The flaky, golden crust. The drizzle of white and dark chocolate. The thick slabs inside that were slightly oozing out the corners. *Just one bite won't hurt.*

I stared at the box, then snatched it up while sitting in the parking lot, watching the crowd disperse. I quickly opened it and crammed half the croissant into my mouth. Somehow the croissant was still warm, possibly from sitting in the heat of the car, so a dribble of the gooey chocolate landed on the front of my shirt. I didn't realize this until after I'd devoured the whole thing and sat in shame with crumbs on my lap and the corner of my mouth. I glanced down when my phone buzzed with a text and spotted that dark, ugly spot.

Good thing I brought extra clothes with me. I stripped out of the shirt after wiping the chocolate stain with a loose napkin, then grabbed the mini duffel bag in the backseat, plucking out an ivory shirt. The color of the shirt was close enough to the original white. Dominic wasn't going to notice the difference.

I checked my phone after cleaning up and there was a text from Jim:

**Dominic is riding with security to Fox Trot.
Don't be mad at him. My idea. See you there?**

"Oh, fuck you, Jim," I grumbled, then I started the car and drove away from the rally. Of course, he'd have his campaign manager do the dirty work. I bet Dominic wasn't even going to tell me, but Jim took it upon himself to do so. Jim Pilton knows how much I hate going out to drink with Dominic. He's been in the midst of one of our arguments. Dominic would drink too much, I'd want to take him home, but he'd get angry and tell me to leave him alone.

Now, I'm sitting here, a tad grumpy and slightly buzzed, stewing about the croissant and my absent-ass husband.

"Another?" a peppy voice asks beside me. I turn my head, spotting the waitress, a young twenty-something with porcelain skin, freckles, blonde hair, and blue eyes. She gestures to the empty glass in front of me.

I nod. "Please. But can you make it a whiskey this time? Top shelf and neat."

She bobs her head, taking away my empty glass and returning minutes later with a new crystal glass two fingers deep with amber liquid. I pick up the drink, swiveling my eyes to Dominic who is chatting with Melissa and Jim.

I shift in my seat just as Dominic flips his gaze on me, then excuses himself from Jim and Melissa to walk my way.

"Great," I mumble. He pulls out the chair on the opposite side of my table and sits with a drink in hand. Most likely Jim Beam. I don't understand why he loves it so much. It's a college drink he and his frat boys drank religiously.

"You know you don't have to stay if you don't want to," Dominic says, setting his glass down on the dark oak table.

"Oh, you'd like that, wouldn't you? Get the wife to leave so you can do all the flirting you want?" I glanced at Staci, one of our volunteers. He's been eyeing her lately too.

"Jo, come on. Today was a good day. Didn't you see the news? We went up two percent in the poll projections." He reaches across the table, placing his hand on mine. "We should be happy, not moping."

"I'm not moping," I counter, slowly pulling my hand away. What I really want to do is snatch it, but people are watching. They're always watching. I lean forward and hiss the words, "I saw you flirting with that journalist after the rally."

"Good Lord, Jo." He says the words through his teeth but maintains a poker face. "Look, if you're going to act like that tonight, I'd rather us go home right now."

"Right. Let's do that," I snap, then pick up my drink and guzzle down the rest. Dominic glares at me, picks his drink up as well, and finishes it off.

I'm already at the door as he speaks to the room. "I'm heading out, friends!" he booms. "Thank you so much for all you do. Like I said earlier, I wouldn't be able to do any of this without you! Enjoy a few more drinks on me, alright?" Cheers break out in the room as Dominic walks my way, acting like he's the king of all, the best man in the world.

"Should we follow along, sir?" one of his security officers asks at the door.

"No, no. It's all good, Frank." Dominic claps his shoulder. "The wife should be able to get me home. I'll call if I need you though."

The wife? Fucking asshole.

I storm out of Fox Trot to get to my car as quickly as I can in my heels. I unlock the doors and climb behind the wheel, but my eyes fall to the croissant box on the seat. I snatch it up and toss it behind the passenger seat, just as Dominic opens the door and settles onto the fine leather with a lazy smile.

I start the engine and drive, letting my anger simmer. It isn't until we're turning onto the street of our private home that Dominic says, "You embarrass me, you know that?"

Here we go. "Oh, *I* embarrass *you*?"

"Yes, Jo! We can't even have a damn rally without you accusing me of flirting with someone. And how the hell are you gonna accuse me when I saw you laughing it up with Sanchez?"

"I saw you with my own two eyes, Dominic, and if I did, I know everyone else did too!" I ignore his Sanchez remark. "You're the one making *me* look like an idiot—like I have no backbone. I swear to God if it wasn't for this campaign, I'd be done with you right now."

He chuckles, and I swear I want to stomp on the brakes just so his face slams into the dashboard. The idiot isn't wearing a seatbelt. He thinks he's invincible. He's lucky I don't go through with the action in mind. Plus, slamming on the brakes and breaking his damn nose won't make him look too good in the press.

"Let's not get carried away, alright? We all know you're never going to leave me, Jo. You have way too much at stake. Besides, if it weren't for me, you wouldn't even have that unit near the park. You wouldn't have all your little girlies huddled up every week in your fancy tea shop, gossiping and talking about tea flavors, chocolate cake, and God knows what else you do. It's such a waste what you've done with your dad's money."

"*Excuse* me?" I snap. "It's *because* of my father's money that your first campaign was funded! It's *because* of his money that you wore those expensive suits and traveled to places unknown and were able to network with all those politicians. If it weren't for us, you'd be nothing, Dominic! *Nothing!*"

I'm so sick of this. It's been like this between us for the last two years. We fight, I threaten to leave, he counters it with how much I have to lose. He's right. I do have a lot to lose. If I walk away, Dominic will make the divorce a nasty one. He won't relent and I refuse to walk out of this marriage without being financially secure.

I drive along the cobblestone driveway, fuming. When I park the car in front of our house, I slouch back in my seat and bring my hands to my face. And for the first time in what feels like weeks, I break out in a sob. The sob hurts my belly and everything inside me. I hate crying. I hate it even more so when it's done in front of him.

"Oh, come on, Jo." His hand is on my arm with gentle pressure. "Jo, look, I'm sorry. Okay? I didn't mean it. I'm sorry." His words are empty. Useless. He's only saying them so I won't be upset.

Well fuck that. Those words won't cut it this time. They don't stop the tears and I'm still angry. I drop my hands and collect my purse and keys, pushing the car door open and rushing toward the house. When I'm inside, I slam the door behind me.

TEN

DOMINIC

Jo won't let Dominic into the bedroom. It's his bedroom too, God damn it. He rolls his eyes, turning away from the locked door. She's acting like a baby, like the world revolves around her. He's getting so tired of her bitching and whining all the time.

With a grimace, he marches to one of the guest rooms. He's been spending a lot of time in the guest room lately. His marriage is in complete shambles, and he has no idea how to fix it.

"Do I even wanna fix it?" he mutters.

Truthfully, he can't figure out why Jo puts up with him, but he knows why he puts up with her. She was right that her father's money funded his career. Well, it was more so his death that fueled it. Her father had been stingy with his money, only giving her enough for college tuition and meals. He'd provided a car so she could get around on campus, of course, but Jolene had a job while in college, despite the trust fund he'd set up for her, one she couldn't even access until she'd graduated. Her father wanted her to continue working, to be involved in the real world. When he died, she drowned in an enormous inheritance. He was partner in an oil company, so she'd practically struck gold.

Dominic retrieves a set of pajamas he keeps stored in the dresser of the guest bedroom. His emergency pajamas, used on the nights when Jo doesn't want to see his face. Soft black pants, a white T-shirt. He takes a quick shower, changes into them, then sits on the edge of the bed.

When he'd met Jolene, she was different. She was bubblier, happier. He remembered seeing her coming out of the gym, a sheen of sweat on her forehead. The first thing he'd noticed was her ass in the yoga pants. He couldn't help staring at her. How had he *not* noticed her before? He tagged along with her when she walked out of the gym, and he remembered her looking at him like he'd lost his mind. He'd never spoken to her, didn't even introduce himself. To her, he was some random man taking up her space.

"I work out too, ya know?" he'd said, and he felt stupid for it. Many people worked out. That didn't make him special.

But, oddly enough, it made Jolene laugh. Her head dropped, and she said, "Good for you, bud."

He wasn't sure what it was about her. Her body. Her smoky and enticing voice. The tinkle of her laugh. The softness of her smile. He wanted to get to know this new girl and soon enough he did. They studied together, worked out together, ate dinner together. Everything they did was *together*.

With a sigh, Dominic walks out of the guest room and down the stairs. One of the lights in the kitchen is on already and when he steps around the corner, Jolene is behind the oversized quartz island counter, pouring steaming water from the electric kettle into a mug. Her eyes flicker up to his—puffy, red, and swollen—and he feels awful. He remembers the Jolene from college, the one who loved him with her whole heart, who relied on him. Who *trusted* him.

Damn. He's betrayed her trust so much.

He ambles through the kitchen and doesn't stop until he wraps his arms around her, reeling her in from behind.

"Just get off of me, Dom," Jo mumbles. But she doesn't fight him off. He's not sure if that's because she likes his gesture, or because she's too weak to do so.

"Can I have a cup?" he asks.

She sniffs. "Fine."

He releases her so she can go to the cupboard and take down another mug. When she sets it down, she says, "It's the tea from that woman at the rally."

He frowns. "We don't have any other tea?"

"We do, but I wanted to try it. We are looking for new flavors for the shop. Plus, the name Purple Sky has a ring to it."

Dominic continues a frown, and she sighs.

"Do you want some or not, Dom? No one's forcing you to drink it."

"Fine, yeah," he mumbles.

Jo dumps a tea bag into his mug, pours hot water from the electric kettle, and they both wait while the teabags steep, transitioning the water from clear to liquid amber. She folds her arms and rests her lower back against the counter edge, avoiding his eyes.

"I was just thinking about our time in college," Dominic says with a chuckle.

"Why?" she asks, not a hint of a smile on her face.

"I don't know. I was thinking about when we met. How head over heels you were for me."

She scoffs, pushing off the counter and picking up the string of her tea bag, dunking it a few times. "You mean how you harassed me into dating you?"

"I didn't harass you. I was just very interested." He chuckles.

She smiles. Just barely. He thinks he has her. He's winning

her over again. It's what he's good at, winning people over. Even his wife.

"I miss how we were," he tells her. "I miss holding hands." He reaches for her hand over the counter, and surprisingly she lets him take it. "I know being governor calls for more time away from you, but I'm thinking once the campaign ends and I get this win, we can book a vacation. Get away together. Just you and me. No distractions."

"Your schedule is too crazy for a vacation," she sighs, and she looks away, automatically defeated. "I know it's my fault that we don't get to spend as much time together. I pushed you to run for governor."

"We both agreed it was a good idea," he adds in. "Your father's partner knew people. He hooked us up for the campaign and we chased that opportunity."

She nods, swallows, then turns away, going to the pantry to take out the organic honey. She plucks Dominic's teabag out of his mug, squeezes it with her fingertips, then pours honey into it. She slides the mug his way before drizzling honey into her own, but only a teaspoon or so.

He picks up the tea and gives it a sip. It's surprisingly good. He takes another hot, hefty sip that slightly scalds his tongue.

"You know, Dom . . ." Jolene's voice trails, and she clamps her mouth shut.

"Go on," he murmurs, holding her dark-brown gaze.

Her irises gleam beneath the chandelier as she locks on him. "When I married you, I only asked for one thing." She stares down at her tea. "I asked you to be honest with me at all times."

Dominic freezes. He has no idea what to say to that, so he waits for her to continue.

"What are you hiding from me?" Her voice is so low he almost couldn't hear the question.

He stares at his wife, and for a split second he thinks about telling her everything. It was that summer in New Orleans nearly four and a half years ago that changed his life—almost ruined it.

Galveston Lounge.

The Ritz Carlton.

The *rug*.

He cringes internally at the last thought. Jolene would *never* understand. Plus, she's safer not knowing. If anything ever backfires, she'll be safe. But of course, that's only one of the many things he's hidden from his wife. And sure, the New Orleans issue is grand, but he has a feeling if she ever finds out about the other thing, she'll never speak to him again.

"I'm not hiding anything, Jo," Dominic finally says, and he watches the disappointment sink into her eyes. She purses her lips as he takes another sip of the tea. On the outside, he appears casual and chill, but internally, his heart is pounding, and his pulse is in his ears.

"Kay." She sighs, turning away. "Well, when you're ready to tell me the truth, I'll be waiting. I'm going to bed."

She leaves the kitchen without looking back at him and he hears her tiny feet as she pads up the stairs. He leans against the counter, glancing at her untouched mug of tea.

ELEVEN

DOMINIC

Dominic carries his mug of tea into the office, placing it on a coaster on the desktop. That witchy woman was weird, but her tea is good, he can't lie. Melissa mentioned at the Fox Trot that Dominic had some documents to print and sign, and since he isn't very sleepy yet, he gets to it. He prints the papers and stores them in a fresh manila envelope to take to Executive Mansion, then he leans back, sipping the rest of his tea.

Jolene knows he's hiding something. She's always been good at reading him. He isn't quite sure how to make it up to her. Perhaps if he tells the truth, she'll perk up. She is his wife, after all. His secrets are safe with her, and she's always had his back. Any sticky situation he's been in, she aids him. But this . . . it's different. He has to deal with it himself.

Something appears in the corner of his eye, and he nearly chokes on his next sip when he spots a silhouette approaching the double doors on the other side of the office. The doors lead to one of the patios, and his home is closed off with oversized iron gates, but he's sure that's a hooded figure coming toward the door. And he's damn near positive that figure has grabbed the door handle and is jiggling it to try and break in.

His heart slams in his chest as he freezes in his chair. He's left his cellphone upstairs in the guestroom. His eyes drop to the desk phone, and he rapidly picks up the receiver as the person continues rattling the door handle. The door shakes roughly as he dials the officer parked at the end of the drive-way. There's an officer on duty every night, a safety precaution for him as governor.

"Sir? How is it going?" Stephen answers. He knows it's Stephen by his deeply southern accent, sounding more like *Sir? Haow's it goin'?* It's always either him or a man named Tyler.

"Come to the house now," Dominic breathes into the phone, watching the door rattle again. The hooded person is now raising an arm, as if trying to see through the blinds. "Someone is trying to break in. Come now!"

"Let's get in there!" Stephen orders, and he's thankful the officer isn't alone.

The door handle continues rattling and Dominic shoots to a stand, gripping a paperweight and glancing at the door that'll take him out of the office. Then, just as quickly as the rattling started, it stops, and the silhouette retreats and disappears. He waits a moment, breaths ragged, clutching the paperweight, as silence fills the room. When he doesn't hear anything, his mind jumps to Jolene.

Shit. Jolene.

He bolts for the door and thunders up the stairs. He tries pushing their bedroom door open, but it's locked *again* so he bangs a fist on it. "Jo!" he shouts. "Open the door, Jo!"

The door swings open and Jolene stares at him like a deer stuck in headlights. "Dom, what the hell is wrong with you?" she screeches, wiping tears from her eyes.

"There's someone trying to break into the house," he says, catching his breath. Jolene's shock morphs to sheer terror and she looks over his shoulder, just as a knocking comes from the front door.

TWELVE
DOMINIC

"Perimeter is clear, sir." Stephen looks different. He used to have a beard, but now he has a thick, comb-like moustache. He's dressed in uniform, the brim of his hat low on his head. The other officer is a woman, short but well-built. She goes by Burnell. "We didn't see any foot prints around the house, no open windows, or doors. Nothing outside the home was tampered with. If there was someone here, the intruder most likely got spooked and ran, jumped the fence. We've put out more cruisers, who'll keep an eye on the area and look for anyone suspicious."

"Good, because I'm sure I saw someone," Dominic insists as Jolene rubs circles on his back. His nerves are fried. He saw that person trying to break in. Could it be the same person who left that note in the mail? Anger floods him, but he swallows it down as Officer Stephen says something about more burglaries that have happened nearby. Who is doing this to him? Why now, in the middle of a brutal campaign?

"I want officers here morning, midday, and night," Dominic demands.

"Of course, sir," Stephen responds.

"We'll be keeping an eye, sir," Burnell informs him with a nod.

A sense of pride washes over him. They *must* protect him. They must keep him safe. He should also contact Frank and his hired security team. He reserves them for rallies and public events, but he may have to change that.

Normally, Dominic isn't so keen on keeping security around his private home. He likes his privacy, hence the reason he doesn't stay in the Executive Mansion, but when you become governor, privacy dwindles.

There is one officer on duty every night, and one who arrives in the mornings if he needs to be escorted to Executive Mansion. But with that note from the mail (crumpled in the bottom drawer of his desk), and now an attempted break-in, he can't take any chances. It's almost as if the person *knew* his office doors were the only place on the property without cameras. The officers checked the security camera footage. There was nothing out of the ordinary, and of course no visuals of the office patio. Dominic makes a mental note to have a camera installed by the office door immediately. He'd never had one there. It didn't feel necessary since one was in the backyard. Plus, he smoked a lot of weed on the patio and didn't want any footage of that circulating. There were ways for people to hack home security systems. What would the citizens say when they saw their governor smoking weed? He faced so much flack and hate already, he didn't want to give the people more reason to drag him down. He needs to stop smoking anyway. Now is as good a time as any.

When the officers leave, Dominic locks the doors, sets the security alarm, and meets Jolene in the living room.

"Who would want to break into our house?" she asks, then she retracts the question when he frowns at her, instead going with, "Well, why would they *dare* to?"

"I don't know." He runs a hand over his head and realizes they're shaking. He drops them, sliding them into the pockets of his pajama pants. He can't let Jo see how terrified he is. She'll ask more questions, start prying. He has a gut feeling this relates to that note in the mail.

"You can sleep in the room with me if you want to," she says, moving closer to him.

"Sure. I'll be up in a bit. Just need to contact Frank and make another call."

She looks into his eyes, as if searching for honesty, but it is true. Well, sort of. He is going to reach out to Frank, but he's not going to call the other person. Jo rubs his arm empathetically, then she takes off, walking up the stairs.

When he hears her footfalls above, proving that she's made it to the bedroom, he returns to his office, stealing glances at the locked French doors every so often, hoping the hooded person doesn't return. They'd be stupid to.

He locks the office door then sits in his cushioned rolling chair, removing the keys taped beneath the desk and unlocking the bottom drawer. He takes out the Nokia and it still has a bit of battery.

He fires up a text to Boaz: **Meet tomorrow, 10 a.m. at executive mansion.**

He sends it off. Waits patiently while sipping his tea that's now cold. A message appears, one little word: **OK**

He shuts the phone off, tucks it back into the drawer, then locks it again. After calling Frank and asking him to set up shifts around his private home, Dominic leaves the office. He takes his tea to the kitchen and dumps the remainder of it down the drain, but, when he looks up, he drops the mug, and it shatters in the sink.

Taped to the window from the outside is another note in permanent marker:

SHE WAS PLEASURE THEN SIN.
ONE YOU PUT TO AN END.
WHERE, OH WHERE, IS YOUR LOVE, BRYNN?

THIRTEEN

BRYNN

I'd never been inside the Ritz Carlton. Are you kidding me? The place was clearly for the rich and your girl was far from it. As I entered the lobby of the hotel, I realized how completely out of place I was in my tight red dress and strappy heels. What the hell was I thinking wearing this? Other women wore elegant gowns or vibrant work suits, while I came in dressed like a damn prostitute.

I felt the eyes on me, heavy and judgmental, but kept my gaze ahead and made my way toward the lounge. To my luck, the lounge was much darker. The lights were dim, and music flowed soothingly. Men on stage played saxophones, drums, and the piano while a woman stood in the center in front of a mic, singing delightful blues. Her makeup was dramatic and heavy with copious amounts of eyeliner, highlighter, and blush, and she wore a shimmery gold cocktail dress with pearls draped around her neck and wrists. In a way, she was like a sad masterpiece, and she sang straight from the soul.

I shifted my gaze to the people sitting on luxury, uphol-stered sliver sofas, drinks in hand as they mingled. It took me a minute to find the man I was looking for. But when I saw him, he was all I could see, standing exactly where he said he would be.

In a far corner at a two-top table was Dominic Baker. He wore a white button-down shirt tucked neatly into brown, creaseless trousers. His dark-brown shoes shined beneath the dim lighting, and a warm, inviting smile was on his lips. A drink was in his right hand, and he tipped the glass at me, which made me bite a smile. I walked in his direction and stopped short of the table as he stood.

"Wow," he breathed. "Look at you, Brynn. All grown up."

I grinned at that. "I can say the same to you. You look incredible, Dom. And clearly doing well for yourself if you can manage to afford *this* place." I gestured around the lounge.

"Ah, well." He smirked, still eyeing me. His eyes dipped to my cleavage, and I felt heat creep to my neck. "Let's sit. Please," he said quickly, gesturing to the chairs. It was as if he realized he was staring and had snapped out of it. "Would you like something to drink?"

"Sure."

He slid the menu my way and a waitress materialized within a matter of seconds. I went with a watermelon cocktail, Dom ordered another bourbon, and when she took off, I focused on the band. The woman was singing a more upbeat song now and revealing a full set of white teeth. A nice transition.

I focused on Dom again. "So why did you *really* leave your number behind?" I asked.

"For this moment," he answered. "To see you."

"Are you sure it wasn't because you felt bad that I was your waitress? Thank you for the generous tip, by the way."

He chuckled. "It's not because I felt bad." A pause. "Would you like the truth?"

"Please."

"It's just that when we stopped talking, I didn't think I'd

ever see you again, but when I did, I wanted to make sure it wouldn't be the last time."

"Aww." I looked into his eyes, as he studied his now empty glass.

"I know. Sappy, right?"

"Not sappy. Really cute," I said. *And romantic.*

The waitress returned with our drinks, and I took a large sip of mine. It was perfectly sweet and fruity. A man with a cape walked through the lounge with white gloves on his hands. I realized he was a magician, based off the oversized top hat on his head and the cape on his back. There were always people like him around—folks who pretended to know magic or read minds, or what have you. The magician stopped at our table, holding a deck of cards.

"Pick a card," the man said, holding the deck toward Dom.

Dom quickly waved a dismissive hand and said, "No, thank you."

"Aw, come on! It'll be a quick little trick!" the magician boasted.

"I don't like tricks," Dom said with more ice in his voice. I couldn't help frowning, and Dominic cut his eyes at me before focusing on the magician again, clearing his throat, and saying, "But thanks."

"Suit yourself." The magician walked off, and I'm pretty sure he'd whispered the word "jerk" under his breath.

"What was *that* about?" I asked.

Dom's head shook. "Nothing. I just don't like magicians or people who believe in magic or do all that witchy stuff. It's silly."

I shrugged. I didn't believe in magic or anything either, but it did serve as good entertainment.

"Did I ever tell you my mom was overly superstitious?" he asked. I nodded. I remembered him constantly talking about it in high school, and now he was bringing it up again. I felt bad about his mom—she died when he was seventeen and it changed his life. He would never tell me the details, but he often said someone was hunting her and wanting to kill her—at least, that's what his mom told him.

"I remember fragments of it, yes," I said.

"There was one time when I was about thirteen or fourteen, I think. She'd found a dead crow in our backyard and went hysterical, Brynn. Swore up and down we were cursed—hexed, even. She said it was proof she was being stalked and hunted by whoever had taken her."

"Your poor mom," I murmured. "You have to chalk that up to her abduction, though. Right? Everyone talked about that for months—how she was taken then brought back?"

The story about Beretta Baker had been all over the news for weeks. Though I hadn't met Dominic yet, I recalled my mom watching the story unfold from the kitchen. She'd burnt my toast one day because she was too busy watching the news. When Dominic's mom returned, she claimed she'd been taken by a religious cult. And apparently that cult "performed spells" on her, used her blood in potions, then sent her back into the real world. I remember thinking maybe those people were treating her like an experiment. They wanted to see how she'd do in the world after pouring all of their witchery into her, but she didn't last long. According to the reports, she'd hung herself and Dominic was the one who found the body.

"Yeah." His throat bobbed and his eyes saddened. I wanted to hug him, but it would've been inappropriate. "Sometimes I feel like it was true—the things she said. Her hallucinations were real to her."

"Perhaps they were," I murmured. And we were interrupted by the waitress again, who brought back a bowl of truffle fries I'd ordered. That was the end of talk about his mother.

The night progressed, the singing lady swapped for a male singer in a sharp tuxedo, and despite how great the music was, our focus was on each other. No more talk about superstitions or abducted mothers. Just us.

I leaned in closer to him, inhaling his cologne, loving the way his teeth glittered in the light, the way my heart raced when he threw his head back to laugh. His throat was so . . . *manly*. I yearned to kiss it, lick it, suck on it.

But then I remembered . . .

My eyes fell to the ring on his finger, and I'd had my third or so drink by then, so the next question flew off my tongue. "Why would you want to spend time with me if you're married?"

The smile that was on Dominic's face disappeared, his eyes more serious. For a second, I wanted to tell him never mind, that he didn't have to answer that question.

But then he said, "We're just two friends meeting up and chatting, Brynn. That's all."

I smashed my lips together. I would've been lying if I said his words didn't sting a little. Then I became curious about who his wife was. What did she look like? Was she sexier than me? Younger? Older? Why wasn't she here now . . . or was she around and due to arrive soon?

Oh, God. I wanted to run away. This was so embarrassing—well, that's what I thought until Dominic leaned in and touched my thigh. My eyes flickered up to his and his mouth was close, the heat of his hand causing a delicious stir in me.

"But perhaps more can come from two old friends wanting to reacquaint themselves again. I'm staying in a private house not too far from here and I'll be frank with you, Brynn. I'm *dying* to be inside you right now." His words came out slow, that honey dripping all over me now, running down and pooling in my chest. "I remember how it was when we were in school. Do you remember? The way you arched your back so perfectly. How you opened up like a flower in bloom. Is it still like that, Brynn? Still warm, wet, and ready for the taking?"

I struggled to swallow and felt an ache between my legs when he pulled his hand away. He drained the rest of his third bourbon and smiled behind the glass, then he placed it down and said, "Gonna run to the men's room. We can head out of here and discuss things further in the car if you're cool with that." He winked on his way, meanwhile my heart was thumping faster than a bunny's foot.

FOURTEEN

JOLENE

Dominic didn't come to bed last night. I waited until well after midnight for him before shutting off the nightstand lamp and forcing myself to sleep. I hoped he would come. Knowing someone was trying to break into the house was terrifying, however the police were around, and we made sure to lock up tight. With that in mind, I eventually dozed off.

When I wake up and prepare myself for the day, I venture down the hallway to take a peek inside the guestroom Dominic sleeps in when we're at odds. He's there, sprawled out on the bed, one leg hanging off as if he'd thrown himself down after more late-night shenanigans.

I don't know what he did last night after the attempted burglary. He said he had to make a call after speaking to Frank, but to who? And why so late? He has so many secrets and it's boggling my mind. It's like I don't know my husband at all. Perhaps I never have.

I leave him be and go to the kitchen to start breakfast: whole grain toast, a freshly juiced fruit, and possibly a scrambled egg or two. I start with getting the fruit ready, slicing into oranges and lemons, and taking turmeric capsules to reduce some of my inflammation. I felt the effects of the croissant all night. I bloated like a whale and tried covering up with baggy silk pajamas. Fortunately, today is a new day and I can cleanse it away.

It's as I'm cracking eggs when Dominic enters the kitchen. I toss the eggshells in the trash bin as he approaches the island counter.

"Wow. You look awful," I say, picking up the whisk.

"Yeah, thanks," he grumbles. "I feel it too."

I look him over in his button-down shirt and creaseless black pants. "Why don't you sleep in?"

His head shakes before I even complete my sentence. "Can't. Lots of work to do at the mansion."

Oh, right. Executive Mansion. He goes there at least three times a week, signing executive orders, for meetings, or to deal with people face-to-face. We were asked if we wanted to reside in Executive Mansion and that was a big *hell-to-the-no*. I refused to live in a place that reminded me of *The Shining*. Not to mention the mansion was so *public*. Besides there being days scheduled for tours, anyone could stand on the streets beyond the wrought iron gates watching us work out, eat, sleep—hell, even have sex.

Staying there would've made me feel like a zoo animal, and it was enough being the wife of a governor and literally no one taking me seriously, despite how hard I work for everything I have. A lot of people like to think that because my dad was rich, I didn't work for a single penny I have when the truth is my father didn't give me access to a trust fund he'd created for *me* until I was twenty-six. And prior to that, while in college, I worked a part-time job at a donut shop while studying because he wanted me to have a grasp on the "real world". He didn't want everything handed to me, and that was fine. I wanted it that way too. I didn't want to be like my mother, who sat around with her hand out and her bottom lip in a pout if she had to lift a pinky.

When my dad died, he left my mom five and half million

dollars plus the house, all their cars, and a few hundred shares from True Oil Co. As for me, he left ten million dollars, on top of my two-million-dollar trust fund and double her shares of the company. I was also left with a major stake in the company, in case all else fails.

Dad died a year after I'd received the trust, and only four months prior to my wedding day. My mom has been pretty pissed ever since and she has not let me live it down. It wasn't *my* fault daddy had little respect for her. She'd made it that way by being so materialistic and sleeping with every man she could whenever he was away. To this day, I don't understand why my dad left her anything in his will. All she did was use him, lie to him. But I suppose she produced me, and I was his most prized creation, so he felt he owed her something.

I'd worked hard, unlike my mom. I didn't sit around judging people or calling them names. I *worked*. I was now owner of a beautiful tea boutique called Regal Tea Boutique. It's a high-end tea shop dedicated to the English tea traditions. We offer afternoon tea sessions every day, and we have a serving counter open just in case someone decides to pop in for a tea to-go. So many people think it's not a real gig, but my business generates hundreds of thousands of dollars. The storefront itself isn't the cash cow, though. We also have a subscription box featuring monthly tea selections with a combination of chocolate, desserts, and recipes.

And when I'm not working at Regal Tea Boutique, I'm attending business seminars and meetings at True Oil Co., my father's company. It was part of the requirements in his will, in order for me to inherit the money. Despite me not having interest in the company, he still wanted me to have a hand in it, make sure things ran smoothly. I visit True Oil in Texas once a month and give them three days of my time. I have an accountant I share with Dominic, who keeps all of our books clean.

"What's wrong with you?" Dominic's voice catches me off guard, and I realize I'm whisking the eggs a little too hard.

I swing my gaze up and he's frowning, switching glances from my face to the hard scrambled bowl of eggs. "Nothing. Sorry." I clear my throat, turning for the stove to heat the frying pan. I need to stop thinking about my mom, the inheritance, all of it.

Dominic sits at the table, scrolling through his phone. I make the eggs, pop some bread into the toaster, and when breakfast is ready, I prepare a plate for both of us and place his in front of him. When I pour juice into his glass, he frowns.

"What?" I ask.

"A little tired of juice. Do we have any coffee?"

"You told me not to get any for a while. You said it's making you crash too hard."

He continues a frown. "Tea, then?"

I nod, getting up to start the kettle. I check the tea cabinet and pull down the tea from the woman at the rally. He seemed to really like it last night.

I pluck out a bag and drop it into a mug. Dominic eats quietly, staring out of the window as I wait for the water to boil. There are bags beneath his eyes. He looks completely wiped out.

"I was thinking about stopping by the mansion today and changing the flowers," I say, and his head whips up.

"You don't have to do that," he tells me without so much as a generous smile. "We have volunteers who come in to decorate each season."

"Yeah, I know but I kind of want to. I saw this beautiful fall bouquet at one of the shops I passed. I can grab some there. You know this Tuesday the mansion is open to the public. The flowers would add a nice touch."

He contemplates that, chewing quickly. "Okay, sure. Swing by on Monday then."

"I have to work Monday," I inform him. And he'd know that if he actually cared about my business.

"Well, Jo, I don't know what to tell you but there's a lot to do today at the mansion. People will be in and out all day. I wouldn't want them getting in the way of you trying to add flowers and whatever else needs doing." He finishes his food, cramming the last bit of toast into his mouth. Carrying his plate to the sink, he rinses it off while staring through the window. Or maybe he's staring *at* it. I don't know. He's acting so strange.

"Fine," I mumble when he finally turns my way.

He flicks his wrist, checking the time on his watch. "I have to go. Call or text me if you need anything. There should be officers and security around all day."

I start to ask if any security will be at the mansion, but it's a stupid question. Of course, there will be. There always are, especially if they know their governor will be there. I suppose I just want this to last longer—us chatting, him being around. All he does is run off. I'm surprised he even stuck around long enough to eat.

He collects his keys from the foyer, and I dump a teabag into a tumbler, drizzle in some honey, and carry it to him. "Don't forget your tea."

"Oh, right." He smiles at me, then places a kiss on my cheek. He then studies me a moment, eyes softening. "I really am sorry about what I said last night, Jo. I get really stupid when I drink. I *do* appreciate all you've done for me. And your tea boutique is great. You deserve more." His last statement seems opened ended. Deserve more of what? Him? Or someone *better* than him?

I don't get the chance to ask. He plants another kiss on my cheek again and says, "See you tonight."

When he's out the door, my body sags to the foyer bench.

Several seconds later, I peer through the sidelight windows, watching Dominic's SUV leave the driveway.

I turn my head the opposite direction, putting my focus on his office door at the end of the hall. My heart dances to life as I stand, dust off my beige yoga pants and matching shirt, and make way toward his office.

With a twist of the knob, I'm inside and determined to find out what's really going on with him.

FIFTEEN

DOMINIC

Dominic couldn't remember the last time he'd been so on edge. Wait, no. Actually, he could. It was the night he'd hung out with Brynn Wallace.

Dominic takes a gulp of hot tea, hoping it'll shake him out of his delirium. He couldn't bring himself to join Jolene in the bedroom after seeing that letter. Something about it made his heart feel like it was in his throat.

Instead of going to bed, he found the mini bar, lined neatly with any alcohol he wanted. Beneath the bar was a wine fridge containing wines that cost well over ten grand each. He found his favorite bourbon, dumped some in one of the empty glasses on the counter, and guzzled it down. It wasn't until about the third glass when his nerves settled and his head, though loopy, felt a bit clearer. There was only one person who could be tormenting him like this, and he was on his way to meet him now.

Two local officers tail his truck as he drives to Executive Mansion. Once there, he walks straight inside, pleased to see two of Frank's security officers on the grounds. When he finds the office, he takes a seat in the large leather chair behind the desk.

He hates this office with a passion. As a matter of fact, he hates the mansion as a whole. It has a mothball smell and creaks even when no one is walking. The wood paneling on the walls is grotesque and the rugs and carpet—though vacuumed several times a week—appear so *dirty*. He knew way before even running for governor—back when it was only a plan—that he'd never sleep in this place. Not because it was built by the hands of prisoners in 1880 (a fact that often made him cringe because he was sure *most* of those prisoners were people of color) but because he couldn't picture a life here whatsoever. This mansion didn't belong to him. It's never truly belonged to *anyone*. And with the paintings on the wall, all those white men staring down at him, he was sure he'd have taken down every single one of them if he'd been forced to reside here.

Dominic leans back in his chair, pulling out a folded sheet of paper. It's the paper from the window last night, now creased and wrinkled from his rage. He wanted to burn it but remembered he needed something to prove he's not losing his mind.

He gazes out the window, then frowns when he sees something unusual out the window. He gets up from his chair, walking toward one of the windows. The sky looks *purple*. Not blue. Not even a pale, gloomy white. *Purple*. And the sun is like a yellow M&M. He squeezes his eyes shut, opens them again, but sees the same thing.

"What the hell?" he mutters.

A door closes in the mansion, snapping him out of his trance, and footsteps thud through the building. A man in all black appears, broad-shouldered with a bald head. He's dark-skinned and much taller than Dominic's six-foot frame. He stares at Dominic with piercing dark eyes, his mouth formed into a tight line. It's Boaz, but why does Boaz look like a demon? Dominic is certain there are horns on that man's head and that his eyes are literal flames. He blinks several times until a clearer presence of Boaz appears.

Behind Boaz is one of the hired security officers with a nose like Pinocchio who announces, "He says there's a meeting with you today, but I don't see him on your schedule, Governor Baker."

It takes Dominic a second to realize this is Paul speaking. Paul is one of Frank's main men. But Paul doesn't have a nose like Pinocchio. Right now, if he turned his head, his nose would whack Boaz right in the face.

Dominic clears his throat, and despite how shaky he's feeling he says, "That's okay, Paul. He's a squeeze in." Dominic gestures for Boaz to enter. "Please shut the door behind you." Paul nods and does as he is told, while Boaz stands on the other side of the room, an angry demon glaring at him. Good Lord, this is really starting to scare him. He feels like his mother, before she was committed. She always said she saw demons and witches. She said they were watching her.

I'm not my mom.

"Take a seat, Boaz," Dominic insists, pointing to the chair on the other side of the desk. His heart races as Boaz comes closer. But up close, Boaz is just Boaz. Not a demon.

Boaz works his jaw, using one large hand to grip the back of the chair. He yanks it back and sits with an agitated exhale. "Is there a reason we couldn't meet at your *private* home?" he asks.

"We couldn't. Jo is there. She'll ask questions. You know she's never liked you."

Boaz scoffs, looking out the window. "What do you want then?"

"You know why I called you in." Dominic retrieves the crumpled paper again, spreading it out on top of the desk. Then he digs in his pocket for the original note from his mailbox. Both are written the same—dark, bold lettering that practically screams at him. The name **BRYNN** written twice.

As if bored but willing to entertain him, Boaz leans forward and studies the papers. "Okay?" Boaz glares at Dominic. "They're just words. They mean nothing."

"They mean *everything*, Boaz," Dominic hisses. "You don't understand. There is someone out there who probably saw you that night."

"Not possible," he retorts in a matter-of-fact tone. "I was careful. No one was around."

Dominic sits forward, dropping his elbows on the table. "Well, there are only three people who know about Brynn, and that's you, me, and that weird-ass cleaner. I'm not sending these notes to myself. Are you doing this?" Dominic's eyes fall to Boaz's large fists in his lap. One wrong word and he'll likely blacken his eye, governor or not.

He almost regrets asking when Boaz sits up taller, cocking an enraged, bushy brow. "Are you out of your damn mind, boy?" he snaps. "I came all the way out here to help *your* ass, just like I did out there. Why would I waste my time doing something like this for both of us to get caught?"

"I—I don't know. For more money, probably? Jolene told me True Oil let you go. It could be blackmail."

Boaz's jaw ticks, but nothing further. He sits back in his seat with flared nostrils. "They did let me go, but I don't need their damn money. I get plenty of that from you, and so does my cleaner. Neither of us have ever spoken about our jobs to anyone. We wouldn't jeopardize ourselves with silly notes."

As much as Dominic wants to ask why Boaz has been fired, he doesn't bother. He can ask later. Right now, he needs to know what the hell is up with these letters. "Did you tell anyone else about that night? Anyone at all? Your wife, maybe? Or a buddy you know at some bar or something?"

"No, Dominic. I didn't. I'm not married, and I wouldn't be that stupid. Look, I've done work like that before, not just for you. It's my job. People like you with your status decide to make a mess and I clean it up."

Dominic nods, wanting to be reassured by that, but not being able to. Boaz is too calm about this. These letters should frighten him too, especially if neither of them are sending them. That means someone saw them. Someone knows.

Boaz had done a job for Dominic way before he'd become governor, back when Dominic had attended a seminar with Jolene at True Oil Co. A man robbed Dominic one night after he'd picked up salads and smoothies for him and Jolene to eat at the hotel. The person took his wallet, his watch, and the wad of cash in his pocket. Dominic was upset about it and had informed the police. Boaz overheard the entire thing and told Dominic he'd get his assets back for him. Within a couple hours, Boaz appeared at his hotel room door, returning his wallet, watch, and wad of cash with a stain of blood on it. "He didn't get far," was all Boaz said, and Dominic had been intrigued by him ever since, despite Jolene's warning to stay away from him.

Boaz was the man True Oil Co. paid to clean up their mess. He was Winton Hart's bodyguard, Winton being Jolene's dad. Winton had used Boaz one too many times to clear up situations his wife Naomi created. She was the true definition of a cougar. She had a thing for younger guys, and all of it gave some of those men the balls to sue the company. Many of them cried sexual assault, believe it or not. They'd say Naomi came on to them and forced them into doing things. Boaz was the one who'd take money and an NDA to those young men and give them the option to either take the cash and shut the hell up or face a worse threat. They always signed and took the money.

But Brynn was a different situation for Dominic. It wasn't about money when he'd dealt with her . . . well, not by the end. With Brynn, this was something he couldn't erase at all with an NDA.

"Have you told your wife about this?" Boaz asks.

"Hell no," Dominic counters, frowning. "And I refuse. She's the last person who needs to know about it."

"Well, do you have any idea who might be doing this?"

Dominic leans back in his chair, thinking. "No one I can think of. Like I said, the only people who know about this are you and me . . . and Brynn, but she's dead."

"Right." That's all he says. No added factor. "I'll stick around town a few days, keep my ear to the ground. Let me know if you come up with anything new. It is possible someone saw you with that woman in New Orleans—someone she knows. Did she mention any friends that night? Anyone close to her?"

"No—I mean, not that I can remember." Dominic runs a hand over his head.

"Well, if anything else comes up, let me know. I'll check out news in New Orleans, make sure nothing has surfaced."

"Yeah. Good idea."

Boaz is out of his chair and lumbering out of the office. The door creaks as he leaves, and Dominic sighs, feeling worse than before he'd arrived. If it's not Boaz, who the hell else can it be?

His mind goes back to Jolene. Is it possible that she knows he was with someone that night in New Orleans and is using that against him? But why would she do that? Why torment him right now? No, it can't be Jolene. She wants him to have the governor's seat again just as much as he does. They've built a life together and despite how often she threatens to leave him, she hasn't. Because she knows he is who she belongs with, and that she'd lose everything if they split apart.

He's felt awful about the times he's cheated on Jolene, slept with other women behind her back. He swore after Brynn he'd never do anything like that again and he's kept that promise—though, it was more for his own conscience than anything. Surely, there's no way Jo knows about Brynn

Wallace? He's never talked about her, never mentioned her. He's purposely avoided bringing up his past with Jolene other than information about his deceased mother. And with the shares, he's careful. He keeps it covered.

No. It can't be Jo. Someone else out there knows the truth. Like that Eden woman from the rally. She knows things.

Something out of the room catches his eye—a tiny person doing cartwheels. He gasps, rubs his eyes, and realizes it's only the mansion's chocolate Labrador puppy, Fred. Someone makes kissing noises for Fred to come to them and he bounds through the mansion to find them.

Dominic can't stand it anymore. He's losing his mind. He shoots out of his chair and collects his keys before leaving the office.

He needs to clear his head.

SIXTEEN

JOLENE

The bottom drawer of Dominic's office desk is unlocked but there's nothing inside it. There isn't even a speck of lint. I don't get it. Why was the drawer locked to begin with if nothing was ever inside? He must've taken it out last night.

Frustrated, I slam the drawer closed and sift through the others, but it's the same thing. Papers, post it notes, sunflower seeds, gum, and a bunch of stationary.

With no luck, I leave the office and find my running shoes in the mudroom. I grab my phone, headphones, and lock the house up behind me. I have to get the hell out of here now before I do something I regret.

Down the driveway, a police cruiser awaits. A woman is in the driver's seat, her window halfway open. It's the officer from last night. Her hair is cut in a blunt pixie cut and her sable skin is smooth beneath the sun. Officer Burnell. She notices me and tosses a wave.

"Good morning, Mrs. Baker!" she sings.

"Morning," I call back, though what I really want to do is walk away and avoid a conversation. That would be rude on my part, though, and I'm not rude.

"Going for a run?" Burnell asks.

"I am. You don't need to tag along. I'll likely run to the coffee shop afterward."

"Okay. Are you sure?"

"Yes, I'm sure. Just keep an eye on the house if you will." I give her my warmest smile.

Her head bobs, proud to make it her duty. "Absolutely."

I place my headphones on and turn the opposite direction, jogging out of the neighborhood. I move along the pavement as cars pass by and the sun beams down on me while Jazmine Sullivan sings about busting her man's car windows. I think about yesterday, my time in the car with that croissant. All those calories. All that guilt.

I jog faster, taking a trail that leads to The Bean Bar. It's my favorite coffee shop and they also serve amazing smoothies. They also have a famous in-house brownie that's topped with powdered sugar. *Ugh.* Why the hell am I thinking about brownies? Wasn't the croissant enough?

I lower the headphones, so they hang around the back of my neck and catch my breath outside The Bean Bar. Once inside, I order myself a blueberry and banana smoothie and pay with Apple Pay. As I wait in the pick-up area, I scan the shop and pause on a familiar face at a table near the windows.

It's that woman from the rally who gave us the tea. Eden, I believe. She's sitting on a laptop, scrolling through it while heavily focused on the screen. Her hair is in two giant dark puffs atop her head, and she wears a black kimono over a dark-green cotton jumper. She also wears boots that have some dried mud around the bottom. Though I'm in no mood to talk, and more so curious what the hell was in that bottom drawer of Dominic's office, I do believe I should thank the woman for her tea.

"Blueberry banana smoothie," the barista calls, placing my drink order on the counter. I collect it, along with a straw, and weave through the tables. Eden's eyes flicker upward, and she does a double take when she notices me. I start to wave but she rapidly shuts the laptop.

"Hi—I'm so sorry to interrupt you. Eden, right?"

"Yes. That's me," she answers. There is nothing welcoming about her tone. I've clearly interrupted something and have now become a nuisance. Knowing it makes me feel icky. I was always a nuisance to my mom—the child often in her way.

I work to swallow. "I was just popping over to say hello. And to thank you again for the tea you offered us at the rally. Dominic seems to really enjoy it."

Eden softens then, the sharpness melting from her shoulders. "Does he?"

"Yes. I haven't had the chance to try it yet, but I will soon."

Eden studies me so long I shift on my feet. In a way, it's like she's reading me, trying to figure out if I'm lying. I'm relieved when she gestures to the chair on the opposite side of her table. "Please, First Lady. Have a seat."

I can't help smiling as I take the seat. I'm still finding it hard to get used to the title of First Lady, even after four years. The sunlight pours through the open windows, bathing my already sticky-hot skin in its warmth. I unwrap my straw and stick it into the lid of my smoothie, taking a long sip to cool down.

"I'm so sorry if I interrupted you," I say again as Eden looks me deep in the eyes.

"It's no big deal. As a matter of fact, you spared me from reading a scathing review about my tea," she replies, and her frown returns. "Someone claimed one of my bestsellers, Honey Chai, tasted like plastic." Ah. So that's why she's upset. I'm pleased to know it has nothing to do with me.

"Don't you hate that?" I ask, sympathizing. "People can be so rude."

"Yeah. It's awful." She picks up her coffee cup, taking a

long sip from it. "It's really nice to see someone so official in a simple place like this. Do you live around here?"

I nod, though I shouldn't really answer that. Especially after the attempted break-in last night. "A few miles away, yes."

"Nice." She looks me all over. "Were you working out before coming here? You're a little sweaty."

"Yep. Took a jog. Had a few calories I needed to burn." I force a laugh and shift in my seat as remnants of the croissant sing in my gut.

"Hmm. I can't tell. You look great."

I can't help smiling at that. If only she knew the exterior doesn't match the interior. I still feel like that chubby girl, the one no guy ever wanted. The one whose best friend was donuts and cakes and chocolate chip cookies. Instead of letting her know all that, I say, "Thank you. I work hard to maintain myself."

A silence passes between us, then Eden leans forward and asks, "Can I do a palm reading on you?"

That catches me by surprise. I peer around the coffee shop, then look at her again. Her eyes are bigger, brimming with curiosity. "In *here*?"

"Sure. Why not?" she shrugs. "It only takes a few seconds."

I always pictured palm readings in tiny shops, behind closed doors so no one could hear. "Um . . . okay." I lift a hand and place it palm-up on the table. Eden straightens in her chair, taking my hand in hers with a whirl of excitement. She studies my palm, lightly tracing her fingers over the lines.

"You've always wanted to be married," she says, not taking her eyes off my hand. "But you're not happy with your marriage right now."

My heart drops with its next beat. I watch her face, how she frowns, and her full, pinkish-purple lips slightly purse.

"There is something hidden in your marriage—a secret that prevents you from achieving happiness. Whatever it is, it will drive a wedge between you and your husband." Eden's dark eyes flicker up to mine and I can't help staring back into them. She releases my hand and I pull it away, dropping it in my lap.

"Why are you not happy, Jolene Baker? What secrets do you have?" Eden's questions seem harmless, but each one pricks me like a thorn, and each thorn lodges itself into a different area: the chest, the ribs, the heart.

"I—I should go." I'm already standing. I shove my chair in and leave the coffee shop, but as I round the building and pass the windows where Eden sits, she watches me go, and I swear she's smiling as she brings the rim of her coffee cup to her lips.

SEVENTEEN

DOMINIC

Dominic has no idea where he's going. He's contemplated going to the park, taking a walk, but he swears on everything the sky is still purple and there's an M&M in place of the sun. Not to mention, every person he passes in his vehicle appears to be staring at him. His security team asked if he wanted them to tag along but he turned it down. He needs a moment alone.

Perhaps these letters have truly done him in. He was never supposed to turn out like his mother, but her schizophrenic behavior may have bled into him after all. It's in the DNA, really. He thought he could escape it, but he's wrong. And why now? He's so close to winning the seat again. He can *feel* it.

He pulls into the parking lot across the street from The Bean Bar and kills the engine of the car. He drove past his private home and thought to stop there and have a chat with Jolene. There was a time when he could tell her everything and she'd take him into her arms. She'd hug him and tell him everything would be okay and that they'd get through it. But this was something he was sure she'd *never* forgive him for. When that thought occurred, he drove past the house instead.

Now, he sits a moment, closing his eyes and letting the

worries rinse away in the darkness behind his eyelids. But the letters burn a hole in his pocket. He should set them on fire. Or perhaps he should take them to one of the sheriffs or police officers and have them test for fingerprints. But if he does that, won't it spark questions? There are no officers he fully trusts, no bad apples who will do things under the table for him. They're out there, he's sure, but he's a *good* governor. He's for the people and refuses to let the bad apples reign. No, the last thing he has time for is questions. They'll ask who Brynn is. Things could get messy.

He opens his eyes, sitting up in the seat again and gripping the wheel. The sky is blue again, and the sun is a bold blinding blip in the sky. *Normal again.* He should get back to work. He starts the car up, but before he can put it in Drive, he spots a familiar person leaving The Bean Bar.

She saunters out with a laptop case tucked beneath her arm, her hair in two large poofs. She wears dark clothes again that are completely unappealing to him. It's the witch from the rally. What was her name again? Enid? Eva?

His pulse quickens as he whips out his phone and zooms in to get a clear picture of her face. He snaps one, sends it off to Boaz's burner phone with the words: **We need to figure out who this woman is**, then continues watching as an Uber pulls up to the curb and the witch climbs into the backseat.

He's not sure what takes over him. He has more important things to do with his life. He's the state governor for goodness' sake, but nothing feels more important than following this witch.

He tails the car until it pulls into the lot of a retro motel called Scarlet Star. He doesn't drive into the lot, but he does swing onto the road next to it and watches the witch exit the Uber, climb the stairs, and prance into one of the rooms of the motel.

Wait a minute. Why is she in a motel? Why doesn't she have a house or an apartment? Could this mean she isn't from

North Carolina? What Boaz said hits Dominic like a pound of bricks about Brynn possibly having friends who knew about their night together. Had Brynn told anyone about their date? If she had, that person would know who he is . . . but why would they be bothering him *now*? Even if they are curious, why not come directly to him? Surely, they weren't there the night he and Boaz dealt with Brynn. What happened with her wasn't even supposed to happen. It was an honest mistake.

Dominic drives away from the motel with more questions than answers. His phone rings, and it's Melissa calling to let him know about a meeting at 12:30. He tells Melissa he'll be there and along the way, it becomes clear to Dominic that he'd underestimated this witchy woman. Now, he must find out *everything* about her.

EIGHTEEN

BRYNN

It took me a minute to gain my composure after Dominic's invitation to his private rental. When Dom rounded the corner to reach the restrooms, I sat back in my seat and took a huge swallow of my sugary cocktail. As I took another gulp, I noticed a white light emanating from Dom's seat.

His cellphone.

He left it there, or perhaps it fell out of his pocket when he stood.

I glanced toward the restrooms, then at the phone again. I wasn't sure what took over me in that moment. I wanted to see what was behind that screen, get a look at his life and figure out what his wife looked like. I shouldn't have cared at all about this woman. I mean, I'd been flirting with her husband all night and was possibly even going to sleep with him. And perhaps I was a glutton for punishment because I knew beforehand that nothing good would come from checking this man's phone, but I grabbed it anyway.

The phone had a code, one I saw him enter several times throughout the night–060383. His birthday. What? I couldn't help watching him type the pin in. It was hard *not* to look when he sat so close to me.

The phone unlocked, and the first thing I saw was a text message from a person named Jo. I didn't know if Jo was a man or woman, but their message said: **Can you squeeze a call in?**

I scrolled through their texts until an image appeared and at the sight of it, it felt like an elephant had stepped on my chest. Jo was a woman, and not just *any* woman. This was his *wife*.

The photo appeared to be professionally taken of Dominic and Jo. Jo wore a navy-blue dress with mid-length sleeves, while Dominic wore a suit to match. His arm was draped around her waist, while she leaned into him with a hand on his chest as they both smiled at the camera. An American flag was in the background, along with a sofa that couldn't have been comfortable and was clearly there for display purposes. Gold drapes hung from the corners. Below the photo was a text from Jo saying: **Look, babe. Campaign pics came in! This one is my favorite!**

My nose wrinkled as I frowned at it. It wasn't that the photo *wasn't* nice, because it was, but it was his wife who I couldn't stop staring at. She was beautiful, with round apple cheeks and coily dark hair. Her sable skin was aglow as she smiled into the camera, her brown eyes soft and wise. She'd seen things. Been through things. I could tell. But beautiful, nonetheless, so why was Dominic wasting his time with me?

I swiped off the photo and scrolled through their messages, seeing texts like:

I'm so proud of you, Dominic.

You're going to soar, babe. I just know it.

Don't forget to wear the black suit today with the red tie. And the dressing for your lunch is on the top shelf of the fridge.

Chicken risotto or chicken parm tonight? Can't decide. Help?

Love you, Dom Bomb!

Before Dom returned, I put the phone back in place and requested another drink from the waitress. Dom was out of the bathroom but stopped to speak to the waitress while fishing out his wallet. While he did, I whipped out my phone and snapped pictures of the stage, where the performers were, then some of the details on the walls, the portraits. Finally, I took a selfie, making sure to capture Dom in the background as he handed the waitress a credit card. I looked amazing, and I could see him clearly, despite the dim lighting so I sent the image to Shavonne, who responded with: **Wait . . . isn't that the ex you told me about?**

I huffed a laugh and darkened the screen. I would fill her in later, but for now I loved the idea of her wondering what was going on and I couldn't wait to spill every single detail in a few hours.

I didn't realize Dominic was back until he sat next to me, leaned in, and placed a finger beneath my chin. His hands smelled like floral soap with a splash of cinnamon.

"So, what do you say?" he asked with his lips close to mine. "Shall we go to my place for a reunion?"

NINETEEN

JOLENE

I take a scalding hot shower—one I hope will wash away this morning's conversation with Eden. What the hell is wrong with that woman? How can she poke and prod at my marriage like it's a lump of clay in her lap?

Anger ignites within me as I step out of the shower, snatching down the towel from the rack and leaving the bathroom. I change into new clothes—tan palazzo pants and a silky pink blouse—and apply makeup and perfume before heading to my home office.

When I'm aggravated, I work to distract myself, so I log into my laptop and check my emails first. It's as I'm deep into a supplier's email, that my phone buzzes on the desk. I glance at it and instantly want to bang my head on the glass desktop when I see the name. Mother.

Not Mom.

Not Mommy.

Mother.

I let the phone ring a little longer, then draw in a breath, swiping the green phone symbol and bringing the receiver to my ear.

"Hello Mom," I say, doing my best to keep my voice neutral.

"Jolene, I'm flying in to see you today," she says. No formal greeting. Always so direct.

I frown. "Why?"

"Because I'm your mother and I want to check on you." She sniffs on the other end, but not like she's sick or sad. More like she's annoyed with this conversation and ready for it to be over already. But I know my mother. She does *not* fly all the way from Houston, Texas to North Carolina just to *see* me.

"What trouble are you in now?" I sigh.

"What are you talking about? There is no trouble. Stop being ridiculous. I just want to see my daughter. Is that so bad?"

Yes, it is bad. I don't want to see *her*. My life is much, much easier without her in it. "I'll have to get one of the guest-rooms ready."

"I'm at the airport waiting for my flight now," she continues, ignoring my last statement. "I should be there in a few hours."

She hangs up without a goodbye and I grit my teeth, slouching back in my chair. I try and rack my brain for what it could be this time that she's gotten herself into.

One time, she'd come to me because thousands of dollars had been withdrawn from her bank account, but only because she was stupid enough to give some guy she was sleeping with her account numbers. She'd claimed it was fraud, that she'd been hacked, but was it a hack, really? Or was she just dick-whipped and stupid?

Another time she'd come by because she had a dream that I was pregnant. When she told me, I couldn't help laughing in her face. The last thing Dominic and I were doing was having kids. There was way too much going on with him in office and with my career.

"It's not much of a career is it, though, Jolene?" my mother

asked, and I wanted to push her out of her chair. The truth is, Dominic never wanted children. I'd pushed him once about having kids and he grew upset before finally confessing that he didn't want children because he didn't want them to grow up with an absent parent. He cared too much about his career and wasn't sure he'd be able to make the time. He didn't want the kid to suffer because he was so busy, and I could empathize with that. My father was also busy, and I feel like I'd be a much better human if he were around more.

I close the lid of my laptop and leave the office, finding the guestroom she often uses that faces our backyard and pulling out clean sheets from the closet.

TWENTY

JOLENE

Three hours later, the doorbell rings and I open the door to face Naomi Hart, my mother. It's just like her to be wearing an oversized yellow hat that reminds me of an accessory belonging to Curious George's caretaker.

Her dark hair falls in thick curls, giving her a wet-and-wavy look. She tips her head, and I can tell she's had more cosmetic work done to her face. Her light-brown skin looks too tight around the cheeks and mouth. And of course, she's dressed in all white. Her signature color, as if she's prepared to be someone's bride at any moment.

"Hi, mother." I step back to let her inside. She brings her Saint Laurent purse closer to her chest, her nose turned up as she peers around the entryway. I hate when she does that, like *I'm* going to steal it away from her. I have more money than she does and can buy a closet full of those bags if I wanted to. I swear she only does it to spite me.

She continues a careful sweep of her surroundings. She's never been happy with my house. She thinks I've settled and that it's not what I wanted, but the truth is all she cares about is designer clothes and jewelry, foreign cars, and giant mansions. Our house is more than enough for us. Five bedrooms, four and a half baths, a kitchen I adore with copious amounts of natural light, and two home offices so Dominic and I can work in peace when we need to. We have a terrace we love to use on spring and autumn mornings, especially for brunches. Not to mention our living room is to die for, and one of my favorite places of the house with its suede brown furniture and cream walls.

When I close the door, I notice her lock on something, a painting I bought firsthand from a local artist named Judo De-Santis. It's an abstract piece of the Raleigh skyline, with splashes of orange, lavender, and blue, as if the sun has set over the city and drowned everything in color. I had the portrait framed in gold.

"How much money did you waste on this?" she asks, turning her head a fraction to eye me.

"Do you want some coffee?" I walk past her to get to the kitchen. I am not about to play her games.

She follows along, her stilettos clicking on the marble floors. I start the coffee maker and steal a glance at her as I go for the crème and sugar. She removes her large hat, placing it on one of the barstools and then fluffing her hair. *So superficial.* When the coffee is ready in the pot, I pour two mugs and carry them on a tray to the dining table. I would offer to share it with her at the nicer dining area that overlooks the deck in our backyard, but she doesn't deserve it.

Mom sits in my usual chair, so I take the one Dominic claims. I start to reach for the crème, but she swats my hand. "Dairy will make you bloat," she snaps.

I stare into her light-brown eyes and how stern they are. Those eyes used to intimidate me. Not anymore. I gently push her hand away and grab the crème, pouring a hefty amount into my mug and then collecting the tiny jar of zero calorie sweetener. She cocks a brow at me, then shakes her head, clearly repulsed. Who cares? It's sugar free.

"Why are you here?" I ask, stirring the milk and sweetener.

"If this was a matter that could have been discussed on the phone, do you think I would be in this God-awful place?" she counters.

I avoid a frown, stirring faster.

She sets her purse down on the table and fishes through it until she pulls out a set of folded papers. She slides them across the table to me and I study her a moment. Could this be another court order on her behalf? Someone else threatening to sue True Oil Co.?

"What is it?" I ask.

"Just open it." She purses her lips, picking up her coffee mug and inspecting the rim.

I roll my eyes, collecting the papers and opening them. None of it makes sense at first. They're just numbers—money, clearly. Connected to bank accounts, possibly?

"What am I looking at here, Mom? Come on, stop beating around the bush."

"Those, Joey dear, are offshore accounts in your name."

"What?" My eyes flicker to hers. "I don't have any offshore accounts."

"Really?" She narrows her eyes. "Do you not remember what your father said in the will about illegal or suspicious activities with his money? All of this is being funneled into these accounts because you sold some of your shares from True Oil Co."

I slide the papers back to her. "Well, that's impossible because I don't have any offshore accounts and I haven't sold any shares to anyone. Why would I do that?"

Mom studies my face a moment, searching for the truth. I suppose she's been good at that when it comes to me. She can tell when I'm lying, but for some odd reason can't tell when *she's* being scammed by some twenty-year-old guy she's sleeping with.

"I spoke with Anita. Our stockbroker, remember?"

"I know who Anita is," I mutter.

"Well, she informed me that the money you got from selling one of your shares is now being invested into two accounts. One of them is in Italy. Another is in Mexico."

My heart thumps a bit as I pick up the papers again, reading the numbers. The amounts range from $10,000 to $15,000. All sent in increments every three or so months.

"Well, it must be a mistake. I don't have any offshore accounts."

"Are you doing something illegal with this money, Jolene? Because if you are, what you received will come to me. I'll have control of your finances since you'll be deemed unfit to handle it."

My heart races a smidge faster as I study the numbers again, then I look at her and she folds her arms across her chest, a smug grin twisting at her mouth. This can't be happening. Of course, my dad left a clause like that in his will. Always the man to make me face the real world, reminding me even from his grave that he's in control of my money and that one fuck-up will leave me broke.

"That is . . . unless *someone else* is doing this," Mom says, and her voice has a lilt to it, like she knows something I don't.

I shift my gaze to hers, hands shaking as I hold her eyes. Her grin transforms into a deep frown. "What's that husband of yours been up to lately?"

"H-he wouldn't do this," I whisper. But of course, it'd crossed my mind. The only person who has access to my accounts and my shares is Dominic. In fact, we have a joint-brokerage account that we decided to set up when I received the inheritance from my dad, but how didn't I catch this? And why the hell didn't Anita tell me? Unless Dominic went to her personally and approved the money transfers . . .

One thing about my mom is she will double check *everything* when it comes to me. Never have I met a person so determined to see my fail. In no way should she be allowed to even *look* at my accounts, but she and Anita go way back, so

I'm not surprised Anita gave her this. For all I know, my mother bribed her for it.

"How can you be so sure he wouldn't do this?" she demands. "I told you from the beginning there was no way a man like *him* could be that interested in *you*. He clearly only hung around for the money, now look at him. Governor of an entire state, living in an overpriced house. Prancing around and doing whatever he wants with your money." Her eyes narrow, and I'm shocked to see crow's feet form around her eyes with how much Botox she receives. "You opened a brokerage account with him, didn't you?"

"He's my husband," I inform her. "It was a mutual decision, and I want it to be that way in case anything ever happens to me."

"And that is my point. Say something does happen to you, *daughter.*" She says the latter word with so much ice it causes goosebumps to break out on my skin. "Where will all that money go? You have no children, no siblings—it's just *him*. And I'm starting to think it's that way for a reason." A smirk claims her lips as she leans back in her chair, taking a long sip of black coffee. She's delighted to see the panic swirling in my eyes, the uncertainty, the sheer despair.

She finishes her coffee, then collects her purse and rises to her feet. "I won't need the guestroom. I booked a hotel in the city for the night. You should speak to your husband, though. Clear all of this up and figure out why he brokered that share. Otherwise, I will have to step in, take this to the family lawyer, and I'm certain you don't want that."

Through my peripheral, I see her pick up her big hat. Her heels click on the floor again as she trots away, and as if her visit isn't bad enough, she says, "Oh, and lay off the milk and sugar, Joey dear. Your face is getting pudgy again."

TWENTY-ONE

BRYNN

I felt sick during the drive to Dominic's place. He mentioned it was some place he was renting not too far from the Ritz. He sat behind the wheel of a beautiful Audi, chin up, cloaked in confidence. Golden streetlights flashed across his face, accentuating his firm jaw and sharp nose. Jazz music spilled from the speakers, and I was momentarily soothed by the saxophones and bass guitars swelling inside the car.

My belly was full of liquid, and my head was starting to hurt from one too many drinks, plus I'd hardly eaten a damn thing but truffle fries in the lounge, but riding with Dominic was nice. For a moment, I pretended I was his wife and that we were on a getaway trip to pour love and attention back into our marriage.

I needed to sober up a bit, so the throbbing in my head would pass. I suppose it is true that once you hit your thirties, your body can't handle all that crazy stuff or partying like before. I used to be able to down a whole bottle of vodka in one night. Now? Vodka was completely out of the question. I was lucky if I didn't wake with a hangover from a bottle of wine.

The car slowed to a creep as Dominic stopped in front of iron gates belonging to a neighborhood. The letters **MV** were built into the gates. He typed in a code on the box, the gates split apart, and he drove until he'd approached a smaller gate.

Withdrawing a black device from the cupholder, he pressed a button on it and the gates swung open with ease. He took the driveway up until a two-story European cottage appeared. I tried not to gawk like a loser as I drank it in. The exterior was cream with an even addition of gray stone. Brown shutters lined most of the windows on the first floor, and a two-car garage was attached to the left. Gold lights rose from the ground, highlighting the house and making it appear like a luxurious castle. This was definitely a place only the upper-class could afford to rent. I couldn't even imagine how much Dominic was paying a night to stay here.

I climbed out of the car, staggering on my heels as I took in my surroundings. The house was on a single-laned street. Other houses were nearby, gated just like this one. Gates inside of an already gated neighborhood. Interesting.

"You've rented *this* place?" I asked as Dominic locked the car and headed for the front door.

"Oh, yeah. One of my good friends let me rent it for the weekend. Gave me a discount." He winked at me over his shoulder. "Pretty nice, right?"

"Nice? Please, it's stunning." I could never afford a place like this, whether it was bought or a rental.

Dominic opened the door and flipped a light switch on in the foyer to illuminate the area. He smiled as he walked deeper into the house, and I followed him. We stopped in the kitchen. It was spotless, with thick white quartz counters, chrome appliances, and little signs on the walls that I was sure the buyer had gotten from Hobby Lobby. They were the cheesy kind—signs that said things like:

Rise & Shine It's Coffee Time, Let's Eat, and **Yum.**

He showed me the living room, which was set up beautifully with ivory furniture, a beige rug, and a wooden coffee table that I was sure cost a fortune. A wide flatscreen TV was mounted to the wall and on either side of the TV were shelves filled to the brim with books and trinkets. Dominic then showed me where the minibar was and prepared us drinks from it.

"Any requests?" he asked.

I shouldn't have, but there was something about being in this house alone with him that pushed me into a dangerous zone. "Vodka," I said.

He prepared it for me, and I guzzled some of it down.

"Wait until you see the master," he murmured, and it was now that I realized how close he was as he stood in front of me. I could smell the bourbon on his breath, feel the heat of his body on mine. He escorted me upstairs with a gentle hand pressed to my lower back, and when we reached the landing, he stopped at double doors at the end of the hallway.

He pushed them open, and luxury screamed from every corner of the room. The bed was made with white sheets and a plush brown duvet. Behind the bed was an upholstered wall, bordered with iron designs on each side. I had the urge to lay on the bed, cozy up with the pillows. Off to the right was the master bathroom. One of the lights was on, revealing a rainfall shower, a clawfoot bathtub, and white marble.

"Is that drink okay?" Dominic asked, gesturing to my almost empty glass of vodka.

"Yeah, but I probably need some water right now," I told him. I needed to sober up.

"You've got it." Dominic left the room for only a moment and while he did, I sat in a single upholstered chair in the corner and started unstrapping my shoes. He returned with a glass in hand containing yellowish liquid, while I was halfway unstrapped.

"Hope you don't mind. My feet are killing me."

Dom laughed, turning to me with the drink in hand. "Make yourself as comfortable as you want." He offered the glass to me and said, "Apple juice."

I would've preferred water, but this would do.

"Here. Let me help you." Dom set his drink down on the dresser and lowered to his knees. I couldn't help smiling as he unstrapped the shoe I hadn't gotten to, undid the buckle, and removed it, setting both shoes aside. Once done, he stood and collected his drink, taking a swig.

I sipped my apple juice, mildly annoyed by yet another sweet and fruity beverage, but it was better than taking in anymore alcohol. My eyes turned to Dominic, who was already looking at me. There was heat in his eyes, flaming with lust. He sipped his drink, and I did mine, but couldn't help fidgeting.

"The Brynn I know didn't waste time getting to the point," he said with a hint of a smile. He moved in closer so that his groin was practically in my face. He was referring to high school Brynn, the one who didn't know a damn thing about sex and didn't care about the consequences.

I huffed a laugh. "Things change, I suppose." And they had. Though I was having a great time, I wasn't so quick to drop my panties for anyone, even if they were my ex. Plus something about this entire night niggled at the back of my mind. A warning was more of what it was. If I crossed into this forbidden territory for him, there wouldn't be any going back. This was a *married man*, which meant I would never come first to him and that did not sit well with me.

He stood. "Perhaps some music." He fished his phone out of his pocket and went to the stand near the TV, where a speaker was plugged in. Once he'd connected the Bluetooth, Ginuwine played, and I wanted to throw up—not because of Ginuwine's voice, but because the nostalgia struck the hell out of me. My vision blurred a bit as Dominic snapped his fingers to the beat then spun around to face me. He took a swig of his bourbon, then undid the top button of his shirt. "You remember this song?" he asked, chuckling.

"Of course, I do." I forced a laugh. "Differences" by Ginuwine. It was a song we played on repeat while acting like horny teenagers in my bedroom whenever my mom worked third shift.

I couldn't believe he was playing it. He truly was treating this like some high school reunion. Like, okay, I get it. We were high school lovers and all, but let's not make this childish.

He approached me, bringing me to a stand and collecting me in his arms. I tried smiling and enjoying the moment, but I couldn't bring myself to do it, and I was pretty sure that was my own fault. I'd allowed the niggling in the back of my mind to swim to the forefront.

I couldn't stop thinking about his damn wife and ever since reading those messages and seeing her photo, I only felt regret. While he was sitting next to me in the lounge, flirting and being charming, she'd been texting him all night. He hadn't responded to any of her messages, and I figured that was a courtesy to me. He was married, and his wife assumed he was happy. She had no idea he was showering another woman with drinks and attention . . . or that he was now alone in a house with said woman.

I realized in that short moment in the lounge—when he'd run off to the bathroom and I filled myself with dirty knowledge—that he'd likely done this before. Found a woman he was interested in while away from his wife, paid for drinks, then took her to his rental or hotel room. I instantly felt shame and then pitied myself for ever coming here to meet him. It didn't matter that I was his high school love. To him, I was just another woman he could get lucky with.

At first, I didn't care that he was married because the wife was unknown. I had this stupid notion in my mind that I was there first, so he'd choose me. He'd fall for me again and leave her, whisk me into his life, ease my troubles, and give me everything I ever wanted. It was such a stupid idea to have because he'd been married to this woman for *years*, while he'd only known me for two while we were young. Plus, the way you get a man is exactly how you lose him. I of all people should've known that.

It's so much easier to detach yourself from anonymous things because they don't mean shit to you, but because I *saw* his wife's face, because I *saw* how happy she was with him, how excited she was for him to come home so she could share a simple dinner with him, and how she supported his career, I realized I couldn't be that person who sabotaged their marriage. Because at the end of the day, all Dominic would do is throw me under the bus to save his ass if he got caught and, frankly, I was worth more than that.

We'd already taken things too far by meeting at the lounge and even further by venturing to this fancy house to be alone. I would be ruining someone's life because of my selfish decision to ignore that wedding band on his finger. It was almost like he *wanted* me to know he was married—like he knew it would make me want him more. Most men hide their rings, but not Dominic, and I couldn't help wondering why.

I knew what it was like for someone to be cheated on through my own mother. All my father did was lie and cheat. It drove her crazy. It made her thin, depressed, but she couldn't do much about it because he paid the bills while he was around. He ran the show. But for some odd reason she was still surprised to know he was leaving her for another woman. As if she hadn't seen it coming. As if she weren't aware that he was a total piece of shit who had no respect for her.

I refused to be the other woman—the homewrecker, the destructor, the manipulator. Did I want out of this poor life of mine? Yes. Did I want more for myself? Absolutely. But this wasn't the way to do it. It felt dirty and lousy and cheap, and you don't think about the consequences until you're forced to face them.

What my mother went through was literally enough to kill her. She drank herself to death, choked on her own vomit. I found her body when I visited from college for winter break, and the only reason I visited is because she wasn't answering her phone. No one had heard from her, so I bought the cheapest plane ticket I could find on such short notice and flew back.

Is it so bad to say I didn't want to pass that energy to someone else if I didn't have to? This Jo woman seemed nice, and I didn't want her turning into a drunk and choking on vomit too.

Certain about what I had to do next, I turned to Dominic as he finished unbuttoning his shirt and said, "I'm sorry. I can't do this."

TWENTY-TWO
DOMINIC

Dominic doesn't go back home that night. He'd received a notification that someone rang the doorbell and when he checked the doorbell camera, he saw a woman he couldn't stand being around. His mother-in-law, Naomi Hart, in a big banana hat. He wasn't sure what Jo's mother was doing in North Carolina or what she wanted, but one thing was for certain. He did *not* want to see her.

Instead, he lied to Jolene and sent her a text saying he had business to finish and would likely be all night. He doesn't, really, and instead goes to Fox Trot for some drinks and to read over his speech. He needs to decompress after the week he's had. Fox Trot is the only place around that isn't open to the general public. You must have a membership to join, so not many people here bother him. Most of the members venture into Fox Trot to do the same thing he does: drink and avoid socializing. That's why he likes it.

He does have to go to Greensboro tomorrow afternoon to show his face for some marathon in support of heart disease, and for all Jo knows, he's decided to leave tonight so that he can be better prepared tomorrow. He's glad he at least keeps extra clothes stored at Executive Mansion. Might as well make use of the place somehow.

As he sits at a table sipping bourbon, he receives a text from Boaz: **No face ID in NC. Will check NOLA.**

Good thing Boaz is onto the witch. Comforted by the update, Dominic sinks into the back of the burgundy leather bench, taking another long sip of his liquor. He'd contemplated the idea of Boaz blackmailing him but realized it wouldn't benefit Boaz at all. He was the one who'd done the dirty work, not him, and Dominic was willing to lie if it meant saving his own ass.

After replying **OK** to Boaz, Dominic opens the Instagram app and logs into the account he uses under a fake name. He doesn't post on this account, and his other is his official governor account, but Melissa handles that more than he does so he doesn't bother with it. His fake profile doesn't even have a picture, but that's perfect for when he needs to check things out, like the profile of that Eden woman. What did she say her username was again?

Dominic clears his throat as he types the name *goddesswitch* into the search bar. It yields some results but none of them are her. He taps a finger against the edge of the phone, thinking. Then he types in mysticgoddess. Still, none of the users show Eden.

"I'm on Instagram under the name mysticcgoddess. Two c's."

Eden's voice runs through his mind again, and he types in the previous username, but with two c's this time.

"There you are," he murmurs under his breath. She's the only person on the app with that username. He taps her profile, glad it's public. The profile picture is an unsmiling, moody selfie. Her lips are a dark plum and her hair is a wild afro. Black eyeliner is heavy around her eyes.

He scrolls to check out her pictures and mixed between

posts about the benefits of her teas is a photo of *him*. Dominic's heart beats faster as he taps his photo. It's him on the stage at the rally he had two weeks ago. He's speaking to the crowd, microphone gripped in hand. He wore the Carolina blue shirt and white tie that day. Jolene picked out the shirt. If this was taken two weeks ago, this woman has been lingering for a while.

The photo is shocking, but it's Eden's caption that makes him uneasy.

THIS MAN IS A FRAUD.

"What?" he gripes. He scrolls to see if there are more photos of him but there aren't. Aggravated, he logs back out of the app and drops the phone on the table.

Who the hell does this woman think she is? *He's* the fraud? She's the one pretending to be some voodoo tea-selling witch. None of what she believes in is real.

He rolls his eyes, picking up his drink and taking a big swallow. His carries his gaze toward the bar, focusing on a woman in a tight-fitting maroon dress. She's standing at the counter, slightly bent over as she speaks to the bartender. Dominic's dick pulses to life as he studies the woman's ass. He takes another slow sip as the woman finds her table. When she sits, her eyes connect with his and a smile sweeps over her lips. A sigh escapes him as he peels his gaze away. He's promised himself to be good. To stay out of trouble. Dealing with other women is why he's in the mess he's in right now.

He polishes off the bourbon, collects his iPad, and leaves the bar after dropping a tip on the table. As he approaches his truck, he notices something stuck beneath one of the windshield wipers. The sheet of white paper flaps with the breeze and his throat instantly closes in on itself when he spots the dark ink bleeding through the back of it. Snatching the paper from the windshield wiper, he surveils the parking lot. Two men stand near Fox Trot, smoking cigarettes and eyeing him. One of them waves with bright eyes, as if aware that it's the governor, and he nods at them before climbing into his truck right away.

He sits behind the wheel for a second, the paper crumpled in his shaking hands as he watches the men finish off their cigarettes and head back inside. When they're gone, he drops his head and finally finds the nerve to open the paper. His mouth goes bone dry when he reads: **CHECK YOUR TRUNK, BAKER**

"Shit." He shudders a breath as he balls the paper up and places it in one of the cupholders. His eyes venture to the rearview mirror, as if someone will be waiting for him in the backseat, but there is nothing but leather seats and a slash of orangey-gold light from the streetlamp.

He steps back out of the car, taking cautious steps toward the trunk. When he pops it open, he's aware of the gray gym bag and tall sack of golf clubs, but there is something back here that doesn't belong. Something he's *never* placed there or seen before.

A small black grocery bag is tied loosely by the handles. He picks his head up again, looking for the person who could've done this. How could they? His truck was locked.

Wiping his hands on the front of his shirt, he reaches forward and unties the bag. He spreads the bag open wider, the sound of swishing plastic colliding with his thudding heartbeat, and when he sees what's inside it, he cups his mouth and stifles a shout.

Inside the bag is a dead, bloody crow. Its beady eye stares up at Dominic, allowing him to see his own blanched reflection. But it's not the crow that makes him want to sink into the earth and never come up for air.

It's the photo attached to it.

He lifts the bloody photo and it's an image of Brynn at Galveston Lounge. And standing behind her, face clear as day, is *himself*. He's looking off a bit in the photo, like he's speaking to someone else, but it's definitely him.

Hands shaking, he flips the photo over and written in black ink are the words: **SIN AFTER SIN. LOOK HOW DEEP YOU'RE IN.**

TWENTY-THREE

JOLENE

Dominic is away, wasting time at the Fox Trot. How do I know? Because about six weeks ago, while he was sleeping, I turned on the location sharing on his phone. I know exactly where he is, and when I saw him pinned at the Fox Trot, I had every urge to drive there, curse him the hell out, and demand answers about these offshore accounts.

I couldn't bring myself to do it, though. After the visit from my mother and checking all of my accounts with True Oil Co., I gave Anita a call and she confirmed that a stock had indeed been sold. She gave me the name of the banks the money from the sale are going to, but the accounts can only be accessed in person.

"So, you're telling me I have to fly to Mexico and Italy just to figure out where the hell my money is going?" I paced the living room with an early glass of wine in hand.

"I'm afraid so. There's nothing I can do from my end other than put a freeze on the deposits."

"I never did this, Anita," I told her. "There is nothing in Italy or Mexico for me! Hell, I've never even traveled there." Unfortunately. Italy was on my bucket list though.

She sighed on the other end. I could hear her children in the background, yelling as they played. I hate that I'd interrupted her day off, but I needed answers.

"Listen, Joey." The way she said my name gave me a zing of nostalgia and I paused mid-sip. Only Daddy and Mom called me Joey. It was more endearing from Daddy. More of a patronizing thing from my mother. But Anita was basically like family, so she called me by that name too on occasion. It made me feel like a real person again, not just a shell of who I was. "Talk to your husband, okay?" she insisted. "I'm not sure if you're aware, but he's the one who contacted me about setting up the deposits for the sold share. He told me this was something you two had planned because you were struggling financially. Said you wanted him to handle it because you were ashamed. Your signatures were on the papers for the company approval and with him having joint access, I figured this was something you wanted. I realize now that I should've called to triple check. I'm sorry."

"But I . . ." I stood in the middle of the living room, blinking back tears. I refused to cry and instead drew in a breath and closed my eyes to cool the burn behind them. "Put a freeze on the money until I figure out what's going on."

"I will tomorrow." She paused. "And by the way, he cashed in a few bonds too. That money plus the money from the brokered share are going into *three* accounts, Jolene. Not two. I didn't tell your mom this, but the third one goes to an account in South Carolina."

"South Carolina?" I repeated.

"Yes. Have a good night," Anita said, and the call ended.

That was hours ago. I went to bed with a bottle of wine, finished it off, then cried myself to sleep. I'd sent a text to Daphne asking if we could meet on Monday, and she said to swing by for lunch.

Now I'm at my best friend's house, seated on the plush

brown sofa in her living room. One of the two casement windows ahead is open, letting in a fall breeze. The breeze is soothing as it brushes across my skin. I wish it could calm my nerves, but it's useless. All I can think about is Dominic, his lies, the accounts, even the attempted break-in. There is so much chaos going on and I feel like I'm in the middle of it all, yet I'm blind to what's really happening. I'm watching the hurricane spin toward me, threatening to rip everything I've built apart. I have a bunker, but I'm the idiot standing outside, waiting to be swept up because I want—no, *need* to know more about how dangerous it is.

I sit with my arms folded, leg bouncing just as Daphne walks my way from the kitchen. I watch her as she places a tray of tea and miniature sandwiches on the coffee table. She looks really pretty today in a pink dress, hair pulled into a neat, braided ponytail. She pours tea into each cup then offers one to me on a saucer. I unfold my arms and take it, avoiding her eyes.

"You ready to talk now, or what?" she asks after pouring a drizzle of honey into her cup. I suppose it was rude of me to come inside with a measly *hello* and saunter straight to the living room. She knew I was upset before arrival, but still. I have more manners than that.

"I'm sorry for how I walked in here, girl," I murmur. "I don't know if I'm ready to talk about it yet." I sip my English tea as it is. No need to sweeten up my already sour mood. I want to cling to this anger, so that I can confront Dominic just as I am when he steps through the doors of our house. He went to Greensboro on Sunday and returns today, likely in an hour or two. He has a meeting around four but should be home afterward. I only know about the meeting because I called Melissa to see what his schedule was like.

"It's just . . . the money, Jo," Daphne murmured. "He

spoke to Anita behind your back. Forged your signature. Sold a whole share and cashed in *your* bonds right under your nose. He's using *your* money and doing whatever he wants with it."

"I know." I finally look at her, and her lips are pressed, sympathy swirling in her brown eyes. "He told Anita we were struggling and that I was ashamed and wanted him to handle selling that share. He fucking lied. I just don't get why he'd go to such an extreme. If he needed money for something, he should've talked to me."

Daphne sighs, crossing her legs and sitting back with her teacup raised in front of her. "I know it's not my place, but I don't think it was wise of you to open a joint brokerage account with him. As soon as you told me he'd asked about it, I just had this feeling, you know? I mean, even back in college, JoJo. The way he was suddenly so intrigued by you. He'd never noticed you before—not that it's a bad thing. It just came left field is all. It was always like he was after something with you. I don't know."

"He had no interest in me before because I was unattractive and chunky. Literally no one noticed me."

"Well, there was one person. And it wasn't for the better."

"Ugh. Yeah. But that's different." I place my tea on the glass coffee table, trying to ignore the thought that I too felt like Dominic come out of nowhere. This gorgeous man with a bright smile and delicious body. I figured I was blessed, that I deserved the attention after all my hard work in the gym and in school.

"Stop talking about yourself like that, Jo. You've always been beautiful, no matter what size." She pauses, and her brown eyes become more serious as she studies me. "How much do you think you know him, really?"

"How much do you know your husband?" I counter, and I instantly regret it because she flinches, as if I've slapped her.

I drop my head, the shame swallowing me whole. "I'm sorry, Daph. I didn't mean that. I'm sorry." Her question has triggered me, reminding me of my mother's visit yesterday. Interrogating me, my marriage, my life, but it's not Daphne's fault any of this is happening. It's mine. All my mistakes have amounted to this. She's only trying to comfort me.

Daphne clears her throat, setting her tea on a saucer, then picking up one of the sandwiches. I've struck a chord with her, I can tell. She's doing that pursed lips thing—the one that makes her look slightly like a fish because she's trying to fight whatever words are rolling around in her brain.

"You're right," I tell her, placing a hand on her arm. Her lashes flutter as her eyes find mine. "The more time goes on, the more I feel like I don't know Dominic at all."

"You need to get to the bottom of what's happening." She picks up a plate and collects another sandwich. "Are you hungry?" she asks before biting into the one in her hand.

"No." And I'm really not. After my mother said I looked pudgy, I don't want to eat a thing. And to punish myself further, I stepped on the scale this morning (something I've not done in *months*) and have gained four pounds. It could be water weight, but still. I have to do better.

"I should get going," I tell her. "I'm supposed to select flowers for the mansion today."

Daphne makes a gagging noise, like she's going to vomit, and I laugh.

"Stop it!" I can't fight my smile. "It's my job, okay? Being the state's first lady and all."

"I know, I know. It just seems so *pointless* for you. Don't y'all have volunteers to do that stuff?"

I stand with my purse. "We do, but the public loves to see stuff like that. They like to be reminded we're regular people too."

She raises her teacup to me. "To each their own."

"The mansion will be open to the public on Tuesday, that's the *only* reason I'm going."

"Do you, girl." She stands with me, seeing me out.

I open the door, but before I go, I ask, "You won't mind me reaching out to Ricardo so he can work on something for me, will you?"

Her eyes stretch for a fleeting second. Then her head shakes, and she says, "No, I don't mind. Do what you have to do."

TWENTY-FOUR

JOLENE

When I'm inside my car, my phone rings in my purse and I dig through it. When I find it, there's an unknown number on the screen with a location in South Carolina.

"Hello?" I answer.

"Hi Mrs. Baker. This is Angelique from Charleston Credit Union." The woman has a southern accent that's so thick I almost can't discern it, but when she says the name of the bank, I light up. I found a point of contact for the South Carolina bank Dominic is having some of the money sent to. They were closed for the weekend, but I sent an email to have someone contact me. "I'm calling because you asked for access to an account?"

"Hi, Angelique. Yes, that's correct," I say, pulling out of Daphne's driveway.

"Okay. I will be able to help you with that. For verification purposes, can you please tell me your date of birth and account number? If you don't know the account number, I can look it up by your social security number."

I give Angelique Dominic's social security number and birthday and within seconds she speaks again. "Are you the spouse of Mr. Dominic Baker?"

"I am."

"Oh, okay. I'm afraid that I cannot give you access to this bank account, ma'am. There is an internal note stating that the account is private and only to be accessed by Mr. Baker himself and one other person, however this person can only make in-person withdrawals."

"Who is the other person?" I ask, gripping the steering wheel tighter. "Shouldn't it be me? I'm his wife."

"I understand that, ma'am, however I cannot give out the account holder's private information."

"You've got to be fucking kidding me," I mutter.

"If you would like access, the account holder can add you as a joint member at any time."

"Angelique, is it possible that I can at least know the name of the person who makes withdrawals in person?"

Angelique hesitates and I push harder.

"Look, I'm not sure if my husband has told you, but the money being deposited into his account originates from one of mine and I did not approve any of these transactions going into your bank. I would hate for your bank to get into any legal trouble because of a minor mishap."

"I understand, ma'am. Please hold while I connect you to my manager." The line clicks to bubbly Muzak, and I continue driving, working my jaw.

"This is Hiro Marietti," a deep voice says after a few minutes tick by. "Am I speaking to the wife of Mr. Dominic Baker?"

"Yes, you are."

Hiro apologizes for the inconvenience, and after several holds, gathering information from me, and confirming that the money *is* originating from my share account with True Oil Co., he apologizes again. I ask for him to add me as an account holder, to which he tells me, "I can certainly do that, but I will have to confirm this with Mr. Baker. Is that okay?"

I hesitate, but only for a second. By the time they get to

Dominic, I'll have all the information I need and there will be no denying it. It'll be a good thing the bank calls him—a wakeup call, so to speak. He'll know I'm aware of his little secret. Well, one of his little secrets. Who knows what else that man is hiding. "Sure, that's fine."

"Very well. Is there anything else I can assist you with?" asks Hiro.

"Can I have the name of the person making physical withdrawals from the account?" I request, parking in the lot of the flower shop.

"Let me have a look." Hiro pauses a moment, and then he's back. When he says the name, I'm confused as hell. The name sends a burst of cold through me and for a second I'm paralyzed in my seat, staring blankly through the windshield. "Is there anything else I can do for you, Mrs. Baker?"

"N-no. It's fine, Hiro. T-thank you for your time."

I hang up quickly, then google the name Hiro just offered me. When I find their social media, my heart sinks to the pit of my belly.

I've had the urge to scream since my mother's arrival, and this time nothing can stop it. I belt one out in the confines of my car and slam a fist on the steering wheel.

TWENTY-FIVE
DOMINIC

Dominic still can't bring himself to go home. It's been two days and not a word from Boaz after sending him the photo of the witch. He sinks back in his chair behind the desk at Executive Mansion, eating a sandwich Jim brought to him. He's done with his meetings for today, fortunately, so he just sits and waits for time to pass.

It's nearing six in the evening and he's certain Jolene will be expecting him home soon. She doesn't usually work on Mondays either, so he can bet she'll have a dinner ready, along with a bottle of wine to share. Then he'll hear her talk about her mother, and she'll most likely complain about some rude thing Naomi has said to her. She'll cry and he'll console her while trying not to roll his eyes the whole time.

He picks up the waxy paper his sandwich was on and balls it up, tossing it in the trash bin before leaning back in his chair to gaze out the window. He spots joggers and dog walkers, mothers pushing strollers, and he finds delight in knowing he governs every single person walking the streets. They all pay the tax dollars that fuel his dreams. He's in control and damn, is it amazing.

But there is one little thing to fix. His stalker.

He's not sure who is doing this to him, but the dead bird in the trunk has been tormenting him. He tried forgetting about it yesterday while in Greensboro, but as soon as he rode to Raleigh with security tailing his car, that bird and photo weighed heavily on his mind. He wasn't sure what spooked him more, the dead animal in his trunk that only meant bad luck, or the fact that someone had broken into his car when he *always* kept it locked, and without so much as a broken window or tampered lock. Keeping the doors locked was not only common sense, but a superstitious thing his mother had engrained in him. *Never leave a door unlocked or you'll be kidnapped, Dominic. Look at what happened to me? Taken then returned. It can happen to you too.*

His mother was a lot of things, but she wasn't a liar and though she'd gone off the deep end, she always kept his best interest in mind . . . for the most part.

It made him wonder what else this stalker could break into. He checked security cameras around his private home while out of town, and other than Jo coming in and out of the house, no one else lingered around. The police were still on duty morning, afternoon, and night, so he had a feeling his stalker wouldn't bother him at home for a while.

It was being in public that was the risk. While he was at the marathon, he felt like he was being watched by *everyone*. Truthfully, he was. Everyone loved seeing the governor, chatting with him, taking pictures with him. But beneath it all, he felt the scrutinizing stares from the people who clearly hated him and all the decisions he'd made for the state. And how could he know if any of them were the stalker? Watching his every move? Waiting to strike?

It's easy to know where the governor will be these days. People eat that shit up like candy, wanting to know every detail, what the governor had for lunch, if he worked out, if he drinks coffee or tea. Dominic is no president of the whole country, but being governor still has its heat. Which is why he has to get to the bottom of the mysterious notes.

His eyes venture out the window again. The sun is setting, and the sky is now a burnt orange with whispers of blue. At least it's not purple anymore. He lowers his eyes from the sky to the people again, but his heart lurches in his chest when he notices a person standing on the other side of the street. They wear all black and stand near a speed limit sign. A hood is on their head so he can't see their face at first, however when they lift it, his heart nearly fails him because the face is familiar.

Dominic rises out of his chair and hurries toward the window, nearly tripping over the rug, but as he does, a bus rolls past, blocking the person from view. When the bus is gone, so is the person. He steps back, gluing his back to the wall, and sucking in deep breaths. His hand goes to his chest, and he feels the thundering beat of his heart against his palm.

He's losing it, just like his mother. Doctors told him schizophrenia is genetic, that he can develop it too. He's losing his mind and seeing shit, that has to be the case, because there's no way in hell he just saw Brynn Wallace standing on the other side of the street looking at him.

She died four years ago.

And it's all his fault.

TWENTY-SIX

BRYNN

"I beg your pardon?" Dominic's voice was closer. I couldn't figure out how he'd gotten across the room so quickly, but he was there, and I gasped. I told him I couldn't do this—sleep with him. I had to get out of this house before I made a major mistake. "Wait a minute. Where are you going, Brynn?" he asked as I slid my feet back into my shoes.

My throat felt thick and my head heavier as I leaned over. I tried focusing on strapping the shoe, but my hands were being stubborn, and my fingers felt too loose.

"Do you think you can take me back to my car?" I asked.

I sat back up and picked up the shoes instead. I could put them back on later.

"Why?" he asked with a dry laugh. "I thought you wanted to be here."

"I know, but . . . I . . . I can't do this, Dom." My words came out slurred. When I looked for him, he was in front of me and despite my vision being blurred, I could see that his head was in a slight tilt.

"Oh, come on. You gotta stay," he insisted. His hand was on my hip, but I shook my head, snatching myself away. As I did, I stumbled backward and the backs of my knees hit the edge of the bed, leaving me no choice but to fall. "Look at that. That's better," Dominic murmured, then he was on top of me.

"Dominic, no. I said I can't do this. I have to go." I pressed a hand to his chest, but it was such a weak attempt. I couldn't understand why my body was working against me. I'd had a few drinks, sure, but not so much that I couldn't control my own body.

"You don't have to go anywhere," he said, cupping my breast, groping it. "You want this, right, Brynn? You want me, yeah?"

I blinked up at him as he gripped my wrists and forced them to the bed. I had the urge to fight, to kick, to scream, but I couldn't. My throat was dryer, my head spinning. It felt like there were two versions of him above me.

And then it hit me—something I thought would *never* happen to me. Something no woman ever thinks will happen to her.

"You . . . you spiked my drink," I mumbled. "You did. You . . ." Why else would he have given me apple juice instead of water? God, I was so stupid.

Regardless that I was dizzy, I couldn't ignore the smile on his face. "Just a precaution," he murmured, then he shoved my dress up to my waist. I heard a door creak open, and Dominic got off of me to look back.

"I see you made it," he said.

"Oh, look at that," another man rasped. "Look at those thighs. Lace panties. She's ready for some fun, huh?"

"Brought her here, just like you asked. You'll speak to Reba, right? I need her in my corner—if she doesn't back me, I'll lose the campaign."

"Yeah, yeah. You've got it. I'll talk to her," the other man said hurriedly.

The room kept spinning. The bed dipped and someone appeared above me. A white man. I couldn't make him out at first, I was so dizzy, but some of the features were familiar. I'd seen him before. The man at Franco's. He was sitting with Dominic. John—that was his name.

Rough, sweaty hands tore at my clothes, then yanked my thighs apart. A deep growl erupted from the man's throat and his fingers pushed my panties aside, poking and prodding at my vagina.

"How does that feel? You like that?" John asked, leaning forward until his mouth was near my ear. He smelled like stale whiskey and cigars. "Women like you are my weakness. A *sin*, really. A man of my nature shouldn't want a little brown thing like you, but I can't help that I do. There's just something about you—something about *all of you*—that makes my dick as hard as rock."

I turned my head, spotting a person standing in the corner. It was Dom.

"Please, Dom," I croaked.

"Shh, shh, shh." John cupped my mouth, pressing his body down harder on mine. Dominic turned to face me, eyes glimmering, a smile on his lips. "I'll take care of you."

I wanted to scream but my body wouldn't do a damn thing I needed it to. I tried lifting my leg to kick the man off, but he kept groping, touching, *licking*. His hot, disgusting tongue circled around my earlobe before sliding down to the bend of my neck.

I laid there while he poked and prodded, then he took down his own pants. He flipped me over like I was a ragdoll, hoisted my hips upward, and that was the last thing I could remember about that night before the drinks and the drugs took over and everything faded to black.

When I woke up, my mouth was tacky, dry, and sweet. I released a groan as a strip of light blazed on my face. It was still dark outside, and the strip of light was coming from the bathroom where the door was cracked open.

It took a few minutes for it all to come back to me—the lounge, the watermelon drinks, *Dominic*.

I gasped and sat up in the oversized bed. My head throbbed when I tried to move and there was an ache between my legs and in my ass. Then I remembered coming to this place. The apple juice. Dominic on top of me and then . . . *someone else*. Some man . . . who was it?

I told Dom I had to go—that I couldn't do it. Someone else came in . . . I passed out.

My bottom lip trembled as I climbed out of the bed. I was completely naked but couldn't remember how any of my clothes got off. My dress was in a puddle next to the bed, so I picked it up, throwing it on quickly and then scanning the room for my purse.

I gasped when I spotted a figure sitting in a chair in the corner. A side table had been pulled in front of him.

Dominic.

He was shirtless with black sweatpants on. His eyes were locked on me like I was a target.

"Dom," I said, aiming to keep my voice steady. In the dark, his eyes were dark and serious. The look he wore *terrified* me. Where was the smiling, upbeat man from earlier? The fun, charming one? "What are you doing? Why are you sitting in the dark?"

"Just waiting for you to wake up." He had something in his hand that was long, thin, and silver. I reached for the lamp on the nightstand, switching on the lightbulb, and saw a pen in his hand. On the table in front of him was a small stack of papers.

"I need you to sign these," he stated, pointing the end of the pen at the papers. There was no life to his voice. It was empty and without sympathy. It made my skin crawl.

"Sign what?"

He slid the papers across the table, and I approached cautiously, wrapping my arms around myself. It hurt to walk. My ass was so sore. I wanted to cry because I'd never felt so much pain in one place. I scanned the paper and the words **NON-DISCLOSURE AGREEMENT** popped out in bold font.

"What the hell is this?" I demanded.

"For you to sign. Not sure if you're aware, but there will be big things happening for me soon. I can't have mild affairs interrupt that."

I narrowed my eyes as he placed the pen down on top of the papers. "*Mild affairs*? What the fuck are you talking about, Dominic! You drugged me and had someone come in to rape me!"

"Lower your voice." It was a command, one that felt threatening.

"You don't tell me what to do, motherfucker. Where is my purse? I'm leaving!"

He eyed me a moment before rising from the chair. I backed away as he walked around the table with the papers to open the top drawer of the dresser. I'd never put my purse there. He must've hidden it on purpose, so I'd wake up to this—forced to face him.

Withdrawing my purse, he carried it with him to the table and sat with it on his lap. "You'll get your purse when you sign the papers," he said,

"I'm not signing shit," I snapped.

"Damn it. I knew you'd make this difficult. It's like high school all over again. You're so fucking annoying." He pinched the bridge of his nose and shook his head. "Just sign the goddamn papers, Brynn. Once you sign, I'll hand you fifty thousand dollars and it'll be a done deal. We'll never speak of this night again."

The fifty thousand dollars made me pause. My mind went back to Franco's, how Dominic smiled at me, charmed his way back in, left his number. He sat across from John, who didn't seem to have the least bit of interest in me at the time. What did these men discuss when I walked away? Was John asking about me, pushing Dom to reel me in and liquor me up so that *he* could have his way with me? It made no sense that they'd dragged me into this. I had nothing to offer them. I was just a waitress.

I swallowed, remembering Dominic say someone else's name before I blacked out.

"Reba," I whispered. "Who is Reba?"

Dominic grimaced. "Don't worry about it."

"I'm not signing those papers," I said. "I don't even know what they're for."

"It's to protect myself and second parties in case you decide to go around blabbing about the events from tonight."

"I will be blabbing, asshole. Right to the cops." I felt my eyes watering, but I bit back the tears because I was not about to let this asshole see me cry. "Give me my purse so I can go."

"Sign the papers."

"Does your wife know you go around drugging women and letting men rape them? Does she know you throw fifty grand at them then hide behind nondisclosures?"

That calm demeanor of his faded, only a little. His mouth twitched, eyes more like steel. Talking about his wife struck a nerve. *Good.*

"Sign the papers," he said again.

"Fuck you," I spat. "You think you're some kind of god—that you can do whatever you want to people now because you have a little money in your pocket? I don't know who the hell you think you are, Dominic, but I'm not rolling over and taking your shit!"

"You wanted to be with me, Brynn. *You* agreed to meet me at the lounge. *You* shared drinks with me. *You* agreed to come with me to continue the night and there were plenty of people who witnessed it who will happily attest to it. Whatever you say to the police won't be enough for what everyone saw a few hours ago."

I swallowed hard and wanted to drop to my knees in that

very moment and weep. He was right. He was so right. I'd even told Shavonne that I was meeting someone. There were waitresses, staff, bartenders. Even the clerk in the hotel lobby saw us together and spoke briefly with Dominic before we left.

"Why would you do this to me?" I cried, voice hoarse. "Why? That man, Dominic. *That man*—you just stood there and let him do that to me!"

"Nothing happened that you hadn't done before. Don't take it personally, Brynn."

"The drugs are still in my system," I reminded him. "Whatever you put in that juice is probably still there. I can go now."

"You're not leaving until you sign." It wasn't a challenge. It was a threat. I saw it in his eyes.

Anger took hold of me with a vice grip. It was hot and throbbing and uncontrollable. I could've cried, could've wept, could've begged him not to make me sign those stupid papers just to get my purse back, but I was *livid*. And I couldn't just walk out of there without my purse. Say I did go to the cops and tell them everything, he could hide it, lie about it. My purse had my phone inside it, my wallet, my ID, my credit and debit cards—hell, even my car and apartment keys. And he was keeping my belongings hostage, just so he wouldn't get in trouble for being an accessory to rape.

Why couldn't he just let me leave? Why didn't he have sympathy for me? Why did he drug me before I even had the chance to refuse? How many women had he done this to, just so he could walk away squeaky clean and like a saint?

My rage was hot and unfiltered, and it was with my rage that I rushed toward him to fight for my purse.

"What the hell are you doing?" he snapped, trying to push me off as I struggled for the bag. I slapped him with one hand, and it stung my palm, but I was glad because if it hurt me, it *definitely* hurt him.

That seemed to piss him off. His eyes locked on mine and were on fire. His lips were tight as he fumed. How dare I slap his delicate, handsome face? *The asshole.*

I gripped the strap of my bag, but he held on tighter. He managed to stand up, tower over me, but I kept fighting, kept hitting. I even landed a punch to his chest.

"Stop fucking hitting me, Brynn!"

"Fuck you!" I screamed, and he snatched me up, cupping a hand around my mouth.

"Just sign the fucking papers!" he growled, but I kept kicking and trying to scream because making a scene and getting the police here somehow was better than signing those damn papers. Perhaps someone would be walking by and could hear me? Sure the neighborhood was big, but it was also quiet. All I knew was signing that nondisclosure would've been like giving my soul to the devil, and I refused. This man, once a childhood love, had drugged me, let a man rape me, manipulated me, and I was *not* about to go down without a fight. I didn't have much to live for, but I damn sure wasn't letting him steal my dignity.

I bit the hand he had cupped around my mouth, and he hissed and cursed beneath his breath. "You stupid *bitch!*" he hollered, and he shoved me away with so much force, my forehead slammed into something sharp and hard.

I wish I could say I got back up and fought harder, but instead, everything went black again.

TWENTY-SEVEN

JOLENE

I jump in my seat when a door slams.

I'm sitting in the living room with a glass of wine in hand. Papers are on the table with all my proof to blast Dominic for what he's done. I want to be calm, collected, but of course the slam of the door catches me by surprise, and I spring out of my seat.

I peer around the corner and spot Dominic in the foyer, furiously flipping through the mail. He tosses the envelopes on the table and shrugs out of his blazer. I stand and wait for him to notice me, and when he does, he frowns, then shakes his head and ventures to the kitchen.

Fine. We'll have this discussion in the kitchen.

I collect the papers from the coffee table and walk down the hallway in my bedroom shoes. Dominic's head is buried in the fridge as he asks, "Why didn't you cook?"

"Because I didn't know what time you'd be home. You never got back to my text from earlier."

He retrieves a sparkling water and shuts the fridge. "Busy day."

"Yeah, I bet."

He cracks the drink open, eyes slightly narrowed at me. I

place the papers on the table as he gulps down some of the bubbly water. "We need to talk, Dominic."

His eyes shift to the papers briefly before sliding up to me again. Then he turns for the fridge once more, opens it, and takes out leftover chicken and green beans. He opens the microwave and it's now that I've realized my error.

He pauses, staring at the box in the microwave—donuts from Sal's Donuts. Wendy, the florist at BeeKeep Flowers, gave the donuts to me. She wanted to thank me for choosing her shop to select flowers for the mansion and I took the box out of kindness. I didn't eat a single one . . . not that I didn't want to. And I suppose that's why I'd left them in the microwave—because maybe I would indulge in one just for the hell of it. The donuts were the least of my concerns when I got home though. I literally threw them into the microwave so I could run to my office and print off the information about the accounts Anita sent me.

My heart beats faster as Dominic takes out the box and turns with it in his hand. "What is this?"

I wet my lips with my tongue, searching for words, but they all fail me.

He steps around the island counter, and I know when his switch goes off. It wasn't this way when we first met. I didn't see this switch go off until after we were married, when we lived in a condo in downtown Raleigh together.

The signs are all here right now.

His eyes darken.

His nostrils flare at the edges.

His jaw ticks repeatedly.

He was clearly angry about something before arriving home, but this discovery has fueled it. He's trying to change the subject, shift the blame on me somehow. He knows I have something on him. He *must* know. Surely the bank in South Carolina got in touch with him by now but I had the leverage, so I didn't care.

"I know you sold several hundred of our shares from True Oil," I say, and am surprised my voice remains steady. Perhaps the wine has allowed me to perform that miracle. "Why didn't you tell me you'd do that?"

"Shares? You really want to talk to me about shares when you've got a half dozen box of *donuts* in our microwave?" He says the words donuts like it's a drug—like I'm doing meth or something. Dominic opens the box, studying the contents. "Got a little bit of everything in here, don't you, Fat Jo?"

The nickname causes a stir in me. I haven't heard it since college. That name was like having bricks thrown at my face. I shared the detail of that name with Dominic because I thought I could trust him, that he'd understand. Instead, I'd given the information to him like a loaded gun, and he uses that weapon against me every chance he gets.

"Dominic, they were a gift from a florist. I didn't even eat them."

"But you wanted to, I bet." He takes one of the donuts out, a powdered one. Some of the white powder sprinkles to the waxed floor as he raises it in the air. "How about this one, huh, Jo?" He chucks the donut at me, and it hits the center of my chest. "Or this one?" he takes out a chocolate glazed donut, chucking it. I duck just in time to miss it, but that sparks his anger even more because he marches toward me with the box and dumps the entire thing on my head. He smashes the box and donuts down so that it meshes into my braids.

"Stop!" I shout, but of course that's not enough. He's now swiping his hands inside the box, collecting leftover glaze and powder on his fingertips. He grips my face with his other hand, clutching it tight and then shoving the glazy-powdered fingertips into my mouth.

"That's what you wanted, right, Jo? Sure, you want to talk about selling shares and finding a fault in me, but don't want to talk about how much of a *pig* you are." He shoves his fingers down my throat, causing me to gag. I try snatching my face out of his hand, pushing against his chest, but he holds onto my face tighter, forcing me back until I'm wedged between him and a wall. "Do you want to be a fat bitch again, huh? Do you want to look like a disgusting sack of shit? Because that's what you'll be if you keep eating this shit, Jo. Trying to hide it won't hide the fat that takes you over! We have a reputation to uphold and if you are going to be *my* wife, you will not be some fat, sad, dumpy bitch! I will *not* walk around with a big-ass wife, do you hear me?" He drops his hand to my throat, clutching tight and blocking my airways.

I claw at his hand. "Dominic. Stop."

But he doesn't stop. He holds on tight, and I can't breathe. Darkness seeps around the edges of my vision. I struggle to say his name, while he watches me with a wicked glint in his eyes. Then, when I think he won't relent, he lets go and I sag to the floor, sucking in breath after breath.

"Get your shit together, Jo," he grumbles, and he may as well have spit in my face. He doesn't look back as he walks away. Doesn't care that I immediately drop my face into my hands and sob.

He flips the switch for the kitchen light and leaves me behind in total darkness.

TWENTY-EIGHT

DOMINIC

Jolene is curled up on the couch when Dominic leaves. He can't stay in this house with her. She wants to be a reckless fat-ass, so be it, but he won't tolerate it.

He collects his keys from the foyer and leaves. He and Jolene have an apartment they rent out from time-to-time in the city. The whole month is blocked off for renting due to the campaign. Sometimes he'll invite a lady friend over to help reduce his stress. Jolene just doesn't do it for him anymore, and it's not that she's unattractive or anything. No, his wife is stunning. But she's a true pain in the ass. He'll stay there for the night, but it'll be best to spend it alone and with no distractions.

He feels he should apologize, but what for? She knows how important the campaign is and how much appearances matter. She can't go around eating every single thing she sets her eyes on. How will that make him look? What will people say when they see her big behind in a dress? No, the woman he's with *has* to look the part—she has to be worth all the sacrifices.

As much as Jolene will cry and be sad, she'll get over it within a few days like she always does. Because that's Jolene

Hart-Baker. Quick to forgive, always wanting everyone to be happy with her, to praise her, to treat her like some abandoned puppy. She doesn't realize how great she's had it growing up. She had a rich father who invested money in her future. All he had was a mentally ill mother who was kidnapped when he was ten, then returned on a random day when he was thirteen. That was the first time he'd lived with his uncle in Greensboro. The second time would be when he turned seventeen.

She popped up, Dominic's uncle Ben called the police, and she told them everything. A man had abducted her after a shift she had at the gas station and a cult sunk their claws into her. On top of that, they fed her all kinds of bad, processed foods to fatten her up. He almost didn't recognize her when she came back. She had to have been fifty pounds heavier and she looked absolutely *disgusting*. When she miraculously returned, the story was all over the news. The police never could find this cult she spoke of and sometimes Dominic wondered if they were even real, or if his mother had made it all up in her head. He wanted to believe her story, but sometimes he thinks she purposely abandoned him and only came back because she had nothing left.

Regardless, Dominic felt like his life would change for the better—that his mother would get book and movie deals, that they'd get a snazzy car, move into a mansion, and make a shit ton of money. But the reality is *none* of that happened. His mother was too chaotic to bother with the press because she was too stuck in her own head. She refused medication and wasn't admitted to a psychiatric detention until she ran a woman off the road because she assumed the woman was being attacked by a red demon.

No, Jolene has had it so easy. She should be glad that he found her. Bettered her. Gave her a reason to live. He was there that day on campus when she was crying in the library. He heard her on the phone as she spoke quietly, moaning about her weight. He saw her the next day when a luxurious Range Rover pulled into one of the parking lots and she climbed in the backseat. It was then that Dominic took it upon himself to look into this girl. He found out her name, then he found out whose daughter she was. Jolene Hart was a walking money bag. He didn't jump on the opportunity quickly, of course. He played it cool, kept a distance, and when the time felt right, he wanted it to feel like happenstance for her—that they'd stumbled into love and that she was all he could see. Plus, she really did have a nice ass, even before she'd lost a bit of weight.

He kept her going at it, shedding the pounds, blossoming into a beautiful woman. He told her his goals, his plans, all of which involved money, and she was there for it all. She wanted to succeed with him, to be at his side, to watch him win. She never cared for copious amounts of attention, but he did, because a specific type of attention could get him paid. Many would consider Dominic a predator. He wasn't that. He just knew what he wanted, and he went after it.

He considers this as he walks into the studio apartment and flips a light switch on. He drops his bag on the bed against the wall, scanning his eyes around the space. Jo had hired someone to deck out the apartment—pale blue walls, a large flat-screen TV, a sparkling kitchen made of silvers and marble. The little center pieces on the coffee table and dining table are Jo's touch.

He strips out of his clothes and makes his way to the shower. He lets the hot water run over him and when he feels thoroughly clean, he gets out and wraps a towel around his waist. He pours himself a bourbon and carries it to the patio, focused on the skyline. It's beautiful at night.

His eyes fall to the parking lot of a gas station across the way. The neon red sign of the station beams in the night. An old silver Beetle is parked near the end of the lot. Two people sit on the back of the vehicle, dressed in dark clothing. He sips his bourbon, realizing how out of place the car is. His apartment resides on the classier side of the city, so this car shouldn't be hanging around. It doesn't belong.

The people sit still for a long time, and it takes him a minute to realize they're looking right back at him. A frown takes hold of him as he watches the people toss a hand up and wave.

"What the hell . . ." He backs away, entering the apartment again. Must be some randoms. Of course, if he can see them, they can see him.

He goes for his bag on the bed to take out clothes, but it's as he's taking a shirt out that he sees the envelope on the pillow. It wasn't there when he first walked in, and knowing this causes his chest to tighten.

He sets the bourbon down to pick up the envelope. There are images inside it—pictures of Jolene . . . and *him*. In one of the photos, his hand is closed around her throat, and he's visibly angry while Jolene stares up at him, veins on her forehead, her hand clutching his as she chokes.

He wheezes, dropping the glass on the ground. It shatters into pieces, but he doesn't move. This image was taken from outside their house, right through the kitchen window. He snatches out another picture of Jolene standing on the terrace, sipping from a coffee mug. Then another of her sitting in a coffee shop, but this image is what terrifies him most because she's not alone. She's sitting at the table with that witch from the rally. All the images are small, as if printed on a portable printer.

He notices black marker bleeding through a sheet of paper in the envelope and snatches it out to read the words.

THROUGH THE WINDOWS I CAN SEE.
HOW YOU TREAT YOUR WIFE SO MISERABLY.
HOW CAN YOU BE SO CRUEL, MR. BAKER?

WHEN THE TRUTH COMES OUT, I'LL SAVE HER.

"No." His throat is dry, hands shaking as he reads the words again and again. Then he freezes and looks up when he realizes the person got into his apartment. *They're probably still here.*

He places the envelope down and steps over the broken glass to get to the kitchen. He pulls out the largest knife from the knife set and holds it in front of him. The only doors belong to the bathroom and laundry room. He checks the bathroom first. Nothing.

He faces the sliding laundry door next and his heart drops. He's not sure how he hadn't noticed the streak of blood on it when he passed by it the first time. The wooden paneling of the doors could hide so much behind them. They give a clear view for someone to wait, to *watch*.

He grips the door handle, heart beating madly, and wastes no time swinging it open. There is no one inside, however there is a dirty beige faux leather purse with streaks of blood tied to the upper rack, dangling by a broken strap. Dominic sucks in a sharp breath, knowing for a fact it's the same purse Brynn Wallace had the night he was with her in New Orleans.

TWENTY-NINE

JOLENE

I normally don't have people visit me so late at night. I like to think that any time after ten o'clock is an unholy hour. Not that I'm very religious, or anything. I do believe there is a higher power overseeing us all and that they determine how our lives are strung together. And whomever this higher power is, I find myself quite upset with them, because the way my life has developed is far from a dream.

It's rude of me to even complain. After all, I have a life much better than others. My time on earth has been fruitful thus far, albeit difficult. I've suffered bullies all while living in a broken home and no matter how positive I try to be, it seems the world is built to suck the positivity right out of me.

The only reason I think of a knock this late as unholy is because it means bad news. Nothing good can come from a knock on your door when it's bedtime. However, I'm expecting these people.

Daphne and Ricardo.

They enter my house and Daphne immediately wraps her arms around me, smelling like toasted coconuts and vanilla.

There are no words I can use to express how I feel as she hugs me tight. I want to tell her how I feel, to pour it all out, but this is beyond hurt, beyond shame, beyond *anything* I've ever subjected myself to. How do you explain the horror you faced as your husband stared you in the eye and *choked* you? How do you tell anyone that he used your flaws and weaknesses against you, called you names, berated and belittled you? How do you tell anyone that after all this time—when you thought your romance was happenstance and that you were the luckiest woman in the world—it is possible, that the man you love has been using you the whole time?

I lead the couple into my living room and Daphne says she'll go to the kitchen to make tea. Ricardo sits across from me on a single recliner, eyes trained on me.

"Are you sure about this?" he asks. His voice is different at night. Gravelly. *Dangerous.*

My phone pings, and there's a message from Dominic: **Why are the security cameras off? Not safe to have them off, Jo. Make sure the house is locked up.**

I ignore his message, listening to Daphne clank around in the kitchen. I don't want him knowing Daphne and her husband are here, and I'm glad he's left like the selfish bastard he is. It's not safe, yet you've left your wife at home alone and without protection? Sure, there are the police at the end of the driveway, but they can't see much from there. Hell, Daphne and Ricardo parked on the street behind our house, and I allowed them access through the back gate so the police wouldn't spot them.

I put my attention on Ricardo, whose gaze hasn't left mine. He's always been a good husband to Daphne. He's always been there for her. I feel a slight pang of envy at the thought, but also relief because Daphne is my best friend and she deserves someone who loves and protects her . . . as well as her friends. I know it wasn't easy for him to agree to come here, and as Daphne told me, I *must* be sure. If I'm to bring Ricardo into this, I have to do it wisely.

"I'm positive," I say.

Ricardo nods, and though it feels like blood is swimming in my ears and that I might faint, there is no turning back now.

THIRTY

DOMINIC

Dominic stirs awake in the bed, panting raggedly as his eyes bounce around the hotel room. His hand is on his chest, the white comforter sloppily draped over the lower half of his body. He's not sure when he dozed off.

He didn't want to sleep at all, but he drank more, drowned himself in bourbon, and curled under the covers as he thought about the events that'd transpired over the past week.

The witch.

The hallucinations.

The dead crow.

The pictures.

He's sticky with sweat, and curses for even closing his eyes. How could he be so stupid after knowing someone was *inside* the apartment? They could've followed him to the hotel and broken in there too. Whoever this person is that's tormenting him, why haven't they killed him yet? What are they waiting for? Because at this rate, death seems more peaceful than all the harrowing questions.

Perhaps they don't want to kill him, he considers. They want him to suffer, to wonder what's next, to second-guess himself and throw him off his game. The biggest rally of his campaign is coming up and he's not even close to being prepared for his speech. He has to figure out who's behind this so he can end it.

Dominic supposes that, in itself, is torture—knowing someone has something over you that you can't snatch away and bury. Knowing this person is anonymous makes it more of a threat. It could be anyone. He's wronged so many people in the past for his own personal gain. He never thought he'd become this sort of person, but he has, and he can't go back now.

His eyes shift to the table in the corner where the bloody purse is. He's almost positive the blood on it is Brynn's and he shudders, unsure what to do with it. He could take it somewhere and burn it. He could toss it in a random dumpster and forget about it. But for some reason it seems safest to keep it with him. Keep it close and deal with it later once the stalker is put to rest.

A vibrating noise sounds off behind him, and he realizes this is why he woke up. His phone was ringing. He snatches it up and answers.

"Boaz? What do you have?" Dominic climbs out of bed, heading to the mini fridge and retrieving a bottled water.

"Found an ID on that woman in the picture you sent. She goes by the name Shavonne Peters, attended Loyola University, and was an intern for a kids' summer camp in 2015. That's the last thing I really have on her up until 2020, where she takes a job in North Carolina as a waitress in a diner called Pop's."

All of the words Boaz says swim away from Dominic but two. *Loyola University.* "Wait. She attended Loyola?"

"That's right."

"How old is she?"

"Thirty-eight."

Dominic's eyes bulge out of his head. "She's the same age as Brynn. She went to the same college. She must know her."

"Could be a friend wanting answers," Boaz states.

"But how would she know I was involved?" Dominic snaps. "Why would she be asking *me* anything?"

"Well, if the woman you had at the rental never went back home that night, this friend probably had questions, asked around the lounge about her. They must've been close. It's possible the woman you had over told her friend who she was going to see."

Dominic's back hits the wall and his body sags to the floor. "No, no, no. Boaz, this *can't* be happening. This woman can't be sniffing around right now. Everyone knows if you search for answers, you'll find them. Tell me that body can't be found, Boaz," he pleads.

"I went to New Orleans, poked around. No one has said anything about a body and no missing person reports were filed with her name. As far as you and I are concerned, she's gone. She was hardly breathing, and I buried her near a marsh. There was no surviving that."

"What about her belongings? Her purse? The phone?"

"Buried it with her. No one will find it."

"So how the hell was that same purse inside my apartment last night, Boaz? There's blood and dirt all over it. Someone is fucking with me, and I bet it's that friend of hers!"

"Calm down," Boaz snaps. "Anyone can buy a bag, get dirt, and make fake blood. If it is this woman, you need to put a pin in this straightaway and burn the evidence. Do you want me to handle it?"

"No." He thought Boaz had it handled years ago but clearly, he didn't. Now, he's certain that *was* Brynn standing across the street from Executive Mansion, staring back at him. What if she's not dead? Boaz said he drove for miles with her body in the trunk until he ventured to a forest near a marsh, dug a hole, and dumped her. He said the place was often infested with gators, and that even if she did miraculously wake up and dig her way out, she wouldn't survive it, not with her wounds.

Now, Dominic is having a hard time accepting any of what Boaz told him. There is a possibility Boaz is in on this, that he wants to see Dominic fail. Maybe he was pissed that he'd been dragged into it, so he set Brynn free and told her to never speak a word of it, paid her off or something, but she's thought about it all and now she's back. He could have lied about it just to save face. Sure, it was a risk on his part and, no, Boaz didn't like loose ends, but people change. And if there was one thing Dominic knew about Brynn, it's that she was smart as hell. She'd conquered many odds with quick thinking and this could've been one of those situations. Say she woke up, saw what Boaz was about to do as he dumped dirt onto her body, and begged to be freed. Would he have let her go?

"Just give me the night to think," Dominic finally says when Boaz clears his throat. "I'll let you know what to do when I figure out more."

He hangs up, then chucks his phone across the room.

There is no one he can trust.

He has to take care of it himself.

THIRTY-ONE

DOMINIC

Four years ago

Dominic had made a lot of mistakes growing up, but none of them could amount to this one. He stood in the master bedroom of John's rental home, mouth ajar and body stiff as he stared at the body on the floor.

He'd shoved Brynn a little too roughly and she'd hit her head on the sharp, wooden corner of the dresser. She was face-down on the ground, and blood was pooling around her head. He started to bend down, flip her over, but didn't want to touch the body.

Fuck! What was he supposed to do? He couldn't just let her lay there and die. Why couldn't she just sign the damn papers? Why did she have to make the situation so difficult?

He hurried out of the room to collect his phone from the den. It had twenty percent battery left. He hustled back up the stairs and was tempted to call the police, but then he remembered the NDA. This woman's body was on the floor and if she woke up and remembered what'd happened, everything he'd worked for would be thrown in a bin.

He wracked his brain, searching for a solution. It didn't hit him what to do until he thought about a conversation he'd had with Winton Hart. This was a year before Winton died. He'd called Dominic, demanded that he come to Houston so they could discuss his proposal to Jolene. He remembered being nervous as hell to be with her father one-on-one. He'd never sat with Winton alone. He had Jolene as a cushion, and she often covered for Dominic whenever Winton began interrogating him. But not this time. No, Winton wanted to speak to him *alone*.

He met him at an upscale soul-food restaurant and when he'd approached the table, Winton had ordered without him. A plate full of fried chicken, collard greens, mac and cheese, and a buttery roll of bread was in front of him, and Dominic couldn't help thinking that was how the man would die—all that fatty food going down the hatch, clogging his arteries, increasing his cholesterol. He'd kept the comments to himself, of course, and took the seat across from Winton, requesting a water from the waitress who wasn't too far away.

Winton looked Dominic from head to toe, then said, "I'm going to make this very clear to you, Dominic. I see you. I see you more than you see yourself."

Dominic's throat thickened. "I'm sorry. How do you mean, sir?" he asked, trying not to shrink under Winton's glare.

"I looked into your history after Joey told me about your past. You told her your mother was in a psychiatric detention. You said she was unwell and so mentally ill that it wasn't safe to visit her. Far from the truth, isn't it?"

Dominic swallowed but held Winton's gaze.

"Don't answer that," Winton muttered, waving his fork. "I know she's not in one. She's dead and the state handed her house over to you."

Dominic blinked, stunned by his future father-in-law's knowledge. A smile spread across Winton's lips, and he pointed his greasy fork at Dominic as he said, "You aren't the only person who does their research. You think I don't know that you're marrying my Joey for the money? I could smell it all over you when I met you."

Dominic chose to feign ignorance. "I love her, Mr. Hart. I'm not understanding where this is coming from."

"Please be aware, Dominic, that if you *ever* think about hurting Jolene in *any* way, your life will be ruined. Whether it's by me, or someone who knows me." Winton's dark-brown eyes grew even darker as a frown creased his forehead. "She loves you and I don't know why. But what I do know is that if you mess up, it will be handled." He turned his head a fraction, peering over Dominic's shoulder. Dominic looked with him, and spotted Boaz sitting in a booth. His hands were folded on the table, eyes hard on Dominic's as he nodded his head. "I have people who take care of business for me," Winton continued, grabbing Dominic's attention again. "And if there is ever a need for me to make someone disappear, it will happen. And I *won't* be to blame." Winton glared at Dominic—*into* him, really—like he could see everything he was made of, his rapidly beating heart, organs, and the thoughts in his head. Then, just as quickly as he'd glowered, he straightened in his seat and said, "Try the sweet potato pie. It's good."

Winton's words haunted Dominic. "*. . . if there is ever a need for me to make someone disappear, it will happen. And I won't be to blame.*"

Boaz had ways of making people disappear. Houston wasn't too far from New Orleans, and he still had Boaz's number saved in his phone when he'd found the guy who'd stolen his wallet. He lifted the phone and called.

A few hours later, Dominic stopped pacing when he heard a car door close. He rushed toward the window, peered out, and spotted Boaz in all his dark-skinned massiveness glaring up at the house. Behind him was a black Chevy pickup truck. It was broad daylight out and Dominic worked hard to swallow, glad the house was surrounded by trees.

There was a knock at the door, and he hurried to open it. Boaz entered the house, moving right past him. He noticed he was wearing cloth booties over his boots and his hands were gloved. The brim of his hat was low on his forehead.

"Where is it?" Boaz asked.

It? It took a second for Dominic to realize he was referring to Brynn. "Oh. Master bedroom, up the stairs to the left."

Boaz turned, heading for the stairs. Dominic followed him, and when they made it to the room, he watched Boaz flip Brynn's body over and press two gloved fingers to her neck to check her pulse.

"Pulse is faint. She's still alive."

"*What?*" Dominic blanched. He thought surely Brynn was dead. She hadn't moved an inch. He thought so—then again, he hadn't really checked. He'd left her body in the bedroom and waited in the den until Boaz's arrival. He assumed she was dead with all that blood on the wooden floor. The blood had rolled toward the rug, staining the oatmeal-colored carpet.

Something buzzed, and Dominic looked across the room, at Brynn's purse on the side table, next to the NDA. Boaz glanced at Dominic before moving toward the purse. He pulled out the phone with his gloved hand and pressed a button to turn the phone off before stuffing it back in the purse.

"What the hell am I supposed to do if she's alive?" Dominic asked, but Boaz ignored him and stood straight, lumbering out of the house. He stomped down the stairs and Dominic rushed after him, making sure to jump over the puddle of blood as he went. "Where are you going?" he asked.

Boaz didn't answer and instead went to his truck, climbed inside, and started it up.

"Fuck." Dominic was sure Boaz was leaving. Brynn wasn't dead. This would be his problem. He watched as Boaz put the car in reverse and straightened up, so the back of his truck was facing the porch. He'd parked at an angle so that the front of the truck blocked the door. Then he climbed out, squeezed between the truck and one of the porch columns, and stepped inside again.

"Stay down here," Boaz commanded, then he disappeared up the stairs. Dominic stood in the foyer, listening to the sound of heavy scraping and thumping. Was he moving furniture? He had the urge to go up and see what was happening but knew better than to make a move.

After what felt like an eternity, he finally heard Boaz's footfalls on the stairs, but he wasn't coming down empty-handed. He had the bedroom's rug in hand, rolled into a cylinder, and was grunting as he dragged it down. There was a body inside the rug—he could see the hair sticking out the top corner.

Boaz stopped, dropped the heavy rug, then fixed his eyes on Dominic. He dug into his pocket, pulling out a pair of plastic gloves and tossing them to him.

"Put those on and help me put the rug in the bed of the truck."

Dominic did as he was told, and as Boaz picked up the heavier end of the rug, Dominic went for the feet. They ambled out of the door, Dominic grunting as he moved, until Boaz slid his end of the rug onto the bed. He helped Dominic push the rest of it up then closed the hatch.

"Now what?" Dominic breathed. Because surely this couldn't be it. There was bound to be blood upstairs, his DNA. *John's* DNA.

"That fireplace work?" Boaz asked, pointing to the living room.

Dominic peered back at the cold, empty fireplace. "I'm sure it does."

"Good. Find some wood, burn those gloves and your clothes, take a shower, and put a fresh set of clothes on. I'll deal with the body. Someone will be here tonight around nine or ten. He'll clean up the bedroom, make it look like she was never here. Do *not* leave until I call you." He stepped outside, pointing at the cameras. "You're sure all the cameras are off?"

"Yes. I'm positive."

"Whose house is this?"

"John Bolton. He's a politician here in New Orleans. He was here last night, and he has a lot on the line. Last thing he wanted was to be seen so he made sure to have the security system and cameras off during my stay." Plus, Dominic made sure. He'd called John to double check about the cameras when he'd prepared Brynn's apple juice, and that's when he'd given John the greenlight to swing by.

"Okay, well like I said, don't leave until I call. And if I were you, I'd get in touch with this John Bolton character and tell him not to mention you were ever in his rental."

"Why? Do you think people will know she was here?"

Boaz glared at Dominic. "It's better to be safe than sorry."

"Sure. Yeah."

Dominic watched Boaz as he picked up a tarp from the back of the truck and covered the rug. He strapped it down with bungee cords, lugged out the trunk bed cover, and when it was secure and everything was concealed, he climbed behind the wheel and started the truck. The engine rumbled to life, causing a vibration in Dominic's chest. The truck pulled off and he stood at the door, watching it leave the driveway, move past the gate, and turn onto the street.

THIRTY-TWO

JOLENE

One thing I love about Wednesdays at Regal Tea Boutique is that business booms. This means all my employees are busy, and none of them see me as I enter through the back door of the building, climb the short flight of steps to the loft, and head straight to my office.

I drop my purse on the desktop and sit in the cushioned brown leather chair with an exaggerated sigh. Even a floor up, I smell the freshly baked scones, brewing variations of tea, and lovely petit desserts for our teatime sessions.

Right now, we're hosting afternoon tea and it's a full house. The parking lot was packed and I'm thankful that my business runs so smoothly, even on days when I'm not around. If only I could rejoice in the success, take pride in all that I've accomplished when many thought it wouldn't take off. My mind is all over the place. About Dominic, of course. I don't want to be anywhere near him, and my visit from Daphne and Ricardo last night caused me a lack of sleep as my decision weighed heavily on my mind. A cup of tea or two will do me good right now, so I send a text to Sally, the store manager, and request an order.

I log into my computer and check emails, as well as the schedule to make sure people have been clocking in on time. I check the books, and all seems to be smooth, so I make my way down to the kitchen to grab my tea.

"It's nice to see you in, Mrs. Baker," Sally says in front of a tray. The tray is topped with a matching porcelain tea set hand painted with Japanese cherry blossoms. Along with the set is a glass cup filled with honey, another filled with cubes of sugar, and a mini three-tier tray. I love the three-tier tray the most—gold plates with three levels of foods to choose from. The bottom consists of crustless sandwiches, the middle of scones with cream and raspberry jam, and the top hosts mini desserts like cakes, cheesecakes, and pies. We like to make the trays as regal as possible and stick to traditional English standards, hence the name of my shop.

"A little work will do me good. How is Veronica?" I ask, and Sally beams as she picks up the tray, heading for the swinging doors. Veronica is her three-month-old baby.

"Oh, she's perfect, Jolene. I'll show you pictures when it slows down!"

"Please do!"

Sally leaves the kitchen and another woman pops in. Her curly hair is pulled into a cute mop atop her head, her skin the color of coffee with too much cream. Sleeves of tattoos cover both her arms. She has small freckles on her nose. "Jessica, right?" I ask as she collects another tray set up with tea and food.

"That's me." She smiles, giving me a look. I'm not sure what that look means, but I disregard it when she says, "Busy today!"

"That's a great thing! You're doing an amazing job. Keep at it."

When she leaves, so do I. I return to the office to respond to more mails and make a few calls. The sooner I get this done, the sooner I can head home and get ready for my cycling class. I'm in the middle of calling up one of my suppliers when there's a knock at the door.

"I'm busy!" I call, assuming it's one of my employees, but the door opens up and the familiar head that pops in catches me off *completely* off guard. I lower the phone, watching as North Carolina's lieutenant governor Samuel Sanchez enters my office. He's dressed impeccably, not a stain or lick of lint on him. His hair is dark and curly, cut short just around the ears and full-bodied at the crown of his head. His skin is like Daphne's husband, tan and smooth. He steps inside with a smile gracing his lips and my heart catches speed.

"Sam, what are you doing here?" I ask, rising in my chair.

"Came to see you, Jo. How's everything?"

I swallow. "You couldn't have called first? People probably saw you."

"What's wrong with the LG popping up to support a local business?" Sam tips his head, approaching the desk, and it's now that I feel like my office is too small. There are three floor-to-ceiling windows overlooking a park, where people take their dogs for walks or children to play. Some even have picnics. Couples walk hand in hand with cups of coffee or, luckily, tea from my boutique. Though my windows are tinted, I feel like everyone can see me. *Us.*

Samuel takes a step closer, and I raise a hand. "Please. We can't do this here," I murmur.

"Okay." He stops, but his cologne wraps around me instead. I lift my chin, finding his brown gaze. He's smiling, that same stupidly handsome smile that got me the first time. "You sure that's what you want?"

This time, the saliva feels thick going down my throat, but I suck it up and step around the desk. "Sam, I told you we have to be smart about this. Visiting me at work makes things pretty obvious."

"Don't worry," he says, his fingers casually sliding into his pockets. "I'll be out of your hair in a bit. Just wanted to stop by, see how that plan of yours was working out?"

"Things have changed a bit," I state. "But I have it handled."

"It's a solid plan, Jo." Samuel takes a step closer. One of his hands comes out of his pockets and I assume he's going to run the backs of his fingers along my jawline, like he always does, but he pauses. His smooth forehead creases as his eyes fall to my neck.

"What happened here?" he asks, running a finger over my throat. I remember Jessica in the kitchen, the way she looked at me funny. Did she see the bruises?

"Nothing." I back away, holding my neck. How the hell can anyone even see it? I covered the bruises with makeup this morning. I double checked. I step around him and stare at my reflection in the mirror on the wall. Sure enough, some of the makeup has rubbed off and is now in the collar of my baby blue blouse. "Shit," I hiss, picking up a tissue and dabbing at my shirt.

When I look up, Samuel's eyes flare. "Did he hurt you, Jolene?"

"It's fine, Sam."

"No, it isn't fine. Look at you." He turns me to face him, but I avoid his eyes. Still, I feel his gaze searching, studying. "This has to stop, Jolene. If you don't put an end to it, I will." His hand cups my waist. His touch is hot, even over the fabric of my clothes. I shudder a breath as he reels me into him so that we're chest to chest. With his other hand, he uses his fingers to tip my chin so I can't look at anything but him.

"*This* has to stop," I breathe. "What we're doing . . ."

"Why should it? He doesn't deserve you," he murmurs on my mouth. And then he presses his lips to mine, coaxing my mouth open. I can't help melting in his grasp.

I drape my arms over his shoulders, and he rapidly picks me up in his arms to plant my ass on the edge of the desk. The corner of my computer digs into my back, but I don't care. I kiss him deeper, circling my legs around his waist, indulging in his touch.

"Dominic knows about us," I say when our lips part for a second. That could be another reason why he's been treating me like a backburner woman in his life. He knows I'm pulling away. He senses it."

As if he didn't hear me, Samuel kisses me again and I moan, tugging him closer by the tie. "So let him know."

"There are still some things that have to be worked out," I say as his mouth falls to my neck.

"Then work them out, Jo. I trust you."

His words light a fire in me—the good kind. It's the exact fire I need.

I'm not sure what it is about Samuel Sanchez that I can't resist. When I first met him, I couldn't stand him, but only because *he* clearly disliked Dominic. Now, he and I are in the same boat. I'm not the only person Dominic has stabbed in the back, lied to, hurt, or manipulated. Dominic counts Samuel out of every single decision, just so he can take the glory. There was a time he took credit for a healthcare idea of Samuel's that saved the state millions of dollars, and Samuel has never forgiven him for that.

Burn enough people and you're bound to feel the heat of the flames yourself. Samuel and I, though an illicit duo, agree on this, and because I'm tired of caring and tired of giving my worthless husband the benefit of the doubt, I let Samuel fuck me on my desk.

THIRTY-THREE

DOMINIC

Dominic sits in his SUV, parked along the corner near the lot of the Scarlet Star Motel.

It's the motel he saw Shavonne Peters staying in, and it's a shabby two-story building, which seems a bit more upscale at night with its neon red and orange lights and the miniature palm tree on the sign. He can't wrap his mind around the palm tree or how it belongs in Raleigh, but he disregards that thought as he shovels organic cashews into his mouth and watches each floor of the motel. He's parked next to an abandoned building, tucked away beneath a thick, broken tree branch. His expensive SUV definitely stands out on this side of town, but he's grateful for the truck trailers parked in the lot. They cover him for the most part.

He shouldn't be here and everything inside him screams it as a fact, but with so much uncertainty surrounding him, what else is there to do? He's been here since six p.m. His phone was blowing up with notifications and requests for last minute meetings that he's had to respectfully decline. To avoid another influx of texts and emails, he told Melissa he was having stomach troubles and to set meetings up for another date. That was several hours ago. It's nearing midnight now, and Sha-vonne is nowhere to be found. He's becoming antsy.

Dominic has spent so much time thinking about the bloody purse, and after that call with Boaz in the hotel, he re-alizes it all comes down to Shavonne Peters. She wants to play games? Well, he can play them too. Normally, he's not keen on showing his face with matters like this. It would've been smarter to have Boaz confront her, speak to her, but Boaz clearly messed up once. This time, he'll make sure there's an end.

Truth is, he's come here tonight to *scare* Shavonne, get her to leave him alone and go back to where she came from. All she has are notes and photos. Nothing concrete. And when it comes to that photo of him choking Jolene, he knows his wife will cover for him over a stranger. Boaz is right about the purse. It could be a dupe—a small detail Shavonne remembers from the last time she saw Brynn.

He checks the time on the dashboard. 11:48 p.m. He fid-gets in his seat as he watches one of the room doors open and a couple walk out. The woman clings to the man with a gig-gle. Dominic rolls his eyes, the thought of love and couples making him sick. He picks up his phone, swipes to his mes-sages, and opens one from a girl named Jessica who works at Jolene's stupid tea shop.

Jessica didn't provide a written text, but she did send an image. One of Samuel Sanchez coming down the set of stairs that lead to Jolene's office at the tea boutique. The sight of it causes him to clench his fists again, just like he did the first time he saw it. He knows what Samuel is trying to do—he wants to get him where he's weakest. He thinks by having his wife, that it'll make him fold. He's wrong. He's faced much worse.

Dominic found out Samuel had a thing for Jolene during a charity ball. He asked her to dance, had his hands too low on her hips, and Dominic interrupted and kindly whispered for him to back off of his wife. It made him look bad in public, like he had no control. He was sure Sanchez wanted it to appear that way. He's been after his governor's seat for some time now.

Two weeks after the ball, he found out Sanchez had visited Jolene's tea shop (Jolene had mentioned it over dinner one night, so happy to have had the lieutenant governor pay her a visit) and Dominic had taken it upon himself to speak to one of Jolene's employees when she wasn't there.

He wanted to stay ahead, be in the loop, so he chose the employee with the worst track record and said he'd pay her if she kept him updated on Jolene and any important people who showed up. Jessica was a former criminal, selling drugs for her ex, in and out of jail for little crimes like vandalism and assault. He knew for a fact Jolene hired her because she loved trying to change people's lives. She loved giving them a raft and hoping they'll resurface a better human. He knows because it was like that for him when they met. She pitied Dominic and his tragic childhood. She wanted to give him a better life, new meaning, and it worked . . . for a while anyway.

Dominic is aware that Sanchez is ahead in his role. He'll likely win lieutenant governor again and Dominic will blindly back him because it's better to have two of the same party members as heads of the state than an opposing party member.

He can't help wondering what the hell Sanchez wanted with Jolene today though. The image shows him leaving the top floor of Jolene's shop with a glint in his eyes, a subtle smile, and behind him, cut short at the corner, is Jo. She's watching him go while chewing on her thumbnail, a habit she only does when she's nervous.

Someone knocks hard on Dominic's window and, startled, he drops the phone, and it lands on the car floor. His gaze swings left, and he can't believe who he sees.

THIRTY-FOUR

DOMINIC

"Why are you watching me?" Shavonne's voice is muted by the window. A deep grimace is on her face, and she's in casual attire—none of that witchy stuff he's seen her in. Jeans and a graphic T-shirt with Aaliyah on it, along with a black cardigan. Even her hair has changed. No streaks of gray, just all black and pulled into a ponytail. Not a stroke of makeup is on her face. For a split second, he thinks he imagined her as a witch. It wouldn't be far off, considering the recent hallucinations.

Dominic shuts the engine of the car off and Shavonne steps back, folding her arms over her chest as Dominic climbs out.

"I should be asking you that question," he counters when the car door is shut behind him.

Shavonne scoffs. "What the hell are you talking about?"

"I know it's you leaving notes for me to find. The dead bird in my trunk. Attempting to break into my house. You're trying to ruin my life. Why?"

She doesn't react to his accusations. Her face remains neutral, minus her brows that shift down deeper. "You mean to tell me it's okay for *you* to ruin someone's life, but not for someone to ruin yours?"

"So, you admit it," he counters, and he curses himself for not having his phone to record this conversation.

Shavonne steps closer, eyeing him. "You think I don't see through this whole governor façade of yours, but I do, Baker. I see right through you, and you're made of pure glass. One tap and you'll break."

"Why are you trying to sabotage me? I did nothing to you," he retorts.

"The same way you didn't do anything to *Brynn*?"

Hearing the name fall from her lips sends him into a cold shock. The ice runs through his veins, paralyzing him where he stands. All he can do is stare at Shavonne as her lips deviously curl to a smile.

"Where is she? Tell me. Is she still alive?" he demands.

She leans toward him and whispers, "Just know you won't get away with what you did."

Those words bring him back to life, back to the moment. He can make this stop. He can get her to go away. "What is it that you want? Huh? Money? Is that it?"

Shavonne bubbles out another scoff while narrowing her eyes at him. "If I wanted money, I wouldn't be handling it this way."

"Name your price," he continues as she starts to walk off. "How much do you want? However much it is, I can get it. I have ways."

Shavonne peers over her shoulder. She drops her folded arms to face him again, looking deep into his eyes. "Look at you. So eager to use your wife's money to cover your sorry ass."

He works to swallow.

"I know what you did to Brynn that night, Dominic. You and that other man. She told me all about it and, trust me, she will *not* let you live this down."

His world is spinning. His mouth has become dry and is tacky from the cashews. His heart pumps double the speed as

Shavonne turns away, her chin up and a smirk on her lips. She takes a few steps, but he can't let her go. She knows too much. Brynn is still alive. They're both here to hurt him— *ruin* him. He can't let this happen.

He's not quite sure what comes over him in the moment. One second, he's watching her go, and the next he's yanking her back by the ponytail, spinning her around, and slamming a fist into her face. He hits her so hard she collapses on the ground and the back of her head slams on the black pavement.

He breathes raggedly as he searches for witnesses. No one is nearby. That's the good thing about a shitty motel in a terrible part of town. No one can stop him. No one cares. The neon lights of the motel flash on them, red hues swimming on one half of Shavonne's bloody face. He must be quick.

He picks her body up and shoves her into the backseat of his SUV but not before rifling through her pockets and purse for her phone. When he finds it, he chucks it toward the trees. Then he's behind the steering wheel, his tires screeching as he peels out of the lot. As he goes, eyes flickering to the rearview mirror, he feels around the floor for his phone. When he finds it, he dials Boaz and tells him what he did. He tells him that Brynn is alive and that if they don't find her, they're both going down.

Less than thirty minutes later, Boaz meets Dominic behind an abandoned warehouse.

"Take her to this address," Dominic says, showing Boaz the screen of his phone.

"We'll need to switch vehicles," Boaz states. "Don't want her DNA getting everywhere."

Dominic hesitates. When he realizes he has no time to argue, he mutters, "Fine."

Dominic hands him the keys, and once Boaz has them in hand, he stalks to Dominic's SUV, climbs behind the wheel, and drives away.

Dominic watches the taillights fade, then stares at Boaz's pickup truck—the same one that had Brynn's body stored on the bed—and a sinking feeling buries its way inside him.

He can't turn back now.

He has to finish this once and for all.

THIRTY-FIVE

DOMINIC

Four years ago

Once Boaz was gone with Brynn's body, Dominic did all the things Boaz told him to do. The first thing he did was find wood for the fireplace. He went out back, where a small storage shed was, and found a few logs. He toted them inside, found matches on the mantel, and lit it up. Once he'd stripped out of his clothes and the gloves and tossed them into the raging fire, he went for his phone and called John.

"What the hell's going on, Dominic?" John asked when Dominic told him to get somewhere quiet. "I was in the middle of a hearing."

"That hearing will have to wait. Look, I wasn't able to get the woman from last night to sign. Things escalated and well . . ." He wasn't sure how much to phrase it over the phone. "Just do me a favor and keep my name off your visitation books, alright?"

"Sure, bud, but I never had you on them. As far as anyone knows, the house was vacant this weekend. And what do you mean you couldn't get her to sign? What about the money? Did you offer it to her?"

"Of course, I did," Dominic stated. "She just . . . she wouldn't take it."

"So, what does that mean? She can't remember me, can she? She was hardly awake." John was panicking. Dominic could sense it through the phone, in the lilt of his voice and his breathing. He needed to calm him down. If John felt threatened in *any* way, all would come crashing down.

"I'll get her to sign, don't worry about it. The money is still in my car, waiting for her. I told you she'd be a little fickle."

"Sure, Dom. Alright." But John didn't sound so sure.

"The cameras have been off since yesterday morning, correct?" Dominic asked, just to confirm once more.

"Yes. Off since Thursday night, when you told me you needed a place to crash. Don't worry, I control the security system of that property. You aren't the only person having parties." There was humor in John's tone, and Dominic, though aggravated, was glad to hear it. It meant John wasn't panicking anymore—that he too felt safe since the cameras were off. No cameras, no proof.

"Okay. Thanks, John. Sorry to interrupt your hearing. I'll speak to you later." Dominic hung up and ran naked through the house, going for his duffel bag in the master bedroom. He spotted the pool of blood and took note of the missing body and oatmeal rug. Boaz had left the bed as it was. Other than the blood, nothing was out of place.

He went to one of the guest rooms and showered, giving himself a thorough cleanse, scrubbing his hair, under his nails, his face, then he got out to get dressed. As he slipped into his pants, he couldn't help wondering if people would see the smoke coming from the chimney, or if anyone would wonder why a person had the fireplace going in the dead of summer. He was being paranoid. Plenty of people lit fires for the hell of it.

Boaz was taking care of it. This was his job—to make serious matters or even people disappear. When Dominic had collected all his belongings and stuffed them into his duffel bag, he went to the master bedroom to get the glass Brynn had been drinking from, as well as his. In the kitchen, he washed the glasses with dish soap beneath hot water three times before putting them in the dishwasher. He was glad that, despite his shaky hands, the glasses hadn't fallen and broke.

His phone buzzed in his back pocket, and he nearly jumped out of his skin when he felt the vibration on his ass. He snatched out the phone, spotting a familiar image of him and Jolene on the screen. His wife was calling. He couldn't talk to her right now. Not after what he'd done. He'd done it for them, though, and as badly as he wanted to regret it, he couldn't. The only thing he regretted was that the situation had turned so ugly so quickly. All Brynn had to do was sign and walk away. That was it.

Dominic let the call go on silently, slipping the phone back into his pocket and carrying himself to the den. Crickets chirped and cicadas croaked, and at exactly nine p.m., a knock was at the door.

He checked the peephole first and a thin man stood on the other side, holding an oversized kitbag. He was dressed regularly, but also had protective booties on his feet. Dominic cracked the door open, and the man faced him, wearing an industrial mask. His skin was pale beneath the mask, his gray hair sticking up at all kinds of angles, as if he'd been near static.

"Came here for a cleaning job," the man said.

"Uh, yes. This way."

The man stepped inside, looking all around. Dominic showed him to the master bedroom, and the man made a *tsk tsk* noise as he dropped his large bag on the floor. "What a mess," the man mumbled.

Dominic stood by the door, watching as the man bent down to open his bag. The bag unraveled, revealing three sections with tools, bottles, baggies, and other items he'd never seen before. The man pulled out a black handheld device, unfolded it, and a blue light appeared on one end. He moved the wand around, revealing little white dots and splatters. The light went past the pool of blood and Dominic felt like he was going to be sick as the blood lit up like snow on the legs of the bed and even the dresser. The man was looking for stains in any and all places, and there was much more in the room than Dominic had anticipated. How had this become his life? He felt weak in the knees as the man closed the wand.

"Going downstairs," Dominic announced, but he was already away from the room, gripping the banister and trudging his way down. He sunk to the sofa, shaking while staring at an abstract painting on the wall, until the cleaner popped up an hour later and said, "All done."

"That's it?" Dominic rose to his feet. He noticed the man's kitbag in one hand and an orange hazard bag in the other.

"That's it. Nothing will be found. Did a double cleaning, in fact." The man looked Dominic all over, as if assessing him, and he wanted to shrink. Would this man tell someone about him being here? And where the hell was Boaz? What exactly was he doing with Brynn's body?

"Do you do a lot of these jobs?" Dominic inquired.

The cleaner shrugged. "At least three or four a year."

Dominic swallowed. "And you don't tell *anyone* about them?"

The man smiled behind his mask. "I'd be out of a job if I went around telling people what I do for a living."

Dominic nodded, wanting to find comfort in those words, but they only made him wary. The man left, and he cursed himself for not finding out his name.

Dominic's stomach was grumbling as midnight approached. Boaz specifically told him not to leave, yet he hadn't called or returned to the house. He began to panic, dialing Boaz's number repeatedly and not getting an answer. In between that, Jolene was shooting him text messages. He hadn't answered her call and she was clearly upset about it, and if he wanted things to seem normal, he had to play it cool, so he texted her back. He lied, saying he was golfing with John, then at a bar for drinks. She asked him why he hadn't responded to her last night, and he told her he fell asleep. Another lie.

He was tempted to leave—get as far away from this house as possible—but then his phone rang close to two in the morning. Boaz was calling.

"Get all your stuff, get in your car, and leave," Boaz murmured. He gave him instructions on where to meet him and Dominic hastily collected his keys, duffel bag, and bolted out of the house.

THIRTY-SIX

JOLENE

I'm sitting on the sofa, a glass of wine in hand and my laptop on the couch beside me, *How to Get Away with Murder* playing in the background, when I hear the front door slam. I gasp and nearly spill my wine when I hear footsteps thundering through the house.

"Dominic?" I call.

No answer.

I stand, walking around the corner to check the foyer. It's empty. I look in the kitchen and he's not there either. I hear footsteps above and set my wine glass down on the kitchen counter before making my way up. My red satin robe from Lovely Silk sashays around my ankles as I hurry up and find him in our bedroom. The closet door is open, and he's coming out of it with a set of clothes. On the bed, he has a duffel bag, and he stuffs the clothes into it.

"What's going on?" I ask. "Where are you going?"

"I have something to do," he says before disappearing into the closet again. He comes back out with a pair of tennis shoes and dress shoes and stuffs them into the bag too.

"Dominic, what's going on? Why are you in such a rush?" I demand.

"I'm just—I have to go. I need time to prepare for the rally Saturday."

"And you can't do that here?" Not that I *want* him here, but still . . . it *is* his home.

"No. I have meetings, things in between. Better that I get a head start in Charlotte."

"Okay." I sink down on the bench at the bottom of the bed. Dominic zips his bag up, slings it over his shoulder, then walks toward the door. As if he's forgetting something, he pauses and dumps the bag on the floor. I expect him to rush to the closet or even the bathroom, but instead he comes to me and lowers to his knees.

"Jo, I'm sorry about last night," he says, and I press my lips, instantly fighting whatever emotion tries to take over me. I won't break. I won't forgive as easily this time. He always does this after one of his bad moods takes over. He'll apologize, send flowers the next day, treat me to dinner at one of our favorite restaurants. But today, there were no flowers, and clearly, we're not going out to eat because he's packed up to leave. "I'm just so stressed with the campaign and scared that I might lose." He lets out an exasperated breath, his light-brown eyes swiveling to mine. He takes one of my hands in his and kisses the back of it. "I know I haven't been the best husband to you, and I promise I will make up for my mistakes, but Jo . . . I need you on my side more than ever right now. There are things that . . ." He pauses, blinking rapidly. It's now I notice the bags under his eyes, like he hasn't slept well in days. "Just know that I need you. I can't live my life without you."

"You're scaring me, Dominic. Is this about the call you had a few days ago? You closed your office door and were speaking to someone."

His eyes flicker away, focusing on a spot on the wall behind me.

I squeeze his hand. "Tell me the truth, Dominic. Tell me what's going on." This is his last chance.

He returns his gaze to mine, studying every detail of my face, and for a split second I remember why I fell for him. Those big, brown eyes, his soft skin, his full lips. I remember how he feels next to me, warm and close. Our bond was impenetrable. No one could stop us.

But in a matter of seconds, the reminiscing ceases and I forget who we used to be when says, "It's better that you stay out of it."

"So there *is* something going on? What are you hiding, Dominic? Tell me so I can help! We're supposed to be a team, remember?"

"No." His head shakes and he removes his hand from mine to stand. "Just . . . it's fine, okay? I have everything handled. Will you be at the rally Saturday?"

"Yes," I mumble. Where the hell else would I be? I stand with him, and he starts to turn but I catch his wrist. "Dominic, please. If you love me, you'll tell me what's going on."

His eyes flicker to my hand, then back up to my face. With his free hand, he removes my grasp and disappointment sinks to my stomach. "Trust me, Jo. Let me handle it first, then I'll tell you everything. I promise."

I don't even get the chance to protest. He grabs his bag and leaves the room, jogging down the stairs before I can get another word out.

THIRTY-SEVEN

DOMINIC

Four years ago

Dominic felt like he couldn't get enough oxygen when he spotted Boaz's pickup truck in the dead of night. He was parked beneath a live oak tree, window cracked, cigarette smoke drifting out. Boaz told him to meet behind a deserted restaurant, just across the street from a food mart that was run-down and, oddly, still in business.

Dominic parked next to Boaz's truck and waited. Boaz stepped out of his vehicle, flicking his cigarette before coming to the passenger door of Dominic's car. His heart thundered in his chest and his pulse swam to his ears as he unlocked the door. Boaz sat in the passenger seat, causing the car to tilt to the right. He slammed the door, locked it, and Dominic controlled his breathing as he focused on the man next to him. It was hard to control when the stench of nicotine consumed him. This was a man he didn't know. A man he'd trusted to fulfill a reckless duty and who could turn on him in the blink of an eye.

"The *rug* is gone. Won't ever be found," said Boaz. He shifted in the seat, and Dominic tensed until Boaz stuck his hand out to offer him something. Dominic's eyes fell to the phone in Boaz's palm, a thick, old looking thing with a small screen.

"What is that for?" Dominic asked, eyeing him.

"So you can call me from this phone and not your real one. You're running for a governor's seat, right?"

Dominic stared into Boaz's eyes. "Yes."

"Then you don't want calls like the one you made to me getting listened to without your awareness. Should anything ever come up—which I doubt it will—call this phone. There's only one number stored in the contact list, and you can reach me there."

Dominic took the phone, weighing it in his hand. "Where did you take the bo—"

"The *rug*?" Boaz corrected him with a glare. "Only refer to it as the rug."

"Yeah, sorry. The rug. Where did you take it?"

"Drove over eighty miles across Louisiana until I found a marsh most people avoid. Walked into the woods and *placed* it there."

"Was she—I mean, was the rug still breathing?"

Boaz studied Dominic, his eyes boring into the side of his face. "No."

Dominic released a breath and gripped the steering wheel. "Good." Perhaps she officially died along the way.

Silence swelled in the car. Dominic couldn't bring himself to look at Boaz, but could feel Boaz staring at him.

"I'll let you go," Boaz finally said. "For my time and discretion, I expect two and a half million dollars deposited into this account." Boaz handed a sheet of paper to Dominic, who took it with parted lips. *Two and a half million dollars?* There was no way he would be able to get that kind of money from the accounts without Jolene noticing. She'd ask questions, and he wouldn't have any answers.

"I—I didn't realize you had a fee," Dominic responded stupidly.

Boaz released a dark chuckle. "You think I do shit like this for *free*?"

Dominic shook his head quickly. He didn't care. He wanted Boaz out of the car so he could drive away, get to the airport, and take his ass home. And frankly, he was *scared* of Boaz. There was something sinister in that man's eyes. Not to mention his hands were enormous and one of them could close around Dominic's throat and end him in no time.

"Payment is for me and the cleaner," Boaz said, tapping on the paper Dominic had in hand. "Send it in increments, so you don't ring any bells."

"Sure, I got it. I'll have it sent." And he would. He'd work out the kinks later, when Boaz was far, far away from him.

Boaz nodded, and as if he were satisfied with that, he unlocked the doors again and climbed out of the car. Before he went, he ducked his head back in and said, "Keep Jolene away from this. If she finds out I did any work for you, I'm sure I'll lose my position at True Oil."

Dominic raised a guiltless hand. "The only people who know about this are me, you, and that cleaner. And I'm not going to rat on myself."

"Too much on the line, right?" Boaz chuckled, his teeth glinting behind the blue light of the dashboard. His smile made Dominic shudder. "Don't forget the deposits," Boaz said, then he closed the door and went back to his truck.

Dominic drove away immediately, and though his flight to Raleigh wasn't for another six hours, he headed straight to the airport, returned his rental car, and sat near his designated terminal, eager to get home.

He expected police to barge into the airport, arrest him in front of thousands of people, some of whom would have their phones out to record it. But no one came. He was safe, the body was gone, and once he was home, it'd be impossible for anyone to prove the horrible thing he'd done.

THIRTY-EIGHT

JOLENE

I couldn't sleep after the way Dominic left. Something is going on with him and it's throwing off all my plans.

I have to run into work for a virtual meeting with one of my tea suppliers. We're running low on our lavender honey mix, and they've been having a hard time producing due to shortages. Fortunately, the meeting doesn't take long and after having all the employees gather in the loft to discuss a price increase for lavender honey until the supplier can adjust, I leave the boutique and drive across town.

I checked Dominic's location last night, shortly after he left. It showed him at the apartment we rent out on West Peace Street. I pull into the lot of our apartment complex, taking out my keys and entering the building with my fob. I ride the elevator up to our floor and my heart thunders in my chest as I approach our door. I unlock it and open the door slowly.

The apartment is vacant, and everything is as it should be. The bed is made. Kitchen counters are clean and spotless, the glass panes of the windows are smudge free.

I close the door behind me, setting my purse and keys on the kitchen counter. I've always loved this apartment. I tell myself often that when Dominic and I are over, I'll live here for a while. I don't care about the house. I'll take my car, my things, and stay here. The apartment has a city view and right now the entire living room is bathed with sunlight, courtesy of the broad windows lining one wall. I glance at the kitchen made of marble, pale gray cabinets with gold handles and knobs. Nothing is out of order. It's almost like no one was here, but I know Dominic was. I saw his location pinned here. He'd been at the apartment for hours before riding to Executive Mansion.

My heels click on the wooden floorboards as I venture across the studio, trying to find anything out of ordinary. I check under the bed to no avail. I check the bathroom, shuffling through the drawers and cabinets, but it's all the same things—toothpaste, toothbrushes, wash cloths, towels.

I leave the bathroom, huffing as I step into the kitchen. I check each cabinet, drawer, and even the fridge and freezer. Nada.

Blowing a breath that causes one of my braids to flap, I stand in front of the window and look out at the city. *Why did he come here last night? What was he doing?* I whip out my phone, checking his location again on the app.

He's on a freeway, leaving Raleigh. *But wait.* He's not going in the direction of Charlotte. I frown, zooming in on the map. "Where the hell are you going, Dom?"

I lower the phone, glancing at the TV on top of the wooden stand. Two doors are on either side of the stand, but one of the doors is slightly propped open. I lower to a squat and draw the doors apart. The right side is empty however the left contains a shoebox. Why is a shoebox under the TV? I haul it out and carry it to the counter. When I remove the lid, my heart pumps harder and faster when I spot an old Nokia cellphone I've never seen before, along with a charging cable and folded sheets of paper. But what steals the breath out of my lungs most is the purse with dirt and blood on it.

THIRTY-NINE

JOLENE

I rush to the kitchen, snatching a paper towel from the roll then folding it over my fingers so I can remove the purse by its strap. The purse leaves behind dirt on some of the papers and the cellphone. I press a finger down on the phone and the screen glows. I run my tongue over my lips as I lift it and unlock the screen. The phone has no passcode.

I scroll through it but there aren't any text messages or photos, however there are several recent calls made to one specific number. My hands shake as I press the number to call it. Each ring makes my heart race until, finally, someone answers.

"I told you not to call from this phone anymore."

I gasp when I hear the gravelly voice on the other end but don't say a word. I cup my mouth as the voice goes on. "Hurry the hell up. She's already awake." A stretch of silence. "Hello? *Hello*?"

I hang up, dropping the phone back into the shoe box as if it's on fire. I know that voice. I know it very well. What is Dominic doing talking to *him*? I step away from the box, bile rising in my throat. This is worse than I thought and changes everything.

I rush around the counter, retrieving a cup of water from the cabinet and filling it with water. I guzzle it down, water dribbling from the corners of my mouth and onto my gray blouse. I swipe my mouth with the back of my hand then turn my eyes to the box again. There are more things inside it. Perhaps they'll tell me what Dominic is up to and where he's really going.

I pull out one of the papers from the box. On it are the words: **I KNOW WHAT YOU DID. WHERE'S BRYNN?**

I frown, taking out another sheet.

THROUGH THE WINDOWS I CAN SEE.
HOW YOU TREAT YOUR WIFE SO MISERABLY.
HOW CAN YOU BE SO CRUEL, MR. BAKER?
WHEN THE TRUTH COMES OUT, I'LL SAVE HER.

"What?" I whisper. Who are they talking about? Through the window? *What* window? My mind goes back to the night of that attempted break in at our house. Was it that night? Who is this? Why are they talking about *me*?

My hands won't stop shaking as I lower the paper. I pause when I see the last one, but it's not just a paper. It's a photo flipped on its face. I turn it over and study it with shallow breaths. It's an image of a woman—she's beautiful with straightened hair and large brown eyes. She's wearing red and is clearly holding the camera or phone as she takes a selfie with a smile. Behind her is *my husband*. He seems to be mid conversation with someone next to him, his head at an angle. I flip the photo over and the words **SIN AFTER SIN. LOOK HOW DEEP YOU'RE IN** are written in bold black ink.

I turn it over, study the photo again. All the notes are written in the same handwriting.

I KNOW WHAT YOU DID. WHERE'S BRYNN?

WHEN THE TRUTH COMES OUT, I'LL SAVE HER.

SIN AFTER SIN . . .

This woman in the photo…she must be Brynn.

I stuff all the items back into the box and then shove it beneath the TV again. If Dominic had it there, he's hiding it for a reason. And I don't know who this Brynn woman is, or how she correlates with the letters, but I need to find out. I grab my purse and keys and hustle out of the apartment, locking it up behind me and rushing to the elevator as quickly as I can in my heels.

When I'm inside my car, my phone pings just as I start the engine.

I dig through my purse, tugging it out and checking the screen. There's a message from someone on Instagram. Someone I've been waiting to hear from ever since I found out Dominic was sending them money from the share he sold. Blood wooshes in my ears as I click the notification and it opens the app. I read the message several times, then drop my forehead to the steering wheel to cry because this settles it once and for all. This is the ultimate betrayal and all these years, Dominic has hidden it from me.

When the tears stop, I swipe the pads of my fingers beneath my eyes, clean myself up, and drive home.

FORTY

DOMINIC

"It must be done. It must be done. It must be done." Dominic has repeated the words to himself during the drive like a mantra. He can't help feeling like his mother, who repeated certain sentences all the time when she was alive.

"They're after me. They're coming. They're after me. They're coming."

Now he knows how she feels, to know someone is after you, coming for you. But he's not like his mother. He won't take the losing way out by killing himself. He'll beat this and come out on the other side.

He'd lied to Jolene about his mom. She'd long been dead, her ashes in a vase on his uncle's mantle. He lied because it felt better than telling the truth—that his mother was a psychotic woman who ruined his childhood.

Dominic grips the steering wheel tightly as he pulls Boaz's truck off the road and takes a rocky path. The tires of the truck bump along the dark gray gravel, branches swiping the body of the vehicle. His phone rings in the cupholder. Jolene is calling. She's been calling for the past two hours. What the hell does she want? Why can't she just sit down and let him handle this?

Dominic cracks a window, needing the air, even more so when he spots the brown cabin perched between low-hanging trees.

The cabin is small, with a sagging roof and a chimney. The porch wraps around to the left and a white door is in the center. Tree branches slope over the house, as if shielding it and its secrets from the outside world. Because there are secrets in that cabin—things that must *never* get out.

He parks in front, spotting his Chevy SUV off to the left. A curtain inside the cabin shifts, falling in place. He kills the engine of Boaz's truck and climbs out, making his way toward the front door.

He gives it a knock and listens to the heavy footsteps thumping on the other side. The door swings open and Boaz has a brow cocked as he eyes him. "You're late."

"I had meetings." He's lying. He didn't have meetings. He just paced around in a private parking lot for quite some time, trying to come up with a solution to the mess he'd created. He realized it all came down to this moment. He did stop by Executive Mansion to snag his iPad so he could have his speech with him. Once this situation was handled with Shavonne and Brynn, he'd planned on going straight to Charlotte. Push come to shove, he'd blame it all on Boaz.

He steps around Boaz, focusing on the woman strapped to an old wooden chair. Thick black cables are wrapped tightly around the upper half of her body and several strips of duct tape are around her mouth, but they don't hide the freshly developed bruises around her eye and bridge of her nose. There are no tears in her dark-brown eyes, only pure rage. Shavonne grimaces at him, breathing raggedly through her nostrils, her dark, curly hair unkempt.

Dominic takes a look around the cabin. It's just as he remembers when he was young, only dustier and creakier now. Wooden walls and flooring, dark counters, a stove he's sure doesn't work, along with a rusted white fridge. The door in the kitchen leads to what used to be a backyard but is now crowded with tall grass and trees. Both are small and vacant. A fireplace is off to his right, next to a dusty plaid green sofa. There are two bedrooms in the back of the house, one of which belonged to him.

This cabin used to belong to his mother. Then she managed to kill herself when Dominic was seventeen, and the state handed the house over to his uncle Ben. She had a will, apparently, and wanted all of her assets given to his uncle (her only other relative), so that once Dominic was of age, he could assume the assets. She didn't have much, just the cabin and an old Buick that he used when he went to college. She had no money saved, nothing of substantial use. Dominic thinks about that sometimes—how his mother created a will just to fulfill the duty of hanging herself in her bedroom. The mind is a powerful thing, but hey, at least she considered her son before doing the deed.

He found her the day she committed suicide, a tipped over chair beneath her dangling feet, her neck bent at an odd angle through an extension cord. He remembers the dress she wore too—a pink one with red flowers. She also had a full face of makeup. It was like she'd made a day of it—prepared herself for her own demise.

He can still remember his uncle Ben going at him about being better than his mother. Uncle Ben may have been a country old man, but he knew the way to live. He had money, and he'd worked his ass off for it, but he couldn't take care of Dominic forever. Uncle Ben had his own kids, his own life. He kept him around, just before Dominic ran off to Duke University. To this day, Dominic still can't believe he landed a scholarship there. But being smart and rich was better than being stupid and broke. He wasn't athletic by any means, so that meant he had to use his brains.

He would *not* let his mother's death define him . . . but look at him now. Back in his childhood cabin, facing a woman who has caused him mounting paranoia. He supposes this is worse than being like his mother, because at least she'd only hurt herself physically, and no one else.

Dominic grabs a chair from the table in the corner and brings it in front of Shavonne. He sits as Boaz remains standing by the door. His eyes are on Shavonne's, and he sighs as he says, "It didn't have to be this way."

She scowls.

"Boaz, can you take the tape off?"

Boaz grunts, moving through the cabin and digging into his pocket. He snatches out a pocketknife, flips it open, and reveals a sharp blade. Panic surfaces in Shavonne's eyes as she watches Boaz approach her with it. He wedges a finger beneath the tight tape and slices at an opening. The tape comes off and Shavonne pants as she says, "You're an idiot."

"Shavonne, tell me where Brynn is," Dominic orders, ignoring her rude remark.

"I'm not telling you a damn thing. Like I said," she breathes. "You won't get away with what you did. Now you've kidnapped *me*. You're so stupid."

He hates that word. *Stupid*. He's not stupid. He's smart and excels at everything he does. The word angers him so much that he rises from his chair and grips her face in his hand. The pads of his fingers dig into her flesh and she whimpers, only a bit, but matches his stare.

"Tell. Me. Where. She. Is," he growls.

Shavonne's right eye twitches. "How did you like the tea?"

He frowns, faltering a bit. "What?"

"The tea I gave to your wife. I bet the hallucinations were horrible for you. LSD does that to a person. I bet it's still in your blood stream." She sneers and he shoves her face away, nearly knocking her backwards in the chair.

LSD? What the hell is she talking about? Is that why he was seeing things? Why the sky was purple? Why he was so damn paranoid of every single person? She drugged him without him even realizing it. As if she senses the panic brewing in him, she giggles. Fucking *giggles*, like some child who just pulled a cute little prank.

His breaths come out raggedly as he turns to pick up his chair and launch it across the room. Boaz takes a step back, eyeing Dominic as he fumes, pacing the cabin and dragging a hand over his head.

"This is on you!" Dominic snaps, pointing a finger at Boaz. "You said she was dead! You said it was fine! What the hell am I paying you all this money for when it was never handled?"

"I'm not the one who threw a fit and nearly killed that woman!" Boaz booms. "I came to help *you* out. I did what I was supposed to. She was buried alive—there was no surviving it! This woman is clearly lying!"

"See! You lied! You said she was dead before you buried her!"

Shavonne's laugh catches Dominic off guard and he whirls around, glaring at her.

"Loyalty is powerful, Dominic Baker," she says in a breathy voice.

"What the hell are you talking about?" he hisses.

"I was there that night when you helped put her body in the truck. I saw *everything*."

"How?" Dominic croaks, the blood draining from his face.

She laughs again and it grates his nerves. "You may think you buried her—that she's dead and you left her behind—but she's not. She still breathes. And she *will* find me. *Tick. Tock. Tick. Tock.*" She stares at him with wild eyes. Boaz shifts on his feet. "You hear that, Baker? That's the sound of your time running out."

FORTY-ONE

JOLENE

I don't know what to do. Dominic isn't answering his phone, there was a bloody, dirty purse in a box beneath the TV, and those notes I saw are terrifying. I have no idea why he isn't answering, but what I do know is I'm pissed off. After reading that message on Instagram several times, I can't stay in this marriage.

My phone rings and I check the screen. When I see who it is, I ignore the call. I'm not in the mood. I stop by a wine and spirits store, grabbing three bottles of wine to take home. I missed my cycling class but couldn't give a damn right now. Who cares about staying in shape and working my ass off for a man who doesn't care about me?

When I'm home, I dump my things on the table and crack open the first bottle of wine. I give Samuel a call, wanting to hear his voice, but it rings several times before reaching his voicemail.

I find a glass and fill it close to the brim, taking a long, hefty sip as I leave the kitchen and carry it upstairs with me. I turn the faucets to start a bath, ready to soak and call it an early night when I hear the doorbell ring.

I frown, realizing I can't check the cameras because my phone is still in my purse downstairs. I rush down with my cup of wine, making sure not to spill any on the stairs.

When I round the corner, I check our home security system's video screen attached to the wall behind the door. A woman is on the screen, wearing all black with her head down. I can tell it's a woman because she has breasts beneath the hoodie she's wearing. With her head down, I can't see the upper half of her face but, regardless, the sight of her makes my heart drum a faster beat.

"Can I help you?" I ask through the speaker in the system.

"Open up."

I pause, studying her in the camera again. She's looking over her shoulder now. She's fidgety. I don't like it. I glance toward the kitchen, where my phone is inside my purse.

"I'm sorry," I call into the speaker. "I can't help you. I don't know who you are and I'm not expecting visitors."

"It's Brynn," she says rapidly, and my eyes nearly bulge out of my head as the woman lifts her head. There. I see her. The woman from the photo. She's still beautiful but something about her face is different. A slanted scar is on the right side of her head, running from her hairline and through her eyebrow. The scar is deep, as if it'd required stitches in order to heal.

I unlock the door and snatch it open, prepared to ask her a hundred questions. What does she want? Why was she in that picture with my husband? Where the hell is he? But I don't get the chance to ask any of them because as soon as the door is open, she withdraws a gun from her hoodie pocket and points it at my face.

PART TWO

FORTY-TWO

BRYNN

Do you know what it feels like to be buried alive?

I remember it very well.

The dirt drops in fat clumps, weighing your body down.

It's heavy and you lose oxygen second by second.

For a moment, you think this is your fate—that you will die, and no one will find you. A darkness shrouds you when you realize your life is coming to an end. You begin to pray, begging the Lord Almighty or whomever you believe in to make this all go away, to absolve you of your sins, to welcome you into their eternal presence. It's a scary thing, facing a death like that.

I lay in a hole in the ground and through eyes that refused to stay open, saw a large man who was hastily shoveling dirt in the ground. It took a minute for me to realize he was throwing the dirt onto my body. There was a pain at the front of my head, so sharp and intense that I didn't want to blink for fear that it would hurt more. I don't think he saw my eyes as he shoveled the dirt in with heavy grunts. I had no clue who he was, or how I'd gotten to this point.

I tried remembering what'd happened but couldn't. It was all so fuzzy. I attempted to move my hands, my feet, and even roll. Nothing worked. I felt cold. Weak. I may not have known where I was or how I'd gotten there, but what I did know for sure was that I was going to die. When a pile of dirt landed on my face, I knew it to be true. The dirt kept coming down as a steady *plop, plop, plop*. The man's grunting softened. Dirt filled my ears.

As good as dead, I thought as I drowned in darkness.

But the end is never definite when breath still fills the lungs . . . or when you have a best friend like mine.

FORTY-THREE

SHAVONNE

Four years ago—New Orleans

Shavonne was worried.

Normally, when it came to Brynn, she didn't have to worry. That's what she liked about having her as a best friend. They were great communicators and if one of them had an issue with the other, they hashed it out like adults. If one of them was short on rent, the other would try and help out. If one of them needed to borrow tampons or pads, they had each other's backs. If they wanted to kick back and watch a movie and drown in popcorn and wine while pretending to be Olivia Pope, they did it together. And they always, always, *always* texted each other back. No matter if they were working, out late, or whatever—they always did.

It was such a priority that Shavonne had to break up with a guy who got jealous that she and Brynn were so close. He kept calling them secret lesbians. She hated that. What was so wrong with having a friend you trusted and relied on? What was so wrong with making them a priority in your life when they'd practically saved yours? Sure, she and Brynn had gotten into an argument the day before over a mess Brynn had left in the kitchen, but it didn't matter. Brynn *always* got back to her, even when they were annoyed with each other.

So, yes, Brynn not responding to her texts for well over ten hours was sign number one that something was wrong. Sign number two was that Brynn hadn't come back home that night. If she was staying with a guy, cool, but she would normally inform Shavonne because it was a rare occurrence. They'd made a pact less than a year ago that they'd never sleep at a guy's house again unless the relationship was serious. They wanted to get their lives on track, which meant focusing on themselves first. But Brynn had met up with her ex, and Shavonne figured this ex had triggered Brynn and made her disregard their pact. Not that Shavonne really cared about her breaking it. It was going to break eventually, when they each found the loves of their lives, but Brynn didn't mention staying the night with this ex of hers. It's not rare that someone hooks up with a past fling again, but something about *this* guy being in New Orleans struck Shavonne as odd. She specifically remembered Brynn saying her last real relationship was with a guy from North Carolina. Brynn had some flings in college, but nothing that was ever serious. What was this ex doing in their city in the first place? Had Brynn been talking to him all this time and not telling her?

At first, Shavonne figured Brynn needed a night to be wild and reckless. But see . . . that was the issue. There was a night when they were wild and reckless, and Shavonne had almost been sexually assaulted in an alley. She and Brynn were having a night out barhopping and Shavonne had decided she could walk to an ATM by herself for some quick cash so they could order more drinks. Her short walk out of the bar turned into a nightmare. A man grabbed her, shoved her against a wall, and groped her. He went under her skirt while choking her, so she'd be still and quiet. Brynn found Shavonne in the alley and maced the hell out of that man, sparing Shavonne heaps of trouble and possibly a sexually transmitted disease. After that,

Brynn bought Shavonne a protection kit (bear spray and a pocketknife) and promised to *never* let Shavonne out of her sight and vice versa when they went out. New Orleans, just like any other city, had its dangers, but so long as they stuck together, they'd survive.

Shavonne and Brynn were more like sisters, really. They always said so. Both of them came from shitty childhoods. Both attended Loyola University where they were dormmates for all four years before graduating and becoming real-life roomies. They had their moments where they'd bicker and, sure, Shavonne could be a little overbearing, demanding, and a bit of a neat freak, but regardless of all that, they meshed. Brynn was laidback and chill, where Shavonne was more alert and hyperaware of everything.

Ever since she was a child, Shavonne envisioned the worst-case scenarios. She couldn't help it, really. Her parents died from a worst-case scenario when she was sixteen. They'd gone on a winter cruise and her mother accidentally fell off the boat. Her father jumped in after to save her. There was a whole rescue situation but neither her mother nor father survived.

When her parents passed, all she wanted was to speak to them again, to hear them. She believed in spirits and the afterlife and had even dabbled in witchcraft here and there. She believed that certain crystals let off good and bad energy, and that superstitions were true.

Shavonne was living with her aunt Trudy on 7th Ward when she paid a visit to a psychic in Garden District. She'd saved money from her job at a burger joint just to see this woman, despite Aunt Trudy's warnings.

"Mess with people like them, and they'll mess with you," Aunt Trudy scolded when Shavonne mentioned going to see her.

The psychic's name was Krystal, a plump black lady with bushy gray hair and a smile that reminded her of the Cheshire

Cat. She owned a little voodoo shop that was more like a hole
in the wall called Magic Hour. Shavonne paid Krystal $75 to
have Krystal "call" her parents in the afterlife. The room they
were in was closet-sized and stuffy, with trinkets lining the
wall and incense wafting about, but Shavonne swore she felt
the energy change when Krystal closed her eyes and called for
her parents.

"They miss you," Krystal said with a smile. "Oh, Shavonne, you look just like your mother. She wants you to stop
taking the medication your psychiatrist prescribed to you. She
wants you to heal and grow without them."

Shavonne broke down crying after those words left Krystal's mouth. Truth was, she hadn't cried much since her parents died. She'd been bottling it in, trying to figure out why
them, why her? *Why, why, why?* And now Krystal was talking
about the medication she'd never even mentioned, and it was
proof—proof that the afterlife *was* real, and that all her studies
were true. Well, at first. The truth (and something she later
discovered) was that Krystal had taken a peek inside her purse
when she placed it on the floor before her reading.

Despite it not being real, it gave Shavonne comfort for the
time being, and Krystal took Shavonne under her wing.
Shavonne wanted to know everything about being a psychic,
seeing into other people's minds, knowing their secrets, and
seeing as Krystal was getting up in age and would need someone to take over the shop one day, she let Shavonne hang
around to tidy up the shop and run the register.

Shavonne learned how to palm read, which crystals were
best to wear for wealth and positivity, and even how to feel
other people's energy. The last bit, Shavonne realized as she
got older, was just a gift rooted inside empathetic people. She
felt it all and could sense a negative vibe or a bad person from
a mile away—even a bad situation made the hair on her arms
rise. She felt all of this in that moment and it was those feeling
that had her worried to death about Brynn.

Shavonne paced the apartment then paused by the window that revealed the busy street. She and Brynn had installed an app called The Green Dot on their phones. It was an app that could be used for many reasons—one parents could install on their kids' phones, or for a bitter boyfriend or girlfriend to install on their romantic partner's device to see where they've been without the partner knowing. But she and Brynn used it because it helped them know where each other were, especially on nights when they went out.

She looked up Brynn's location, as she'd done less than ten minutes ago, and it was still pinned somewhere outside the Garden District. If she were still with her ex, she'd be at the Ritz Carlton like she'd planned. She'd been texting Shavonne all night with pictures, bragging about the scene, the singers, the drinks.

Shavonne drew in a slow breath and gave Brynn another call.

No answer.

She fired up another text in all caps: **WHERE THE HELL ARE YOU BRYNN? I'M WORRIED!**

Brynn had a work shift at eleven o'clock and it was already nine-thirty in the morning. She *never* missed work and wouldn't start missing it now over an ex from high school. Shavonne sat on the sofa, blinking at her phone, waiting for a message or a call from her best friend. When a measly five minutes passed, she called Krystal.

"Vonnie?" Krystal answered.

"Hi, Krystal. Do you think I can take the day off? I have a bit of an upset stomach. Probably that crawfish I had last night."

"Oh no! Do you still have some of the peppermint chamomile tea blend I gave you?"

"I do." Shavonne's eyes flickered to the tiny kitchen, where the rack of teas from Magic Hour were. She hated lying to Krystal, but she wasn't sure what else to say. Krystal needed her now more than ever since she was diagnosed with high blood pressure. Krystal, the woman who only ate fruit, vegetables, and drank tea, had high blood pressure. Go figure.

"Well, drink some tea and get better. I'll man the shop today, don't worry about it." Shavonne could tell Krystal was smiling, which made her feel even worse for lying. But she'd feel downright awful if she didn't trust her gut and go after Brynn.

Something wasn't right, and she was going to find out. Worst case scenario, Brynn had been kidnapped then killed. Best case, she'd just forgotten to call or text back and was fucking her ex in every position she could.

When Shavonne hung up, she rushed to the closet and got dressed in dark brown joggers and an oversized T-shirt. She tugged down a black zipper hoodie, just in case, and went for her keys in the key bin.

Inside her car, she checked Brynn's location on the app again, then entered the address of it into her phone's navigation app and followed it.

FORTY-FOUR

SHAVONNE

Four years ago

By the time Shavonne reached the location, her hands were clammy, and she was thirsty. She picked up the plastic bottle of water from her cupholder that'd been sitting in her car for the past two days and gulped some down as she turned onto a street she'd never been on before.

The street took her toward a wrought iron gate with the letters MV built into the iron. She was in Marshview, a neighborhood many people talked about, and a place designated for the rich. She stopped the car and studied the gates, then her eyes wandered to one of the houses behind it. It was massive. All brick, two stories high, with an enormous front yard.

There was a security box to her left that required a pin. She checked her phone again and Brynn was definitely around here somewhere. The Green Dot said she was an eight-minute walk away. But there was a gate and a code required. How was she going to get in?

"Crap," she whispered. She put the car in reverse and drove until she saw a large dirt patch next to a bush. She bet this spot was used for police to park and surveil the neighborhood. She hoped none would come while she staked out.

About twenty minutes went by and not a soul had come in or out of the neighborhood. Fair enough when you're rich during the summer. If you are home and not spending thousands of dollars on vacation, everything you need can be delivered to you and there's really no need to leave home unless you *want* to leave. Fortunately, Brynn's Green Dot hadn't moved.

To her luck, a FedEx truck drove along the back road. It stopped at the gate and a man stepped out of the truck, reading something from his phone before pushing one of the buttons on the security box. The box beeped and the gates spread apart for him.

Shavonne sat up straight, starting the engine of her car and driving behind the FedEx truck. She hoped the gate was the delayed type. When the driver rolled in, she made sure to stick close behind him. Cameras were pitched atop two poles on either side of the gate, but she kept her head down and was glad she wore her hoodie. When she was past the gates, relief sunk in. She pulled to the side of the road after the distance of the Green Dot lessened. The app was now telling her that Brynn was less than two minutes away by foot.

She climbed out of the car, taking a thorough look around. No one was out. Not even a person walking their dog. Shavonne walked along the sidewalk, following the app as Brynn's Green Dot glowed. When the app told her she was less than a minute away, she hustled forward. She threw her hood over her head and stood in front of a gate to one of the houses.

This house was the last one on the end of the street, swallowed up in trees and holly shrubs. From the end of the drive, she couldn't see much, just the tips of the house and a square chimney. She checked for cameras. There was one, but it was pointed down at the ground instead of near the front of the gate, which she found odd. That camera would only catch someone's feet as they passed by—if the lens was wide enough.

Shavonne's gaze swung left and there was a brick column attached to the gate. In the brick column was a built-in mailbox. She opened the mailbox, lifted a foot, and stepped on it. It gave her enough leverage to swing her other leg over the brick wall and hop down. When she landed, she rushed forward, and that's when she noticed the luxury sedan parked in front the house. Someone was around. But Brynn's car wasn't.

She hid behind a tree trunk, checking Brynn's location again. The Green Dot was now telling her she was on top of Brynn's dot. That meant her best friend was somewhere around this house. Or inside it.

Panic rose in Shavonne's throat as she contemplated what to do next. She could've just knocked on the door and asked if Brynn was there. But what if this person lied? What if they'd done something to Brynn? Shavonne was all about instinct and trusting her gut, and something about this did not sit well in hers. Brynn wasn't the type to risk it all for a one-night stand. She had priorities and she often kept to them.

Instead, Shavonne crept along a grassy path to the right of the house until she approached a window. The window revealed a kitchen. It was vacant but in pristine condition, all chrome and white marble. She went to another window. The living room. No one was there. Her heart raced a bit faster as she rounded the back of the house, expecting to hear people gathered and chatting, or Brynn with this random ex of hers, but as she popped her head around the corner, no one was in the back. All the outdoor furniture was covered up with gray weatherproof fabric, pollen, and fallen leaves. It was almost like this house wasn't used much at all.

She spotted a trellis clad with ivy attached to the house. It was tall and white, leading up to the second level. She rushed for it, climbing it carefully, thankful there was nothing behind or next to her but trees and sky.

There was a window to the left, at the top of the trellis. She stopped when she was high enough, gripping one of the slats with one hand and leaning over a bit. The trellis creaked beneath her weight, and she prayed it would hold her hundred and fifty-six pounds.

From this window, she could see an oversized landing. Lights were on inside, and she spotted a bedroom. A person moved back and forth in the room, his phone in hand. It was the guy from the picture Brynn sent. Her ex. She couldn't remember his name—Donte or something. But it was him. He was running his hands over his face, clearly in distress. He stopped pacing to check his phone, then paused, bringing the phone to his ear.

When he walked away, Shavonne couldn't breathe. Because in that bedroom behind him was a pool of blood and a body in a red dress. It wouldn't take a genius to know it was her best friend.

Shavonne's fingers trembled as she withdrew her phone, went to the camera, and snapped a picture of the scene because men like him didn't get caught unless there was proof. This ex of hers had clearly become somebody based off this fancy house and the car parked up front. There was no telling how long Brynn's body had been there, or what he'd done to her. She stared a moment longer, hoping this was some sick prank or game—hoping Brynn would roll over and start laughing (she did have a dark sense of humor) but she didn't. And her worst-case scenario had proven to be true.

Through tears, she climbed down the trellis and ducked around the house. She jumped the brick wall again and hurried to her car, slamming the door behind her with wild breaths.

She needed to call the police, but she couldn't stop herself from breaking down and sobbing first.

FORTY-FIVE

SHAVONNE

Four years ago

Shavonne sat in her car, ready to call the authorities. She had to pull herself together. She picked up the phone, hands trembling, and pressed the numbers in the keypad slowly.

9 . . . 1 . . . 1.

But before she pressed the call button, a black pickup truck drove past her, stopping at the gate of the house she'd just run from.

She sucked in a breath and lowered in her seat, watching as the truck waited for the gate to open. When the gates were spread, the truck drove straight in and moved out of sight.

Wait a minute. Was someone returning to the house? Did this mean they'd find the man who hurt Brynn? Find her body? Perhaps she could corroborate with whoever was in the truck and put Brynn's ex in jail. She waited a few minutes before climbing back out of the car again, jumping the fence again, and landing with a soft grunt.

Hurrying toward a cluster of trees, she watched as a burly man stood on the porch and knocked on the door with a large fist. The man turned a fraction, peering over his shoulder, and

Shavonne crouched behind one of the live oak trees, fingers deep in the tree bark, breaths erratic as she focused on the house ahead.

Mosquitos buzzed around her while gnats fought for her attention. She swatted them away with one hand, and with her hoodie on, she could feel sweat accumulating on her forehead and beneath her bra.

The man faced forward again as the front door opened and she watched Brynn's ex appear on the other side. She couldn't deny he was a handsome man, but it was always the pretty ones with rotten souls. Who just stood around while a body surrounded in blood was near them? The door closed and she waited, pulling out her phone, ready to dial the police. Her fingers hovered over the number. She wasn't sure what was stopping her. To her, none of this felt real. In her mind, Brynn was still alive, and this was all some sick, twisted joke.

She waited.

In less than five minutes, the front door opened again, and the large man walked outside, scanning the area before climbing into his truck and parking backwards, so that the bed of the truck faced the door.

"What is he doing?" she breathed.

He went into the house again and Shavonne waited until the men returned and swung the door open. They were going back and forth in conversation until the burly man tossed something at Brynn's ex. The ex stepped back, so she couldn't see what he was doing, but in a matter of seconds both men bent down. She noticed they both had gloves on.

She tried not to make a noise as the men lifted a rolled-up rug and grunted as they shoved it onto the back of the truck. She bit into her bottom lip and tasted blood when she realized the rug *wasn't* empty—that it was lumpy and misshapen, and pieces of hair stuck out of the ends. *Brynn.*

She pulled out her phone, making sure it was on silent before going to her camera, zooming in, and snapping a picture of them. In the photo, Brynn's ex clung to the end of the rug to make sure it didn't fall. She cursed under her breath. It was a bad picture. To anyone else, it would just look like he was putting something on the truck, not a body.

The big man in the truck spoke once more as he withdrew the truck's bed cover to conceal the body and Shavonne took that opportunity to run back to the brick fence and jump it. She was in her car and behind the wheel when the black pickup rolled out of the driveway. When the man drove past, she started her car, made a U-turn, and followed him out of Marshview.

FORTY-SIX

SHAVONNE

Four years ago

"Damn it." Shavonne dragged a hand over her face as she stared at the mini glowing orange sign on her dashboard. She was running low on gas. She'd been tailing this pickup truck for three and a half hours, making sure to stay several cars back. She was not at all prepared for this journey.

"Please just stick with me. Hopefully it'll only be a few more miles," she whispered, more to herself than her 2012 Toyota.

To her luck, the truck took a ramp off the highway. She followed it, staying behind with no clue where she was. They were still in Louisiana based on all the signs she'd followed, but this particular area was one she'd never heard of.

The truck slowed and turned onto a narrow path. She stopped before the turn as the truck kept driving. She couldn't follow him like she wanted. He'd definitely notice someone tailing him on a solo path—one that clearly led to backwoods or another private house.

She gripped the wheel, staring at the dashboard. A minute ticked by. Then two. Now was good. She turned off her headlights and drove in the dark, passing tall swaying grass and lurking Spanish moss trees that looked like hanging dead bodies in the night. She couldn't see a damn thing, and she nearly jumped out of her skin when her car chimed again, alerting her that gas was low.

The path ended and she cracked the windows, smelling mud and salt. Shavonne waited at the end of the path, looking ahead at the open field of grass and trees. Where did the truck go? She looked left, then right. No sign of it . . . that is until she spotted red taillights ahead, snaking between a cluster of trees. She veered left and drove toward overgrown shrubs, parking along the side of them. No one would see her car. With haste, she climbed out of the vehicle and ran across the field, stopping short of the truck and hiding behind a tree.

The man had the headlights of his truck flashing forward and stood in the light with a thick-handled shovel. With a heavy grunt, he pitched the sharp end of the shovel into the ground and began digging. Shavonne went around the back of the truck as the man continued digging and listened for any sign that Brynn was alive. She couldn't hear a thing.

She moseyed into nearby bushes and waited. She didn't know what the hell she was going to do, and her phone was down to seven percent. She could've called police but there was no cell reception out here. This man had chosen this location for a reason and now she regretted not calling the police at the house when she had the chance. What the hell was she going to do to stop him? She had no weapons on her, other than some bear spray and a pocketknife. That wouldn't take him down though, and if Brynn *was* dead, she would be putting her life at risk for nothing.

She sat with her back against a tree trunk, listening for what felt like hours as the man dug until, finally, he stopped and walked around the truck. A tree branch snapped under her knee as she shifted forward to get a better look and the man's head whipped back. He looked in her direction and she cupped her mouth, trying to make herself as small as possible. Her breaths felt loud as they poured out of her nostrils. The man stared for a long, long time. He took a step in her direction and her heart might as well have shot up to her throat.

Then, just when she couldn't take another second of the still silence, a rabbit scurried past her and hopped across the field. The man sucked his teeth and went back to what he was doing. He opened the bed of the truck and hauled out the rug with Brynn's body. He dragged the rug around the truck with mild grunts and gasps, then he unrolled it next to the hole. He wasted no time dumping Brynn's body into the ground and Shavonne could've sworn she heard a small sound—a whimper or a cry as he did so, but the man acted like he didn't hear a thing. He tossed in a purse with her and went straight for his shovel to start scooping dirt and dumping it into the hole.

Thick tears lined Shavonne's cheeks as she watched him cover her best friend. What she really wanted to do was get into the man's truck and run him over, but she was shaking like a leaf. She'd never dealt with anything like this before in her life and she wasn't brave like Brynn. She didn't fight men or spray them with pepper spray. She just . . . *cowered*. And she sat there while her friend was being buried alive, and the man kept shoveling and scooping until he'd finished. And when he was done, he threw the dirty shovel onto the bed of the truck, along with the bloodied rug, and drove away.

But Shavonne wouldn't let this be it.

She may have been scared to confront him, but she could still try to save Brynn. She waited until the man drove away, taking the path to the main roads. When she could no longer see his taillights, she ran back to her car and pulled out a shovel of her own. It wasn't anything like the man's in the truck. Hers was half the size of his and rusted with a cracked handle. She'd bought it when she and Krystal had gone to the beach to look for shells they could sell in the shop. It was possible the shovel would break on the first dig, but she didn't care. She wouldn't stop. She'd get Brynn's body, dead or alive.

She dug quickly, thankful the dirt was soft. It was a bit moist, but it was fine. She kept digging with heavy breaths. Her shoulders ached and her arms grew numb. Her palms were sore and raw, and she was getting tired, but she didn't relent—not until she saw one of Brynn's hands. It was twitching. Then she heard moaning. It was faint, but it was definitely coming from the hole.

"Oh, God. Hold on, Brynn!" Shavonne wailed. She ditched the shovel and dropped to her knees, scraping at the dirt. It wedged beneath her fingernails as she clawed at it, powering through the numbness and pain until she could see Brynn's face.

Dirt clogged her best friend's nose, and her eyes were closed. There was a gash on her forehead that was so deep she could see some of the white meat. Dirt had wedged its way in there too. Shavonne was positive it'd get infected, but an infection was better than death.

She clawed and clawed until finally, the top half of Brynn's body was visible. Then she grabbed Brynn's arm and hauled her up while using her own body to climb out of the hole. She wasn't sure how she'd done it. Never in her life had Shavonne felt strong. She didn't lift weights and she hardly worked out, yet she'd managed to get Brynn's body onto main ground, and she cried when Brynn's bloodshot eyes fluttered open and looked right into hers.

FORTY-SEVEN

BRYNN

I truly felt like I'd died that night. Perhaps a part of me did—that bright-eyed, kind, and generous version of myself. The woman who gave every person the benefit of the doubt, who cared more than she should have, and made time for people who truly didn't deserve it? She'd been buried. When all the dirt had piled up, filling my nostrils and every other facial hole, the nice Brynn was no more. I'd become a Brynn in *survival* mode.

I moaned as loudly as I could beneath the dirt, eyes closed, trying to move, but completely immobile. I was losing breath second by second. I managed to move one arm to claw at the dirt, but it'd been so packed down that it was impossible. My head still throbbed, and my eyes burned behind my eyelids. This was torture at its purest form and all I could wonder was how someone could do this to another human? How can you hurt someone so much, try to hide it, and still sleep at night? No one in their right mind is capable of such heinous things.

I can remember what it felt like drawing in what felt like my last breaths. But then I heard something. Grunting. Scraping. Thudding. Then I felt humid air hit my face and I could breathe through my mouth again. I sucked in a breath, swallowing dirt and grass. My hand twitched, my feet were shaking. A hand clutched my wrist and a person groaned as they tugged me out of my burial ground, their hands on my face, swiping. There was a familiar voice, but it was muted from the dirt in my ears. My eyes cracked open, and I saw two of the same woman. I knew her but couldn't remember her name at the time. She sucked in a breath and her face was wet with tears as she wept. I wanted to smile at her, to hug her because it seemed like she needed it, but the darkness threatened to steal me away again.

"No, no, no. Brynn, please. *Please*," the woman begged. "Open your eyes. You have to stay awake."

My vision was blurred. I couldn't see her face. She wiped my lips, removed some of the dirt. She resuscitated me and I could breathe. Barely.

She managed to get me inside a warm area. A car. It jostled and bumped along the grass until she hit even pavement. I was in and out on the backseat of the car, streetlights flashing across my face. I remember the sky though, inky and filled with blinking stars. Then I remembered blinding white light and seeing the woman from an upside-down angle as she peered around while standing next to the back door of the car. She was inside again, starting the engine and whispering the words, "Yes. Okay. I'm gonna get you to a hospital now, Brynn. Just had to get some gas. Stay with me."

When the car came to its final stop, I closed my eyes for good. I'd made peace with God and was now ready to accept my fate.

FORTY-EIGHT

BRYNN

Ten days later

"We should go to the police." Shavonne whispered the words to me but they were insanely loud. The room I was in was white and sterile, with blinding lights that forced me to close my eyes. I'd had surgery days ago due to a concussion that caused a subdural hematoma, or in common terms, bleeding between my skull and my brain.

The doctor and nurses constantly told me I was lucky to be alive, and even luckier that I was coherent so soon. Shavonne told the doctors I'd fallen down the stairs.

The doctors have tested my memory, asked me about colors, shapes—simple things kindergarteners would be asked. I recalled most of it. The only thing that'd stumped me was figuring out the name of a cylinder and diamond.

However, I remembered some things, despite the head trauma. I recalled the scent of coffee as it floated through the hallways of the hospital. I remembered the name Jell-O, as it jiggled in the bowl on my tray. I remembered milk, spoons, forks. But, for some odd reason, I couldn't remember much of the night Shavonne was pressing me about. That's another thing I could remember after spending time with her. Shavonne, my best friend. My confidante. The woman who saved my life.

She wants me to remember. I was fully functioning for the first time in days. Prior to that, I'd been in and out of consciousness because of the surgery, But on this day, I was alert. Bandages were still wrapped around my head, and a drip bag infused with morphine was connected to my arm.

"This whole thing is going to go cold, Brynn. I told you what I saw. What *they* did." Someone walked past the room and Shavonne clamped her mouth shut. When they were gone, she focused on me again, gripping my hand.

"I can't even remember what happened, Vonne," I croaked.

"Yeah but look at you. The longer we wait, the worse it'll be. They'll get away with it, Brynn." She removed her phone from her hoodie pocket, swiped through it, and showed me photos. There was an image of me, a selfie—and behind me was my ex-boyfriend, Dominic. "You don't remember spending time with him?" she inquired.

I blinked, and for some odd reason, my heartbeat sped up a notch. Shavonne glanced at the heart monitor as it beeped at a faster pace but returned her attention to me. I stared at the phone so long the image became blurry. I blinked, and tears slipped down my cheeks.

That's the thing about trauma. It festers, and it's a relentless beast that doesn't care how your life is going. It will attack you at any given moment without so much as a warning. There is always something to trigger you—to bring you back to what you think you've forgotten. The body remembers whether the mind wants to or not. And seeing the image of that man caused some of the memories to come back to me like grainy pictures.

The drinks. The laughter. The car ride and streetlights flashing across his face. The taste of apple juice. Hands clasped around my wrists, pinning me down. A slap.

My hand twitched when I remembered the slap. I'd never hit anyone like that before, but something told me he deserved it.

"It was Dominic, right?" I whisper and Shavonne's eyes light up. "That was his name. Dominic Baker."

"Yes! That's him. Look, I took a picture of your body on the floor in that house, and also when they put you in a rug on a truck. We can show these photos to the police and have him arrested. All the proof is here."

My head shook. "He's probably long gone, Shavonne."

"So what? Brynn, we have proof that he hurt you. Look, the police are going to show up again and ask what happened. I didn't know what to say when I first brought you in, but they clearly found your situation strange and said they'd come back when you're alert."

"No, Vonne, all you have is a picture of me lying on the ground, a man holding the end of a rug, and a selfie of me with him in the background. It won't prove anything."

She faltered. "But you didn't get hurt for no reason. They tried to bury you. *Alive*," she reminds me.

"Imagine how it'll sound if I say I was buried alive? Imagine what they'll think if you tell them you followed some random man into the woods and saw him burying my body? No one would believe it, Shavonne," I hissed. "For all we know, they'll think *you* were in on it!"

"But I wasn't!" she exclaimed.

"I know that, but it just . . . it won't add up. And . . . I'm *scared*, Vonne. I—I can't remember what all he did, but I don't *ever* want to see him again."

She pulled her phone away, tucking it into her hoodie pocket. "Brynn, I know you're scared, but this man almost got away with murder."

I swallowed and the saliva was rough going down. "I need water."

"Where's the Brynn who fights?" Shavonne went on, and her question cut me in two. "You can't let him win. You can take him down and get justice."

"I need water," I repeated, more firmly this time.

I couldn't take any more of her optimism. Could she see the state I was in? I'd just had surgery in my head to stop the bleeding. The fact that I even survived was a miracle and she wanted me to go *back* to that horrifying situation with Dominic? She was out of her mind. Plus, I knew how the system worked. Dominic was a rich man with rich people at his side and I was a poor woman with *nothing* to my name. I was worthless and not a single person would care about my outcome but the people sitting in this hospital room. Even my parents wouldn't have cared. My momma, God rest her soul, would've scoffed and asked me, "Well what did you do to provoke them?"

That's why I was so ready to leave North Carolina and make a fresh start when the time came. I would no longer be gaslit or put last. I could flee and put myself first . . . but fleeing only backfired.

If Dominic didn't get away with burying me nearly two weeks ago, he *definitely* would the next time around.

After gulping down the water my best friend poured for me, I turned over and gave her my back.

"Come on, Brynn. You have to fight." Shavonne's voice was laced with hurt, with hopelessness.

I closed my eyes, but that didn't stop the tears from falling.

FORTY-NINE

BRYNN

Two months later

I was lucky to still have a job at Franco's and Nulli's mini mart. Truthfully, I think the managers felt sorry for me. I'd lied and told them I'd gone hiking, fell, and hit some rocks, which caused my concussion. They took one look at the large gash on my head and kept me on their payroll. Pity sucks, but not when it works in your favor.

I'd decided that after that horrible night with Dominic, I would keep my head down. I'd work to fill my hours and avoid going out at all costs. Not that going out was a priority. I was ugly now. The scar on my head had healed, sure, but it was still red and prominent. I looked like half my head had been chewed by some sharp-toothed monster, not to mention the newly developed migraines were random and brutal. I often couldn't finish a sentence because I couldn't think of words. My mind was just so spacey.

Every morning that I looked in the mirror, I wanted to cry. He'd done this to me and I couldn't figure out why. With each passing day, the fuzzy details would come back to me though. They started off muted and vague, like a black-and-white TV show without the volume, so it was easy to dismiss at first. But slowly, like a snowball rolling to create an avalanche, it all came back. My doctor informed me that it would take some time for some memories to return. But I'd hoped some time would be three or four years down the road, when I was better off mentally, not two months later.

Because they'd returned at such full force, I had trouble sleeping. I woke up in the middle of the night screaming, hand clutching my chest as I remembered the man on top of me, followed by the stack of papers and the dark look in Dominic's eyes. The fight we had, a blow to my head, and then cold dirt being shoveled on top of my body. Shavonne ran into my room, eyes wide like saucers. She saw me on the bed, curled in the fetal position, and she laid with me. As I cried, she held me and told me everything would be alright.

But would everything be okay again? The old Brynn would've believed it, but this *new* Brynn? I had no clue who she was. She was cold and bitter and angry. She was mean and tasteless and afraid to even check the mail.

The next morning, Shavonne tried cheering me up. She had a spread of breakfast on the table—eggs, pancakes, bacon, orange juice. We ate together in silence while *Charmed* circa 1998 played in the background. I went to work shortly after to help the morning crew at Franco's prepare for an engagement party that would be booking the entire restaurant for the night.

But when I went in, I saw a man standing at the bar, and my whole body turned to ice.

FIFTY

BRYNN

The man turned around and, just as I'd suspected, it was him. The old white man with the oversized nose who'd sat with Dominic the day he bristled his way to New Orleans. He was speaking to Chad, one of the bartenders, with a to-go box in hand. I couldn't remember the man's name. Jim. Jake? No, John. It was John.

I stood near the door, drawing in deep breaths. I couldn't move my feet even if I'd wanted to. I was stuck in place, and my heart boomed when the man bid Chad farewell and turned in my direction. He walked toward the exit, but his head tipped when he spotted someone in his path. He smiled as if he were a true gentleman and stepped around me.

Before he reached the door, he paused and said, "Wait . . . I remember you."

I peered over my shoulder with my pulse erratically beating in my ears.

"You waited one of my tables before, right? Exceptional service. Keep it up." And with that, he was gone.

I faced the door, watching him climb into the back of an SUV. When the SUV took off, I ran to the bathroom, shoved the door open, and hit the first stall. All the breakfast I'd had with Shavonne went flying into the toilet.

When I was done, I sank to my bottom and pressed my back against the stall wall. I couldn't help crying, nor could I stop. Not for at least fifteen minutes. I finally collected myself, left the stall, and rinsed my face with cold water at the sink.

When I felt I was stable enough, I walked back out and went straight to the kitchen. I immediately went to work, hoping no one would notice my puffy red eyes or how on edge I was.

That stupid man. He was there that night. He was on top of me. He . . . turned me over. Pushed himself into my ass. He didn't even remember that he'd done it.

I swallowed hard, chopping vegetables, my focus on the silver blade of the knife. I wish I'd had the knife when he walked by. I would've stabbed him right in the chest with it, twisted the knife, and smiled on my way to prison.

Trent made his way back, checking things off his clipboard while Victor washed dishes. Sous Chef Eric was behind the stove, seasoning a slab of meat.

Something in the corner caught my eye and I looked up at the TV. A woman was on screen, speaking to someone I knew. I stopped chopping the veggies and felt a tight squeeze in my chest when I saw Dominic Baker on the screen and on the blue bar beneath him in bold font were the words **FIRST BLACK GOVERNOR OF NORTH CAROLINA SPEAKS ABOUT EXPERIENCE**.

It was a popular news channel—a nationwide one, in fact. And he was on it. The TV was muted, however I didn't have to hear him speaking to know every word coming out of his mouth was utter bullshit. I stood behind the counter, knife gripped in hand, staring at his arrogant face on the screen and that deceivingly charming smile. The screen switched to reveal a carousel of images of him standing with citizens, children,

and even shaking hands with the Obamas. Being around the
Obamas was impressive, I had to admit, but what caught my
attention most was the image of him and his wife. It was one
of the pictures in his phone, the one his wife said was her favorite.

Did his wife know that he was a lying, backstabbing piece
of shit? Did she know that he was abusive and okay with mur-
dering someone just to cover his own ass?

It occurred to me then, right in Franco's kitchen, that Dominic tried getting me to sign that NDA because he was running for this role as governor. He'd conned me into thinking
we had a chance, when really he was using me to get whatever he needed from that man John. He'd practically spat in
my face, and now he was making national headlines and smiling proudly, as if he were a saint. As if he hadn't had his ex-
girlfriend raped and nearly *murdered* her!

Oh, I was angry. The rage filled me from head to toe. I
stewed in that rage while fulfilling my duties at Franco's. And
normally after a shift, I was exhausted and ready to sleep, but I
wasn't tired that night because I had a plan. It was only an
inkling of one, but it was enough to push the Brynn boat full
steam ahead.

It was that day when I realized I had the advantage. It was
too late to go to the police. That hole Shavonne dug was
probably a muddy cavern now. The place Dominic had rented
was most likely spotless and without a strand of my DNA. I
once felt like I was at a loss, but quickly realized I could take
him down myself. Dominic didn't know that I was still alive,
and so long as he figured I was dead, I could make his life a *living hell*.

I drove straight home, walked into the house, and waited
for Shavonne to get out of the shower. She screamed when
she caught me pacing on the other side of the bathroom door.

"My God, Brynn! What the hell is wrong with you? You
scared me!" she cried.

"I'm sorry," I told her. "But you're right. I've thought about it, Shavonne. I saw his stupid face on the news. He's the fucking governor of North Carolina now."

"What?" she blinked, confusion filling her eyes.

"Dominic is the governor," I said.

She gasped. "You're joking, right?"

"I'm not joking." I huffed a dry laugh. "We're going to take him down, Vonne. We're going to make him pay for what he did."

PART THREE

FIFTY-ONE

BRYNN

Meeting Dominic was a mistake. I saw the wedding band on his finger and knew he wasn't available, but I went with him anyway. I suppose I can't fully fault him for my decisions.

Though I was eager to meet him, there was something about him that'd changed from the time he was in Franco's, to when I met him at the lounge. Even the way he reacted to the magician and the talk of his mother was unsettling, but I pushed through it.

I didn't notice all the other ways at first either. It took me some time to go over that night, to analyze the smallest details and work out those fuzzy kinks. There was a shiftiness in his eyes as they darted around the club. He was overly aware of *everyone* around us, but in the back of my mind, I figured he was just that kind of person. Considering his childhood and his mom's death, it made sense. Plus, I'd been around people who didn't trust their surroundings. How can you trust them when you live in a country where someone can waltz inside with an automatic weapon and blast everyone inside it to smithereens? It makes sense, really, to be alert and vigilant in a world like this.

But Dominic had no reason to be that night—unless he

had something to hide. And I was the idiot who chose to ignore the signs. Instead, I drank the fruity drinks and grew increasingly comfortable with him. I trusted him to take care of me, like he had when we were kids. But there was still a niggling inside me that pushed me to take extra precautions, whether I saw them as precautions or not. Sure, Dominic Baker had been my high school sweetheart, but people changed as they aged, and sometimes not for the better.

I made sure to take pictures, even when he wasn't looking. I made sure to double check The Green Dot app so Shavonne would know where I was. Best friends look out for each other, you see. And she did.

If Shavonne had never been the worrying type, or the kind of person who assumed the worst in someone before the best, I would be dead. But it's because of her that I'm alive and breathing. We pieced together this entire plan to take down the man who nearly killed me and we knew the risks going into it. Now she's missing, and I'll be damned if my friend dies because of my need for revenge.

I raise the gun now, tempted to press it into Jolene Baker's forehead. I came through their back fence to avoid the police parked upfront.

Jolene opens her mouth, like she's about to scream, but I raise a finger to my lips. "Nah-uh. Don't do that."

Her mouth clamps shut, and she takes a step back as I keep the gun steady in one hand. I step into her oversized house, using my free hand to close the door behind me.

"Where is your husband, Jolene?"

She swallows. "I—I don't know."

"You don't know, or you don't want to tell me?"

"I really don't know," she says in more of a whine this time. Her head turns a fraction to glance over her shoulder. I turn my gaze that way, knowing it's the kitchen. I step forward as she steps back and spot a Saint Laurent purse on the table.

"Go to the kitchen, close all the windows," I order. She turns swiftly to shut the blinds and when she faces me again, I gesture to the table. "Sit down."

She sits, eyeing her purse. I hear water trickling above, running through the pipes of the house. Someone is upstairs. She's lying.

As if she's aware that I hear something, she quickly says, "I started a bath. The water is still running. I—I can show you . . . if you want me to."

I ignore her. I don't give a damn if the bath is running. This house deserves to flood. I gesture to the purse with my gun. "Is your phone in there?"

"Yes," she replies.

"Take it out."

She reaches for the bag, pulling back a clasp and digging into it. I raise the gun, in case she tries to do something stupid, like draw her own weapon. When she takes out the phone, I step forward and snatch the bag away.

"Unlock it," I demand.

Her hands are shaking as she unlocks it. Once it's done, I tuck the purse beneath my armpit then take the phone from her. I go to The Green Dot app on her iPhone and spot Dominic's name. When I tap it, it shows a location—somewhere forty-five minutes from here.

"Brynn," the wife says, and I eye her. "I—what's happened?" She stares at me, eyes glistening. The water continues trickling above.

"He has my best friend," I tell her.

"What do you mean?"

"I mean that he *kidnapped* her. I've tried texting and calling her and she's not answering." I also checked The Green Dot, and her last location was near the motel. I searched until I found her phone near the trees. Dominic must've tossed it before taking her.

Jolene's head shakes. "No. Dominic wouldn't do that."

I narrow my eyes at her. "You'll be surprised to know what your husband will do and the lengths he'll go just to cover his own sorry ass. I know that you know, Jolene. He's done some terrible things to you too."

Her head drops as shame seems to wash over her. "I—I don't know why he'd take your friend, but I promise you, I have nothing to do with it."

"Sure." I put her phone in my pocket. "How about we discuss it on the car ride to his location." It's not an offer. She literally has no choice. Jolene rises from her chair, trembling.

"C-can I at least turn the bath water off?"

I stare at her, and she fidgets. Good Lord, I feel sorry for this woman. It is true—Shavonne and I feel sorry for her. She's gotten the short end of the stick, and it's not her fault that her husband is a lying, manipulating jerk. I draw in a breath, then cock my head toward the stairs.

Her eyes light up as she rushes past me and I follow her up the stairs, keeping my gun on her back. I can't help studying the upstairs area, the landing, abstract paintings on the wall, and many, *many* bedroom doors. Dominic has all this, plus a beautiful wife, and he doesn't deserve any of it.

Jolene enters a master suite that's painted a creamy color with a beige bed spread and disappears into the bathroom. I find her around the corner, watching as she turns off the faucets. The bath water is over halfway full.

Jolene faces me, wringing her fingers together.

"Get some shoes while you're at it," I tell her, and she nods, ducking past me to get to her closet. She takes out a pair of running sneakers, slips them on, and I tell her to take us to the garage.

Once we're in the car, I place her phone in the cellphone dashboard mount so she can unlock it again. She types in the code, and I memorize it—030684. I bet it's her birthday. Typical, just like her husband. I toss my backpack inside the car before sitting in the backseat.

"These are the rules," I say as she opens the garage gate and starts the engine. "You keep your hands on the wheel, ten and two. You follow the GPS and drive only. Don't look at anyone in their cars, don't ask to make a stop to pee or any of that. We're going to drive and get my friend back. If you do *anything* wrong, I will put a bullet in your head and I'm not joking, Jolene."

"But how do you know he has her at this location?" she asks.

"I don't. But I know he took her, and if he sees that I have *you*, perhaps he'll relent."

She swallows hard, shaking her head. "This is ridiculous. God, what has he gotten me into?"

I press the gun to the back of her head and give it a nudge. "Drive."

"This is ridiculous, Brynn. There are officers at the end of the driveway! They'll see you pointing a gun at me and—"

"I'll duck. Now go."

She shudders as she grips the wheel and presses on the gas. I duck and though I'm playing this bad girl role, my heart thunders in my chest as she goes over the hump that takes us onto the main road, right where I know a Sheriff is parked. If they see me, I'm doomed. If she makes even the slightest gesture that someone is in the car with her, I'm dead and I won't be able to save Shavonne. I eye her through the gaps of the seat, and she's focused, hands ten and two like I instructed.

She starts to turn the wheel, but someone beeps their car horn. Blue and white lights flash, and my heart sinks to my stomach.

FIFTY-TWO

JOLENE

"Shit." I look through the rearview mirror and watch as Sheriff Burnell walks my way. Her hand is at her waist, close to her firearm, and she comes toward my side of the car. "They're coming to my window," I whisper. I feel the car shift a bit as Brynn adjusts herself lower. The windows of my BMW are tinted, so Burnell shouldn't be able to see Brynn in her dark clothing on the floor unless she aims a flashlight back there.

Officer Burnell stops at my window, wearing a cordial smile. "First Lady, just want to check in. The governor told me you wouldn't be leaving until the morning to head to Charlotte for the rally. Is everything okay?"

"Oh, yeah! Everything's fine." I try and keep my voice steady, but it comes out overly chipper.

Officer Burnell gives me a funny look. "You're sweating a bit. You sure you're okay?"

"Oh, I was on the treadmill before coming out."

"Ah. I see." Burnell eyes me, then glances at the back window. My heartbeat accelerates, even more so when I feel the hardness of Brynn's gun pushing into my right side.

"Can I tell you the truth, Sheriff Burnell?" I ask.

"Please. Call me Stacey," Burnell says, her attention on me again.

"Right. Well the truth is I'm sneaking away to my best friends' house for a few drinks, Stacey. This weekend's rally will be a big one and I'm a little nervous for Dom. A few drinks will do me some good. I'll most likely crash at her place for the night, though, so no need to wait up."

Stacey smiles at that. "Oh, I hear that, Mrs. Baker. I can imagine times like these are stressful, especially with it being so close to voting day."

"They sure are."

The gun eases off my side.

"Well, I'll keep my eye on the house, make sure it goes undisturbed."

"Thank you so much, Stacey. Your services truly mean a lot."

Stacey bobs her head with pressed lips and steps away from the car. When she turns, I drive off, refusing to give her another inch.

It isn't until I'm on the freeway that I hear Brynn sigh. She climbs over the middle console and sits in the passenger seat. Her gun is still pointed at me, but not as firmly.

"You didn't snitch," she says.

I blink a few times. "You have to save your friend."

"Yeah, but my friend involves your husband."

I let her words marinate in the silence.

"Look, whatever Dominic did for you to have to come to these circumstances is clearly not okay. I just want you to know that I had nothing to do with his plans. He's been out of control for quite some time and you aren't the only person who wants to teach him a lesson."

Brynn sniffs, sitting further back in the leather seat. "You really have no clue about that night? Nothing at all?"

I shake my head.

"He's never even brought up my name to you?"

My head shakes again.

"Figures," she mutters, looking through the windshield. If I'm not mistaken, her eyes are glistening. My chest tightens as I look away.

FIFTY-THREE

BRYNN

My leg bounces in front of me as I keep the gun pointed at Jolene. I feel a migraine coming on, and they've been coming more frequently. My doctor informed me that I was prone to migraines. With head trauma like mine, it was typical.

I grab my backpack from the backseat and unzip the front pouch.

"What are you doing?" Jolene asks, panicking.

"Just keep driving," I mumble, retrieving the orange pill bottle from the pocket. I remove the lid, dumping a hydrocodone into my palm. I swallow it dry then pick up my gun again as Jolene keeps her hands wrapped around the steering wheel.

Her phone rings and I spot the name Samuel on the screen. I eye her as she lifts a hand to decline the call. When she's settled again, she blows a breath and says, "I'll get back to him later."

The car is silent again. The soothing sound of wind rushing past the vehicle and the pitter-patter of rain allows me to relax for a moment.

"So, I take it you're fed up with your husband too and that's why you helped me back there?" I ask.

She glances at me through the corner of her eye as head-lights drag over her face. She won't answer. Fair enough. I *am* holding her hostage.

"I saw what he did to you in the kitchen," I murmur. Perhaps that'll get her to stir.

She almost doesn't react. *Almost*. Her mouth twitches, like it wants to turn downward so she can frown. "Let's just find your friend and deal with this."

"How exactly do you plan on dealing with *this*, Jolene?" I ask. "Please enlighten me. Because the way I see it, your husband not only tried to bury me alive, but he has now kidnapped my best friend."

Her head turns so she can steal a look at me.

I sit back against the seat. "You think he's so perfect."

"I—I don't. I know he's not perfect." Her throat bobs up and down, "God, Brynn. I'm so sorry."

I hate that she calls me by my first name. She's trying to humanize me when the truth is I'm not the one who needs it. Her husband does. Hell, she probably does too. People know when they get married that their spouse has a flaw. Jolene knew from the moment she said *I do* that she'd have to take his secrets with her to the grave. That's what spouses do. They honor and protect and all that extra crap.

"Why are you apologizing for him?" I ask, in more of a snap.

"Because I just—I've sensed something off for so long, but never thought it would be this. *Kidnapping* people. *Burying* them." Her bottom lip rolls between her teeth.

I sigh and look through the windshield. It's now drizzling and the tiny dots on the window glow red from other cars taillights.

"Why did you come here, really?" she asks.

"Because he assumed I was dead. I wanted to show him that he can't escape his past or his mistakes. He ruined my life."

Jolene stares ahead without blinking. "Your life isn't the only one he's ruined," she mumbles.

I keep quiet. I don't care about her sob story. This woman has it made, with her fancy house, car, and the luxury little tea shop she owns. What could possibly be so hard about her life?

"What if . . . what if I can help?" Jolene asks.

My attention switches to hers again. "Help how?"

"Dominic doesn't know that you're with me. Maybe we can use that to our advantage."

I frown, and my eyes shift from her to the screen of her phone. I suck in a breath when I see Dominic's location has changed. He is now twenty minutes *away* from the original location. What the hell happened? That stupid call must've caused the app to glitch.

"Wait a minute," I breathe. "He's not there anymore. Where is he going?"

Jolene pulls to the side of the road, her windshield wipers smoothly swaying back and forth. She peers at the phone too and says, "He's probably going to the apartment we have. Or he could be on his way to Charlotte."

"No." I remove the phone from the stand, shoving it into her hand. "Call him *right now*. Tell him you know what he's done and that you're on the way to his previous location."

"But—"

"Look, if you really want to help me, you'll do this! Like you said, he doesn't know that I'm with you. I can use that! But he needs to be around. He can't get away!"

"Why?" she asks, bottom lip trembling.

I push the phone further into her hand and point the gun at her head again. I could tell her the truth of why I need him around—that I want to face him, shoot him a time or two and make him bleed and suffer—but there's a chance she'll never press a foot to the gas.

I watch her press Dominic's name and call him.

"Put it on speakerphone," I order.

She does and holds the phone up so I can see the screen.

"Jo, what is it?" Dominic's voice floods the car and I try hard not to cringe at the sound of it.

"Dominic," Jolene gasps. Her eyes swing to mine, glistening behind the blue light of the dashboard. I shift the gun forward in warning. If she says anything to ruin this, I *will* shoot her. "Dominic, listen. I—I know about the Nokia at the apartment. I saw the letters. The pictures. Who is Brynn, Dominic? You have to tell me!"

"God damn it, Jolene! I told you I had it handled!" he shouts.

"I don't care! I'm worried about you! I'm your wife! Just tell me where you are so I can help!"

Dominic huffs into the phone. "I'm heading to Charlotte. I can't miss the rally."

"Well . . ." She swallows. "I won't be at the rally."

"*What?*" he snaps.

"I saw your location at Briggs Lane. I'm going there. Whatever you're hiding, I need to figure it out. I can't help you otherwise."

"No, Jo! You can't—"

She hangs up the phone and I want to slow-clap for her and sing bravo. Her eyes find mine and I lower the gun an inch. Seconds later, her phone buzzes with a text.

"What does it say?" I ask.

"He's going back to Briggs Lane too."

I sit up straighter as she places the phone back on the stand, then turns the steering wheel to get back on the road.

"You know what Briggs Lane is, right?" I ask and she shakes her head with an empty look in her eyes. "It's his mom's cabin. The place he grew up."

Her eyes dart to mine quickly and she nearly veers off the road.

"He never told you about it?"

"No," she murmurs.

"Well, now you know."

FIFTY-FOUR

JOLENE

Of course, I know about Briggs Lane. As soon as I saw it pop up as his location, I knew why he was there and I wanted so badly to ignore it.

There was a time, right before my father died, when he told me he'd hired a private investigator to look deeper into Dominic and his past. We were eating dinner—me, dad, and my witch of a mother—and I was so angry to hear him confess this information. *I did it for you, Joey*, he'd said.

He told me there were things I needed to know about Dominic, and that I shouldn't be so quick to marry him. Daddy said Dominic was no good for the family. At the time, I just assumed my father was being overprotective and overbearing and was willing to throw any information at me in order to get me to leave Dominic, so I chucked my fork on the table and left.

I flew straight home to Raleigh that night. Dominic had business in South Carolina. But my father wouldn't have been, well, my *father,* if he hadn't mailed the documents to me the following day. Inside it were news clippings about a woman who'd been abducted for months and then returned. This woman was heavyset and appeared older than her actual age listed in the article. Her hair was gray, and her eyes were big and familiar. There were more news reports about this same woman killing herself. And then a picture popped out of the envelope of a young Dominic and his mother. She had her arm wrapped around him as they faced a camera. He was smiling. She was not. Below the photo were the words: **Missing local woman Beretta Baker reunites with her son Dominic Baker**. More info was inside the envelope, like the title to a house with the address 4951 Briggs Lane in Raleigh, North Carolina.

I couldn't believe what I was reading. Dominic told me his mother was in a psychiatric facility. He said I could never visit her because she was unwell, and he was worried she'd lash out at me. But all this time, she'd been dead, and he lied about it. Why did he lie?

I took it upon myself to find this house on Briggs Lane, so I grabbed my keys and drove to the address, only to find a cabin that was in horrible shape. It was surrounded by enormous trees and covered in vines. Dusty rocking chairs were on the porch. To my surprise, the cabin was unlocked so I took a peek inside. The house was dirtier inside, particles floating in the air.

I stepped into one of the bedrooms, and one of the floorboards wobbled beneath my feet. I found pictures tucked beneath that floorboard as well as a note. To this day, that note haunts me because even though it was a suicide letter, it's written in *Dominic's* handwriting.

When I saw the app pull up Dominic's location at that address, I couldn't figure out why he'd go *there* of all places. Now I'm here, sitting next to a scorned woman and making my way back to that haunting place.

It doesn't take long for me to find it. I drive along a dirt path that winds upward between massive trees, and spot the cabin perched on a hill. I park near a tree and out of sight, like Brynn insists, and we sit for a moment, staring ahead. Lights are on inside the cabin and a husky silhouette passes by the window.

It's Boaz. I know it is.

"What's your plan?" I ask.

Brynn keeps her eyes ahead, focused on the cabin. Then she grabs my phone, pops open the passenger door, and says, "To get my friend back."

I watch her run through the grass and find a footpath that leads to the house, peering around as she goes. Her hood is on her head, making her look like a thief in the night.

When she's far enough, I lean forward and reach under my seat until I feel something hard and cold. I pull my other phone out that only one other person knows about, power it on, and make two necessary calls.

FIFTY-FIVE

BRYNN

I have no idea what I'm doing. I didn't think Dominic would be stupid enough to bring Shavonne here, and being at this cabin has thrown off my entire plan.

When I saw him camped out around the motel, I knew he'd go to drastic measures just to conceal the truth, so we went forward with the plan anyway.

Actually, it was Shavonne who noticed him the very first time. She saw his car parked across the way when she'd left The Bean Bar and pretended not to notice the lurking black SUV. She rode straight to our motel and when she was inside, she watched from the window as Dominic parked on the side of the road.

Then, a few days after planting the dead crow in his trunk, he shows up. I noticed him first when I ran to get ice from the ice machine in the lobby. The Black SUV was parked near a cluster of trees, close to abandoned buildings and trucks. The engine clearly wasn't running, as none of the lights were on, but I spotted Dominic's frame behind the wheel.

"He's out there," I told Shavonne when I went back to the room with the ice.

She pulled her head out of her book, frowning. "Seriously?"

"Yes. I knew it'd only be a matter of time."

"Damn." She swallowed, her eyes bouncing around the motel room. "How long do we make him wait?"

"A few hours," I said, dropping ice into a plastic cup. I cracked open a cherry flavored Pepsi and poured it over the ice. "We need him to be desperate—to get impatient and antsy, like we planned. That's when people make the most mistakes."

And sure enough, he did. I watched from behind the back of the motel as he punched Shavonne in her face. It took everything in me not to scream, not to run out and shoot him with the unregistered pistol I'd bought from some man's trunk in New Orleans. Dominic put her in the back of his truck, tossed her phone, and hauled ass.

Now, I'm at this cabin, my gun in hand, breaths ragged as I walk around the back. One of the windows doesn't have a curtain and I see Shavonne sitting in a chair with thick black cords wrapped around her body. That large man who buried me (or so he thought) is inside too, sitting on the couch. He's rubbing his head, eyes squeezed tight, like he knows this is the end of the line for them. He and Dominic are in deep shit, and it'll all come to light soon.

I walk around the back of the house, stopping just before I turn the corner. I hear something screech, and then a rough sliding noise. When I peek around the corner, the big man steps through the backdoor with a pack of cigarettes in hand. I yank my head back and press it against the wall of the cabin as my heart beats faster.

Okay. Okay. I can do this.

I bring the gun to my chest. I've never used one before in my life, but I'm willing to if it means saving Shavonne. If I shoot this man and weaken him before Dominic shows up again, I will have the upper hand. Dominic won't see me coming.

Cigarette smoke drifts my way and I breathe as evenly as possible. I wait a few moments, facing the backside of the cabin. I can shoot him while he's taking his smoke break and while he's off guard.

Something crunches behind me, like footsteps over gravel, and I look back with a sharp gasp, just before bumping into the side of the house and causing a loud thump. My finger is wrapped around the trigger, so the gun goes off and a bullet flies through the trees. I've never heard a gunshot before, but it's loud, and the gun rattles in my hand, causing me to drop it.

I stare at Jolene, just as the brawny man steps around the corner and catches us both.

FIFTY-SIX

JOLENE

"What the hell is—" Boaz steps around the corner with a cigarette pinched between his lips and a heavy scowl. Brynn is glued to the side of the cabin and her gun is only a few inches away from her feet. I bend down to pick it up, point the gun at Boaz, and shoot him.

My hands shake as I hold the gun. I don't realize I'm staring at Boaz's body—the first person I've *ever* shot—until Brynn runs around him to the back of the cabin. I chase after her as she enters through the back door and spot her standing in front of a bound and gagged Shavonne.

They both stare at me, eyes wide and panicked. I point the gun at Brynn and think about how easy it would be to get rid of her. But, unlike Dominic and Boaz, I'm a good person. And though all of this has caused me a major headache and has sent me on a downward spiral, I'm a woman of my word.

I lower the gun, and Brynn's shoulders visibly relax. Shavonne breathes hard behind the thick layers of duct tape around her mouth.

"Keep her like that," I order. I rush around them to turn off all the lights inside the cabin. The power is on, courtesy of an expensive generator Dominic ordered for this place. What exactly does he plan on doing with this cabin anyway? I can't figure out why he hasn't sold it and am starting to think he has some odd obsession with it. Why else would he have invested in a generator to give it power and light? It makes no sense.

I peer out the window and, on cue, a vehicle with its headlights off rolls toward the cabin. The women freeze behind me.

"Is that Dom?" Brynn asks. Hearing her say my husband's nickname sends a prickle down my spine. It's a sheer reminder that she was once intimate with him . . . but that's beside the point now.

Brynn rushes next to me, peering out the window at the silver pickup truck. "His SUV is black, right? That's not him." Her eyes cut to me as the man in the truck climbs out and shuts the door. "Who the hell is that, Jolene?" she demands.

I finally look at her as the man approaches the house. Brynn's eyes swim with a hint of panic and confusion, and by now, I'm sure she wants to strangle me because I didn't tell her about this part of the plan. I couldn't, really.

Still, I can't help the satisfied smile that sweeps over my mouth as the man walks up the stoop and pounds on the door.

FIFTY-SEVEN

JOLENE

Six weeks ago

I wake up to the sound of running water. The sun stretches across the bed sheets, and I feel a delightful rawness between my thighs. I point my gaze to the bathroom of the hotel, where the door is cracked open, and spot Samuel Sanchez's muscular back as he brushes his teeth. His hair is damp and wavy, and I can't help my smile as I remember threading my fingers through his silky hair.

Last night was incredible. I've never been treated like such a princess, or like I'm the only girl in the world, but here I am with the Lieutenant Governor of North Carolina.

I grab my phone from the nightstand and as expected, no calls or text messages from Dominic. I'm not surprised. He doesn't ask about my whereabouts anymore. That stopped a long time ago. Plus, with the campaign slowly spiking, he's busier than ever.

"Oh, good. You're awake." Sam sits on the edge of the bed next to me, running his palm over my thigh. "I ordered room service." He nuzzles the tip of his nose in the crook of my neck.

"Mmm. That's good," I whisper.

"The room service or what I'm doing to you right now?"

"Both," I laugh.

He chuckles and lays me back, kissing me with his minty mouth. "We'll also have visitors today. And before you decline, I want you to hear them out."

I can't help the frown that takes hold of me. "Visitors? What are you talking about?"

"They're coming to the hotel."

He sits up and I do the same, tugging the sheet up to cover my naked chest. "*Who* is coming to the hotel?"

Sam goes to his suitcase, taking out a pair of trousers and a button-down gray shirt. He pulls out the iron and plugs it in as I stare at him, waiting for an answer.

"Two girls reached out to me, Jo. They're from New Orleans, and they've been in Raleigh for a few weeks now." He goes for the ironing board and unfolds it at the end of the bed.

"Okay?" I can't figure out what this has to do with us? Two chicks from New Orleans? Are they strippers? Is he expecting some kind of naughty fantasy to play out with three women in the room?

Noticing my frown and the way I'm practically gluing myself to the headboard, Sam walks my way and lowers to one knee.

"They have dirt on Dominic, Jolene," he says in a low voice, looking me deep in the eye. "You said you wanted the divorce to be clear and cut, so that you can walk away, and he can't get a single dime from it. These girls can provide that. We get him out of our lives, I make my move as governor, and we all move forward."

"How?" I whisper.

He only smiles and kisses the top of my head. "They'll be here within the next two hours. Just trust me, okay? I'd rather they explain it to you."

And sure enough, two hours later, there's a knock at our door. Me and Sam have already eaten, and now the food is sitting like a rock in my belly. I had some champagne, but it's now making me feel dizzy and off balance. Perhaps I shouldn't have guzzled down two glasses so quickly.

My heart thumps rapidly in my chest as Sam goes to the door as his calm and collected self. And when he opens the doors, it feels as if all the air is sucked out of the room.

FIFTY-EIGHT

JOLENE

There are two women, like Samuel said there would be. One of them has thick hair, braided halfway at the top of her head, and the rest pulled into a puff. She wears big earrings with pink crystals in them and is thinner than her counterpart to the right, who has an icy look in her eyes. Despite the look, she is beautiful. Dark, straight hair, brown eyes, full lips, sable skin. However, I can't help noticing the scar on her forehead. It cuts deep, going from the hairline to her eyebrow. Whatever happened there had to be painful.

"Come in, ladies. Please," Sanchez says, gesturing to the room. I smooth out my skirt, eyeing him as the girls walk inside and surveil the room. I'm not sure what they're looking for, but it's strange how on guard they are.

We all sit at the table in the corner near the floor to ceiling windows. Sunlight pours down on the nape of my neck as I look at the two girls sitting across from me.

"Like I told you, Jolene. These girls have a story to tell about Dominic," Sam murmurs. "Brynn, Shavonne. Why don't you tell her what you've told me."

Brynn and Shavonne look between each other, then at

Sam. "How do we even know we can trust her? She can easily run to him and tell him we're in town," the one with the scar says.

"I wouldn't do that," I reply quickly.

She looks me up and down.

"Who is Brynn and who is Shavonne?" I ask.

"Brynn," the one with the scar says.

"Shavonne." The other raises a quick hand.

"Okay. Well, I'm Jolene Hart." I purposely leave out Dominic's last name. "I'm here to listen. Tell me what's going on."

"It's okay," Sam says, his voice burning with sincerity. "You came to me for a reason, right? I'm here to help. This is a safe space."

The girls seem to loosen up a bit. Brynn scrapes her thumb cuticle with the other thumbnail, dropping her eyes to the table. And when she speaks, I try my best not to react or to reveal how I really feel.

She tells me about the day she saw Dominic in New Orleans. How he was at her job and left his number. She agreed to meet him at Galveston Lounge and went with him to a house a short drive from the city. I try not to be enraged as I think about my husband spending time with another woman. I recall him telling me about his trip to New Orleans, and how he'd successfully landed a golfing weekend with John Bolton. John had the connection he needed, and Dominic was confident he could win him over.

"It's still a bit fuzzy," Brynn says in a thick voice. "But I remember asking for water and he brought me apple juice. And I'm pretty sure he put something in my drink because I couldn't really control my body after that. Everything was blurry and then he was on top of me, trying to take off my clothes." She swallows, and I bite back tears. "I don't think he did anything to me that night *sexually* but someone else did.

Some white man by the name of John." That causes me to flinch. She can't possibly be talking about the same John that Dominic was meeting. "He was with Dominic in the restaurant. He came to that house Dominic took me to and he was on top of me, *licking* me, then he flipped me over and . . . from there it goes pretty dark. I'm glad. I don't think I'd be here now if I remembered what he actually did to me." Brynn swallows, then reaches for the bottle of unopened water on the table. After guzzling some of the water down, she says, "I woke up in the middle of the night after all that and Dominic was sitting at a table in the room with papers. He was . . . he was forcing me to sign a nondisclosure agreement. He had my purse and said he wouldn't give it back so I . . . I got mad and went for my bag. I wanted to fight him, slap some sense into him, but I clearly didn't win because I don't remember much after that. Just being buried alive."

"What do you mean *buried alive?*" I ask, a cold feeling sinking into my stomach.

Brynn goes into detail about how she'd been in and out of consciousness the entire time after Dominic hurt her. She could hear everything. Feel everything. But she couldn't move. Then she mentions a man with a shovel, who I know is Boaz based off the description. And if Dominic brought Boaz into the situation, then I know he was trying to cover something up.

I can't believe any of this and have to steal a look at Samuel who is nodding as Brynn speaks. For a moment I don't believe any of what Brynn says. Sure, Dominic had hurt me a time or two, but *this?* Allowing a rape and then attempting to bury someone alive? It was extreme and I clung to that until Shavonne took out her phone and showed me images of Brynn. The selfie of her and Dominic together. An image of Brynn on the floor inside a house, in a puddle of her own blood. A photo of Boaz standing next to a black pickup truck and Dominic touching a rug. Images of Brynn in the hospital, eyes taped shut and her head wrapped in bandages after what is clearly a surgery.

"I have this scar because of him. I had a severe concussion and bleeding in my head," she says.

The blood drains from my body as I look at all the evidence. And a true wife—one who loves her husband and would do anything for him—still wouldn't believe this for a second. Because all wives think they've hit the jackpot and that their husband is perfect in every way. We're foolish enough to believe our partners are the greatest people on earth and that we're living in some fairytale happily ever after. But the truth is, marriage is hard work and sometimes it sucks. And it sucks even more when you realize your spouse is a monster.

Two nights prior to meeting Sam, Dominic had hurt me too. He revealed an ugly side of himself that I'd seen three times before. I liked to call it The Beast. He often kept The Beast at bay, but when it revealed its ugly head, it was cruel and relentless. I rub the top of my head, where my scalp still stings from when he grabbed a handful of my hair. We'd been arguing about his speech. He was mad that there was a typo, even after I said it was proofread—which it was. I told him I'd fix the damn typo and tried to leave the living room so I could go to my office and contact the proofreader, but he caught me by the hair and snatched me backward so hard I fell to the floor. That doesn't even account for the time before that, when he gripped the back of my neck while I was cleaning the tub. He found out Samuel had come to my tea shop and was mad that I didn't tell him about it. Or the time before that, when he managed to knock the wind right out of my lungs with a fist to my stomach because he caught me eating a slice of cake at a fundraising dinner.

Dominic may have seemed like a charismatic, endearing man, but he was a monster. And here these women were, presenting me with an opportunity to finally take his ass down.

All these stories about wives setting their husbands up to gain freedom were always so farfetched to me, but now that I'm in it, it makes total sense. When your husband has power, you must be careful and you must *always* be one step ahead.

On this day, I agreed Dominic would never hurt anyone again once we were done with him, and we spent the rest of the day formulating a plan.

FIFTY-NINE

BRYNN

The plan was pretty clear.

Me and Jolene knew all about Dominic's fear of "magic" and superstitions. To be honest, it wasn't normal how terrified he was of something that wasn't real. Though it was tragic on his mother's behalf, we were grateful that he had a paranoid schizophrenic mother who filled him with such nonsense.

The man truly did worry himself to death about being cursed. In fact, Jolene mentioned several times in the hotel that if he spilled salt, he dumped some over his left shoulder so no bad luck would be brought down on him. He knew all of the common superstitions, like black cats and ladders, seeing the number 6 in a trio, and broken mirrors.

The plan was so stupid, it was brilliant. Dominic was a narcissistic jerk and believed nothing could stop him . . . so we had to make him stop himself. We wanted to torment him first, drive him crazy, because his biggest fear was winding up like his mother. Jolene said he went to a psychiatrist annually to make sure his mental health was stable. He thought she was unaware, but I get the sense that Jolene finds out many things on her own.

By tormenting him, we struck him where it hurt. We wanted him to feel helpless and backed into a corner. It was Shavonne's idea to present the tea. She and Krystal spoke about what he'd done to me, and Krystal had tricks up her sleeve and ways to make people take a "journey" with her teas. It was illegal, of course, but no one had to know. Krystal provided a tea called Purple Sky to Shavonne. Purple Sky is laced with crushed LSD pills. Our thing was, if he'd drugged me, we'd drug him too. The thought of it almost made me laugh because it was so foolishly simple. The only problem was getting him to *drink* the tea. That's where Jolene stepped in. She and Shavonne agreed that Shavonne would fake an identity and offer the tea to Jolene as a gift during one of his bigger rallies.

"You should pretend to be one of those psychics or voodoo ladies," I said. "He got all hostile about that magician in New Orleans. If he feels like you're into that kind of stuff, he'll instantly become agitated. It'll throw him off his game."

"That's good." Jolene nodded eagerly. "You'll have to make yourself seen. Let him know you're watching—that you know something, even though he might think you know nothing. He has to be paranoid. That's the only way we can make him feel weak. We can set up an Instagram or something, make it look like you've been watching him for a while now. Because he will look you up. He'll want to figure you out and make you to go away to save his own ass."

The next step was to kick the paranoia up a notch. That same weekend, Jolene offered us a key fob to the gates on the premises of her house, as well as a key fob for Dominic's SUV. I had the idea of writing the notes and mentioning my name. Jolene told us to dial it up by bringing out the photos from that night too, so she bought a portable printer for us to use.

"We want him to feel like he's being haunted by a dead woman," Jolene said, and it was crazy to see how into this plan she was.

"Will he really believe that?" Samuel asked. He was shrugging out of his coat with a bag of Chinese food in hand.

"Trust me, Dominic will," said Jolene.

The planned worked for a bit. We saw him spiral, and we did little things to trip him out. We planted the note in their mailbox, and Jolene took care of the note on the window after the attempted "break in". We planted the dead crow, which literally broke my heart. Do you know there are people on the internet who will kill an animal for you and deliver it for a fee? It blows my mind the things you can find these days. Me and Shavonne hate hurting animals, but if we didn't step it up, he'd lose his paranoia, so we unlocked his SUV after following him to Fox Trot and placed it back there along with a recently printed photo.

When he was in the apartment, that was Jolene's bid. She knew he'd run there at some point. She had cameras installed and could see everything he was doing. Her plan was to use the cameras to prove she knew nothing of what Dominic had done, so that when she checked the apartment herself and found the evidence of Dominic's secret, the police would believe her, and it would all be recorded. Or staged, I should say.

Jolene had followed Dominic to the apartment shortly after and while he showered, she went inside with her key and planted the photo of her and Dominic with our note on the back as well as the fake blood with my old purse. She left as quickly as she'd arrived and Shavonne and I sat near a gas station, laughing about it and even teasing Dominic a bit by waving at him when he stepped onto his balcony. He wouldn't be able to make out who we were, but we were watching. We were *always* watching.

With the purse, Dominic would start pointing fingers and trying to figure things out. Who was tormenting him? Stalking him? Planting notes and dead birds? Why was he having so much bad luck recently? Was his past really coming back to haunt him? I wanted him to think a dead woman's ghost was coming for him, so I watched him whenever he visited Executive Mansion. I saw him in the window looking right at me.

Shavonne had already spooked him as her persona of Eden. He was quick to point the finger at her and we wanted him to take the bait. We needed a reason to trap him, get him to be reckless again.

And he did. He took her.

The plan was for Jolene to meet me shortly after I sent her a text saying Dominic had either hurt Shavonne or had taken her. We'd both go after him and get her back, then call the police to report that he'd kidnapped her, but not before I could shoot him once or twice. Then the past would unravel about me, and he'd go to jail. That's all I wanted—to hurt him the same way he'd hurt me, and to get justice for setting me up in New Orleans. I wanted all his dirty laundry aired so that people knew what kind of sick, twisted man he was.

But when I texted Jolene, she didn't respond. I called. She didn't answer. Then I got angry and drove to her house with my gun, parking on the street behind her house and using the fob she'd given me to get through the back fence. I had a feeling she would back out of this—that she'd panic when Dominic took Shavonne, or worse, take Dominic's side.

In my gut, I didn't fully trust her and figured she and Samuel Sanchez would ride off in the sunset, leaving us stranded and having Dominic kill us off, just so he'd ruin his own life.

As an unknown man walks into Dominic's cabin with a ski mask on, I believe it to be true.

Jolene has changed her mind. She wants us gone. I don't know what she gets out of it but what I do know is that this random man was *not* a part of the plan.

SIXTY

JOLENE

Let me make something clear. I am *not* a bad person. I strive to be a good woman who does good things. I wanted to be nothing like my name-calling mother, or even like my father who was money-hungry and obsessed with control. But genetics are powerful. We can't deny the habits in our DNA and no matter how much we try *not* to be like our parents, some part of us becomes them anyway. When a person hits their last straw and becomes fed up, there is no going back. We all have a tipping point, and once we've reached the ledge, we're left with no choice but to jump off and tread the waters.

Well, here I am. Treading.

I've been treading since college. My senior year was when I knew I was more like my father than I realized. He was calculative and he hated mistakes. He also didn't allow *anyone* to walk all over him and had raised me to be the same way. There was a reason he had a man like Boaz around. Boaz wasn't just a bodyguard or security. He was much more. And not only did Winton Hart use him to handle situations, so did I.

I grew up a fat girl. I loved food. I loved sweets. I had a therapist once who told me I associate food with happiness, and this is true. There is one specific memory I love when I was twelve and my dad took an entire week off of work to spend it with me. I'd been complaining about the lack of father-daughter time to him for months, so he moved some things around on his schedule and made the effort.

And during that week, oh goodness, did we eat. He took me to Cape Cod where we soaked up some sun and rotated through new restaurants every morning and noon. Then we'd pop by a bakery, or an ice cream shop and he'd let me get *whatever* I wanted. I'd grab brownies, cookies, cakes, and the likes and I'd eat it all in our hotel room while watching *Family Matters* reruns. This, to me, was joy. But I didn't realize then how loving something so much could ruin my life. I packed on the pounds. I looked puffy and swollen. I didn't notice how much my weight played a factor until I was in high school and tried out for the cheerleading squad.

All throughout high school, I was bullied for my weight. And in college, I thought things would get better and that people wouldn't care so much, but I was wrong.

There was a girl named Michelle Dawson. She was a cheerleader on campus, and she had a crew—three other girls who followed her around like abandoned puppies. Michelle would make snorting pig-like noses whenever I walked by, and she'd laugh and throw fries at me in the library when I studied. I was upset about her behavior—stressed, even. Daphne told me often not to worry about it, but I took it to heart. Even more so when I attended a party and my pants ripped when I bent over. One of Michelle's friends took a picture and Michelle blasted it on one of the student forums. I was embarrassed, devasted, and I hated myself. I remember calling my dad and sobbing so he flew me to Texas for the weekend and Boaz dropped by.

Boaz had always frightened me. I wasn't sure what it was about him, but he had a scary look that made you not want to even peek his way. He saw me sulking on one of the living room sofas as he passed by to meet my dad in another room. And while they chatted, it hit me that Boaz worked for us. He did unspeakable things for my dad. He cleared situations for us, and especially my mom. So, before he left, I caught him outside and asked if he'd take care of Michelle. I didn't care how he did it, but I wanted him to teach her a lesson—to get her to stop messing with me.

Boaz didn't ask for anything but her full name.

That following Wednesday, I didn't realize the snorting noises and fries in my hair had come to an end until Daphne burst into our dorm and said, "Did you hear about Michelle?"

My heart immediately dropped because deep down I knew. I knew something bad had happened and it was Boaz. "What are you talking about? What happened to her?"

"She got hit by a car," Daphne breathed. "Someone ran right into her."

The breath dwindled in my lungs. And when Daphne left to take a shower, I couldn't help the smile that swept across my lips.

Michelle lived. It was fine. She was still breathing and living life now, according to her Instagram, but she had to have one of her legs amputated due to the injuries. The police never did find out who hit her, and though I smiled with relief, I was still worried someone would find out I was the one who wanted her to get hurt, so I avoided Boaz as much as possible after that.

I wish I could say that was the last I'd have to worry about that bullying broad Michelle Dawson, but it's not. Because even though I'd arranged for her to get off my back, she still went on with the last laugh and I've only just found out.

But it won't last long.

SIXTY-ONE
DOMINIC

Dominic grips the steering wheel of his SUV as he stares at the dark cabin ahead of him. Something's wrong. All of the lights are off inside. When he left over an hour ago, they were on, and now Boaz's pickup truck is gone. Something doesn't feel right. He can sense it in his gut.

The trees lurk over the house, the branches scraping the roof like talons. His pulse is in his ears as he reaches into the glove compartment and withdraws a black and silver handgun. Jolene said she was on the way. He isn't sure if she's left home already, but she *cannot* come to this cabin with Boaz and Shavonne inside it.

Pushing the car door open, he steps out and shuts it as quietly as he can. He's parked close to the bushes west of the house and passes an unorderly thorny bush. He remembers when this particular bush was small, and he'd gotten himself tangled up in it after climbing a tree and falling. He had cuts on him for days. This was back when his mother was normal—when she'd tended to his scars with antiseptic, Band-Aids, and a homemade sweet tea.

Dominic walks along the footpath on the side of the house. He won't enter from the front. If this is some kind of setup from Boaz, he'll be prepared. He's not sure why he ever trusted Boaz with any of this. Since the beginning, when he showed up at the door and took the body out, he had a bad feeling about it, but he was desperate and willing to do whatever it took to get Brynn's body out of the way.

And speaking of Brynn, if she's still alive, where is she? She must be in on this scheme with her friend. Perhaps she knows where he is. Maybe she's already here. With that thought hammering in his mind, Dominic raises his gun and rounds the back of the house, and that's when he spots a puddle of fresh blood.

"What the . . ." He draws in a breath and shakily releases it through parted lips. Something is definitely wrong. Did Boaz kill Shavonne? That wasn't in the plans. He walks slowly to the door, careful to avoid the streaks of blood running toward it. When he's facing the door, he grips the doorknob, and twists it open.

He's inside, breathing in the stale, dank air, the stench of wet wood and mold. Blood is still on the floor, a long thick streak leading toward the main room. He should've burned the house down while Boaz and Shavonne were inside it and gotten rid of them. But that still left Brynn. She was out there somewhere, and he was sure she'd come for him. If he can find her and kill her for real this time, he can end this.

Dominic stands in the dark kitchen, peering around the front half of the cabin. Shavonne is no longer wrapped in the chair and there's no sign of Boaz. His heart races when he notices the streak of blood disappears at the corner of the kitchen counter. Brynn might have come here already and saved Shavonne. She must've followed him here right after he took her and waited for the perfect time to strike. Or, as he assumes, Boaz is helping them? But why? For more money?

He takes a step forward and the floorboards creak beneath his weight. His eyes follow the bloody, smeared trail around the kitchen counter that carries to the sofa and fireplace. And that's when he notices the *body*. The person is flat on their stomach, head turned at an odd angle. It only takes several seconds for Dominic to realize it's Boaz. He rushes to him, bending down and grunting as he flips him over.

A sharp breath escapes him when he sees the blood all over Boaz's shirt and his eyes wide open. The whites of his eyes are bright in the dark. Dominic scrambles away, landing flat on his ass as he stares at Boaz's dead body. Whoever did this, they're going to do it to him too.

It's Brynn. It has to be Brynn.

He hurries to stand, ready to leave the cabin and escape the mess he's created, but then he stops when he hears the floor creak. Footsteps come from the back of the house, and a familiar silhouette appears.

Jolene.

SIXTY-TWO

DOMINIC

Relief sinks into Dominic's body as his wife steps into the room.

She's wearing jeans and a chiffon black blouse with sneakers. She never wears sneakers unless she's working out. Her hands are hanging at her sides, but he notices a gun clutched in one of them. His relief vanishes.

"Jo," he breathes, staggering on his feet. He blinks as she steps closer. She's not smiling. Just staring. It's weirding him out. And then it hits him—Shavonne is gone. Boaz is dead. No sign of Brynn? What the hell is going on? How much does Jolene know?

"Did you set that woman free?" he asks.

"No." She purses her lips, tilting her head a bit. Then she points to the dark, slim hallway with the tip of her gun. "She's back there. Shavonne *and* Brynn are."

His eyes stretch wider. "Both of them? Back where?"

"In the smaller room. I assume that was your bedroom when you were a kid."

Dominic blinks, wrapping his finger tighter around the trigger of his gun.

"How did you get them here?" he probes.

"Dominic, I told you I wanted to help. I told you we're a team."

He swallows thickly, looking past his wife to the dark hallway. "Well if you want to help, hand me your gun, Jo." He's not sure why, but he doesn't trust her right now. Something about all of this feels off.

She blinks at him, then shrugs and walks toward him. He tries not to flinch as she offers the weapon to him. He takes it slowly while looking into her eyes.

"Did you . . . did you *kill* them?" he asks in a low voice.

"No. I figured you'd want to. We can bury the bodies in the woods behind the cabin. They don't have much family so no one would ever come looking for them and if they do, they won't find them."

Dominic is shocked to hear his wife say all of this so nonchalantly. Jo has always been the morally conscious person—the kind of woman who'd rather him collect a spider in a cup and set it free than to smash it with a shoe.

"How long have you known about them?" Dominic asks.

"A while now. I had a hunch that something was going on. When I saw Shavonne at the rally, I looked into her. You seemed really disturbed by her presence. I wasn't sure what she had over you, but then she and her friend came to me, trying to get me to side with them." She rubs his arm, strokes it. "We're supposed to have each other's backs through thick and thin. I made them trust me, just so we could handle this *together*, babe."

"I know." He squeezes his eyes closed. "God, I'm so sorry, Jo. I'm sorry I hid this from you. I just—I didn't want you getting involved with any of it."

"But I am now. So, let's go take care of this."

He nods, and the relief anchors him again as his wife leads the way down the hallway. He follows her, and there is only a sliver of moonlight coming from the door at the end. His heart thunders as he passes his mother's old bedroom—that same bedroom where she clawed at the walls and tore up bed sheets. It all circles back to her death and how sudden it was. He had school that day but remembers the house being eerily quiet, just like it is now, minus the moaning of the floor as he and Jolene walk. He had nothing to fear though because his mother was dead. He loved her, but also had never felt so relieved. He still remembers writing the suicide note for her. He could never bring himself to show it to the police, though. They'd ask too many questions, so he hid it in the floorboard.

Truth is, he *wanted* his mother to disappear again. He wanted her to die or be abducted once more because she made his life a living hell. He couldn't stand the screams, the cries, the late-night lurking outside the cabin. She was unstable for a long time and all he wanted was a better life for himself. He had a sip of that better life while spending a few years with his uncle Ben, but then she returned, and it was snatched away.

He still remembers.

She'd burnt her hand on the stove while staring off again, and he wrapped it for her. This was the third time that month she'd burnt herself by not paying attention. She was fidgety. Anxious. Looking all around the cabin and whispering "They're coming. I feel it. They're coming."

Dominic hadn't slept well in weeks and felt his mother was becoming more of nuisance every day.

"Mom, why don't you just go?" he'd said after finishing up with her hand.

Her big, wet eyes focused on him. "Go where?"

"Away," he muttered, exasperated. "Just . . . go away so I can live a regular life. Maybe if you do, there won't be any more voices. You'll be free . . . and so will I."

He didn't think she'd go the route of suicide. He'd hoped she'd run away and never return so he could permanently live with his uncle. He imagined what his life would be like *without* her and the idea of it was bliss. He wrote the suicide letter after she passed as a way to make amends and to better the situation. He didn't want to feel guilty for telling her to go. Writing the letter didn't help, so he hid it. Why didn't he burn it? Why keep it? Is it because he imagined she would be grateful for whatever excuse he conjured up for her? In a way, that letter was his way of making peace with her death and releasing the blame, and perhaps that was why he'd hidden it and kept it all these years.

He shakes the memories away as Jolene enters his childhood bedroom. But it's when he's inside the room that he realizes it isn't just Shavonne and Brynn waiting. They're tied and bound to the chairs, heads hanging and clearly unconscious. But there's another man here and Jolene stands in the corner with her arms folded as he charges toward Dominic and tackles him to the ground.

SIXTY-THREE

JOLENE

It doesn't take long for Ricardo to capture Dominic, take the guns, and knock him out. After all, that's Ricardo's forte. It's why he and Daphne travel so much, and why she can't talk much about his job. It's also why sometimes she disappears without so much as a heads up.

Ricardo was born and raised in Colombia. He does private work for a cartel and moved to the states to become an international hitman for the Colombian cartel, so to speak. He doesn't like to refer to himself as a hitman. He likes to think of it as handling dangerous business and being paid under the table for it. When Daphne first told me what Ricardo was, it sounded unreal—like a chapter out of *Ozark*. I literally laughed in her face by how ridiculous it sounded. In my world, things like that didn't exist. But they are real. Sure, we have the fictionalized TV shows and movies about mafias and cartels, but no one ever thinks a member of those would be so close to home.

If someone steps out of line, Ricardo handles it by making them disappear. And by doing so, he's paid hundreds of thousands of dollars. In a way, he's just like Boaz. Tonight, Ricardo will make Boaz's body disappear for a few hours, right after he ties my husband up. I had to offer him *a lot* of money to do this for me. It's one thing handling random low lives involved with a cartel, but it's another to deal with a *governor*. But he takes care of Dominic with ease, each action a well-performed habit. Dominic is out cold, and Ricardo grunts as he lugs Dominic's body up.

"Where to?" asks Ricardo.

"Kitchen table."

He drags Dominic out of the room with a few bumps, thumps, and some clattering. I glance at Brynn and Shavonne. They're out cold. Ricardo chloroformed them because he didn't want them seeing his face.

This was not part of the original plan, but Brynn's plan was so *stupid*. I'm sorry, but it was. She had this whole idea of getting Shavonne taken by Dominic so she could have a reason to "come out of hiding" and shoot him. She wanted this poetic sort of justice, but it only would've led to holes, and I couldn't have that. If Dominic was going down, he had to *really* go down. He had to be the blame and no one else. I didn't want him to have any outs when it came to this night, so my plan took form.

I leave the room to find Ricardo has situated Dominic on a chair at the table and is now walking out of the cabin. He returns several minutes later with a wide, flat wagon that looks like it could be used at a coroner's office. He stands over Boaz's body that he dragged in after dealing with Brynn and Shavonne. With Dominic's gun, Ricardo shoots Boaz's corpse in the head.

I flinch at the sound.

Ricardo manages to pick Boaz's body up with a grunt, drape it over the wagon, and haul it toward the door.

"Police will ask about the blood," Ricardo murmurs.

"Yeah. Like I told you, once they find out it belongs to

someone outside of this cabin, there'll be no denying what
Dominic did. They'll think Dominic murdered Boaz to try
and keep his past quiet then hid his body a few miles from
here. I'll make sure Shavonne and Brynn attest to this. They
saw Dominic and Boaz arguing before Dominic shot Boaz
outside the cabin. Boaz managed to run into the cabin for his
own weapon but didn't make it far because he was shot
again."

There are streaks of Boaz's blood near the back door.
Some of the streaks have been altered by Ricardo to look like
Boaz was dragged *away* from the living room, not into it. It'll
look like Dominic tried to drag Boaz's body out of the house.
I would feel sorry for Boaz, but I don't. It's because of him
that all of this has happened. Then again, I suppose I should've
thanked him first because he spared me this worthless marriage.

Every detail has to make sense and it has to add up. And as
far as the unregistered gun, Ricardo has wiped the prints off.
I'll say it was another gun of Dominic's so the bullets in Boaz's
body align with our story. It must be clear that my husband is
the threat.

Ricardo asks, "You sure you have everything else handled?"

I nod. "I do."

He stares at me a beat with dark eyes. "Alright. I'll let
Daph know what went down when I get home. Give me
about thirty minutes before you make the call."

"Okay. Thank you, Ricardo. This means a lot. Oh—and
before you go, I need another favor."

I tell him what I need, and even behind his ski mask, I see
his brows incline. "Are you sure?" he asks.

I nod, then brace myself for the impact.

Ricardo's throat bobs and for a hitman, it's sweet that he
worries about hurting me. Daphne is so lucky. I bet he has his

downfalls, but they can't be any worse than Dominic's, and at least Ricardo is honest with his wife. He was honest with her about what he did for a living from the beginning. Daphne was never supposed to tell me about her husband's lifestyle, but she managed to let it slip out a year ago. She was overwhelmed with traveling so much, and I kept pushing her to tell me what was going on. She was always so *vague*, always away from home, and I could never figure out what all the cameras around their house were for, or what kind of job Ricardo had to be making so much money to travel. Daphne said he did something with accounting, but an accountant wasn't getting paid the amount of money it would cost to live the luxurious lifestyle they had. I thought the cameras were so he could watch Daphne, and that perhaps he was a little psychotic, but quickly realized the cameras were so he could watch out for anyone coming after *him*.

When Daphne let it slip out, it was ridiculous to hear, but it made sense. Ricardo wasn't very pleased to know that I knew, but after a while, he stopped caring. I suppose, he figured I had no proof, plus I had Daphne to back me up. I'd never tell a soul, but I would use him for my own personal gain if necessary.

I ball my hands into tight fists as Ricardo reels his elbow back. His gloved fist flies forward and slams into my face. I cry out and fall to the ground. Ricardo bends down but I tell him, "Kick me! In the ribs!"

"Jolene, that's—"

"Do it," I pant, still holding my face.

He does, and his boot slams hard into my ribcage. I cry out again, crumpling over as my rib throbs. "That's . . . that's good," I whimper. And despite the white-hot pain in my rib and my bleeding nose, I stand when Ricardo offers me a hand.

"I'm going now, Jo," he murmurs.

My nose burns, the blood dripping profusely, but I nod

anyway, and he takes off. I go for an old blanket on the sofa and press it to my nose, then close the door. When the bleeding has stopped, I face my husband, who is still out cold in the chair. He'll wake in a few hours and so will the women in the back room. I cling to my rib, sitting in the chair across from him, and waiting for him to wake up.

SIXTY-FOUR

DOMINIC

There's a throbbing on the back of Dominic's head. He groans and blinks several times with his focus on his lap. He spots the dingy wooden floors, smells the moisture in the air that has nestled into the boards. He's still in the cabin.

He tries moving his arms, but only jostles in the chair. If he moves anymore, he'll tip over. He picks his head up and swallows a gasp when he spots his wife on the other side of the table.

Then it all comes back to him.

The way she walked around the corner with the gun.

The way she spoke to him, told him what she'd done to Shavonne and Brynn.

He looks at the object in front of her and it's his gun.

Her elbows are on the table, the backs of her hands propped beneath her chin. He'd think he were in good hands, but she only stood there as he was attacked, and now she's staring at him without a single emotion on her face. He can't tell if she's angry, sad, or happy even. There's blood on her upper lip, crusty and dark. And her left eye is swollen shut.

"Jo," Dominic breathes. "What the hell is going on?" His

mouth is dry, and it's like he's talking with sandpaper in his mouth.

"Aren't you going to ask what happened to my eye?" she inquires. She's still not frowning or smiling.

"W-what happened to it?"

"You struck me," she replies simply.

He frowns. "I didn't lay a finger on you."

"Sure, you did. Maybe not here, or today. But you have."

He gulps and the saliva is rough going down.

"Jo, let me out of these cords. Right now."

"No." She finally drops her hands, and he tenses as she rests one of them on top of his gun. When she brings it up and points the barrel end at him, his heart picks up in speed. "Do you know how hard it is to be a good wife to you?"

He says nothing, just stares at her with paralyzing fear. He's never seen Jolene like this. She's always so soft and quiet, never hostile. He's never seen her with a gun either, yet she holds his as if she's had a lot of practice with one.

"Jo, whatever this is, we can talk about it, okay? I—I know I should've told you about Brynn, but baby . . . I did what I had to do so that I could get the position as governor."

She tilts her head, lowering the gun just a bit and he sees his soft Jolene, the one with questions in her eyes. The one who loves him.

"Tell me everything," she demands. "Right now."

This time, he won't hide a thing. He'll tell her anything to lower her guard and get out of this situation.

"You know how I had a meeting with John Bolton in New Orleans a few years ago? Well, he's close friends with Judge Reba Saxon, and Saxon had major pull in North Carolina back then. I almost didn't win him over, Jo, but then Brynn came to wait our table while we were out for dinner. She was my waitress that day and John . . . he just went *feral* over her. Started licking his lips, asking how I knew her. He told me that if I could get him Brynn alone, that he'd talk to Saxon—tell her to endorse my campaign. And you saw what Saxon's announcement did for me, Jo. It got me the governor's seat!"

"So you coerced Brynn into all of this?" she asks and she stares at him like *he's* the monster. But doesn't she see? He did this for *them*.

"No . . . I . . . well, I left her my number, hoping she'd take the bait and she did. She called me that same night and we met up for drinks."

"Met up for drinks where?" she demands.

"The Galveston Lounge, but that's all it was, baby. It was just drinks."

She shakes her head. "You didn't text me back all night because you were with her?"

"I'm sorry, Jo."

"So, what? Did you sleep with her that night too?" she snaps.

"No, no! I didn't do anything with her, I swear to God! I didn't even kiss her! She wanted to ride with me to John's rental in Marshview. We had a few more drinks at the house and I wasn't sure how to make the proposition to her about John. I needed her to *willingly* do it so that he wouldn't complain . . . so I put diazepam in her drink."

Jo's brows shoot up. "You *drugged* her?"

"The drugs weren't mine! I got it from John."

"So John does this kind of stuff all the time then?" she snaps.

"I—I don't know."

"Clearly, he does! Why else would he have drugs like that to just give to you? Jesus, Dominic! These are the men you surround yourself with? Rapists? Liars? No wonder you're the way that you are!"

"I'm *nothing* like them, Jo. I've never raped anyone," he grounds out.

"But you did lie."

His head shakes and he looks away.

"So let me get this straight. You drugged this woman, then let another man take advantage of her. She and her friend came to confront you about it, so you kidnapped her friend and brought her to this shitty cabin to try and hide the truth? What were you even going to do to her? You should be glad I showed up!"

"I—nothing. I just wanted her to tell me where Brynn was. They were fucking with me, Jo! Playing games with my head!"

"Well, Brynn is here now," she states. "What was your plan after that?"

"I don't know. To have Boaz get rid of them for good this time."

"For good? What does that even mean?" she cries.

"I mean . . . well, just to make them disappear. To fucking kill them! Jo, we have so much on the line. Baby, please? The rally is tomorrow. We need to handle this and get out of here." Dominic rocks in the chair again and Jolene stares at him, head shaking, eyes empty.

"Boaz is dead," she finally says.

The cabin falls silent. Then it hits him, and he stops rocking in the chair. The puddle of blood outside the cabin. The streaks of it in the house. Boaz's body was on the floor. He swivels his head but can't find the body anymore, however there are streaks of dark blood on the floor. Did he imagine Boaz's body? No, he's not crazy. Something else is going on.

"Where is that man? The one who hit me? Did he hit you too?" he asks, and he can't help wondering that if he did, how the hell Jolene is still alive. How is she here asking questions when there is someone else in the house trying to hurt them.

Unless . . .

"Jo," Dominic rasps. "What have you done?"

She places his gun down on the table then lifts something

from her lap. When Dominic sees that it's her phone, his heart fails him. She's on the voice recording app. She presses the big red button to stop recording.

"Jo—what the fuck are you doing?" he hisses.

"Someone had to stop you," she murmurs.

"Why would you do this?"

"Why would you be sending money to Michelle Dawson?"

His chest constricts. "W-what?"

Her good eye narrows. "You heard me."

"I—I don't know what you're talking about."

"I spoke to Anita. She told me about the foreign accounts that I found out are linked to Boaz and some other man named Tommaso Barone. These are the men you had handle the situation with Brynn in New Orleans, right? She told me the story, about how she was buried. *Alive.*"

"No no no no. He said she was dead."

"Well, she's alive, honey. She was still breathing, but Boaz kept piling dirt on her, hoping she'd suffocate. But her friend followed Boaz. Shavonne? She saw the *whole thing.* She has pictures of Brynn on the floor in John's house."

Dominic's breaths become erratic, and it feels like the walls of the cabin are closing in on him.

"While also talking to Anita, I found out that there is a third account money was going to. Money to a woman *and* former bully of mine named Michelle Dawson. It's strange that you'd think I'd be so naïve as to not find out. What, you tell Anita not to worry me about selling hundreds of shares from *my father's* company and that would be it? Do you forget who my mother is? She *lives* to see me fuck up! I never should've trusted you! I mean, what the hell was I thinking making a joint account with you!"

Dominic's jaw pulses. Right now, would be a good time to rip out of these cords, shoot Jo, and salvage the situation. He could lie and say the women attacked him, dragged him and his wife there, then killed her but he shot them before they could come for him. He could make it work. He *could*.

"You know the story about Michelle. She was the one who created the name Fat Jo." Jolene stares into his eyes. "She had the majority of the campus referring to me as that. Some people literally thought I went by that name and that I was *okay* with it. And all this time, Dom, you've been seeing her behind my back. All these years. Trust me, I was very upset to hear what you did to Brynn, but this? This shit with Michelle was my last straw." She chokes on her words. "I'm curious to know if this was her plan? To get you to come after me? To marry me, just so you two could have the life you wanted? I see she has a five-year-old now too. He looks just like you."

"Jo," Dominic rasps. "Michelle doesn't know anything about how the money gets into that account. This has nothing to do with them."

"Doesn't it? You've been stealing money from me and sending it to her. All those times when you told me you had to take a weekend away, or that you had business during some of the most bizarre times of the years, even the holidays, you were with them. All this time, you've had a whole other life. But I thought you didn't want kids. Or did you just not want them with the fat girl from college? Is the amputee better?"

"Jo, it's not like that, I promise you," he pleads. "I love you, okay? I loved you from the moment I laid eyes on you."

"That's funny because you never used to play football by the gym until I started going there. Just like a man to pop up when a woman is finally trying to do right by herself." She scoffs. "Michelle told you to come to me. She told you to use me. I know she did because she confirmed it when I DM'd her. I told her I'd report the money she withdraws from your account as fraud, and she got scared. She told me *everything*!" Jo picks the gun up again and points it at his face.

"Jo, please! Just let me out of these cords and we can work

it all out. I—I won't send Michelle anything else. I can end it all. I promise you."

Jolene stares at him a moment, and it's almost like she wants to believe him. But then she picks up her phone, dials 9-1-1, and puts it on speaker. When he hears the voice on the other end answer the call, Jolene screams to the top of her lungs. "HELP! This is Jolene Baker! I—I need help, please! My husband—he has these girls and now he's trying to *kill* me!" She's hysterical, eyes round, veins popping out of her neck. "Please get here now! I'm in a cabin—uh, I think it's on Briggs Lane! Please he's going to—" Jolene ends the call, and she's calm again.

"What the hell?" Dominic mutters. "What did you do? Why would you say that?" he shouts.

"Here's what's going to happen," Jo says, pushing out of her chair. It's like she didn't hear him at all. "A friend of mine is on his way to this cabin right now. He's coming because I gave him a call and told him I was worried about you and needed his help."

"Who is this friend?" Dominic snaps.

It almost looks like she smirks, but he can't tell in the dark. "You'll see. Brynn and Shavonne are the women you abducted because they have information that can ruin you. My friend will arrive and see the chaos and blood everywhere, he'll punch you in the face and knock you out again. Shortly after, the police will knock the door down and find my friend holding me to make sure I'm alive. When I come to, I will tell the police *everything* that happened. That I was worried, so I found you at this location. I saw what you'd done to those women, how you drugged and chloroformed them, so I called my friend to let him know I was scared and needed his help to de-escalate the situation. I tried to stop you, but you knocked me out and hurt me really badly. You were in the middle of cleaning the bloody mess you'd made with Boaz—the man who assisted you but then turned against you—while I was out cold, until my friend arrived, which caught you by surprise. You two got into a fight, and he won." Jolene steps around him and moves through the cabin to check the windows. Just as she does, headlights flash through the house.

Rage courses through Dominic and he rocks in the chair. It tips over and he lands on his side with a hard slam. Jolene turns to look at him, watching as he fidgets and kicks his feet while calling her all kind of terrible names. Footsteps drum up the stoop, then the front door opens.

When he sees Samuel Sanchez, he knows.

This setup was arranged a long, long time ago and now it's over for him.

SIXTY-FIVE

JOLENE

"Jo, hi," Sam says as he enters the cabin. He's dressed casually—jeans, a T-shirt, and Nike running shoes. My heart thumps double-speed at the sight of him. I want to sink into his arms, let him hold me for the rest of the night, but we have to finish what we've started.

"Hi," I whisper.

Sam walks past me, his footsteps heavy as he makes his way toward Dominic. Dominic is fuming, breathing raggedly through his mouth as he shakes and jerks in the chair.

"Ah, I hate to see you go down this way, old friend," Sam sighs.

"Fuck you!" Dominic hisses.

Sam blinks at him, then he sighs and moves around the back of Dominic's chair to pick it up. When Dominic is upright again, Sam stands in front of him.

"She's just using you," Dominic snarls. "Don't you see that?"

Sam's head tips before he shifts his gaze to me. "Now?"

I nod. "Now."

Taking a step back, Sam reels his elbow backward and

slams a fist into Dominic's face. Dominic grunts, but doesn't pass out the first time, so Sam punches him again, and this time, Dominic's head drops while blood dribbles from his mouth.

Sam flings his hand, hissing from the pain. I rush to him, taking his hand and kissing his knuckles.

His eyes meet mine, and with his good hand, he rubs my swollen eye. "Look at you," he murmurs.

"I'm fine. Police should be on the way." Just as I say that, I hear a *thunk* in the back of the house. Sam leads the way down the hallway, where Shavonne and Brynn are. Brynn is lying backwards in her chair, staring up at the ceiling with a grimace as she jerks this way and that. When they hear us enter the room, they freeze.

"What the hell is going on?" Brynn demands. "This wasn't in the plan!"

I step around Sam to help Brynn back up in her chair. "We just need you to stay like this for a few minutes longer, okay? Trust me."

"No, I *don't* trust you!" Brynn snaps. "Who was that guy earlier? What did he do to us?" She's referring to Ricardo. He didn't want the women knowing who he was, or to remember his face, hence the ski mask. That was the deal I'd made with him. Brynn was so angry, shouting at me about being a liar and manipulator just like Dominic, so Ricardo chloroformed her first. Then he went for Shavonne, who couldn't scream with her mouth taped. "It will be okay!" I'd screamed before Ricardo could do her bidding.

But I see in their eyes now what I did wasn't okay.

"He didn't hurt you, I promise," I assure them. "He only did it so my plan could work. I did it so we wouldn't have any loose ends. The police are on their way, and we have Dominic trapped. Once they get here and see this terrible scene, he'll be put away."

Brynn swallows. "Did you . . . did you record his confession?"

"Yes."

"And he mentioned John Bolton?"

I nod. "Yes."

Her eyes water a bit, but she pushes those tears away and shifts her gaze to Shavonne. Shavonne only stares back at her friend, still mildly confused. She looks like she wants to throw in the towel and go back to whatever corner of the world she calls home.

"I need to see him, Jolene," Brynn insists.

I glance at Sam, who shifts on his feet. "Brynn, you're all tied up. How am I going to make it look real if—"

"If one of us isn't tied, it'll make it look like he wasn't done with his plan and got interrupted by Sam."

I sigh as she stares at me, eyes pleading. If I let her out of the cords, that will undo all the work Ricardo did. The plan was to have them "trapped" and to make it look more authentic. But I realize perhaps my plan would be *too* perfect if they are.

"Please, Jolene," Brynn begs.

I swallow, then turn to Sam. "Sam, bring something to cut her out of the cords."

Sam wastes no time finding a rusty old knife and returning to cut at the bungee cords wrapped around Brynn. When she's freed, she stands up and immediately leaves the room. I follow her out while Sam stays put in the bedroom with Shavonne.

When Brynn walks toward Dominic, he turns his head a fraction. It's a weak attempt of looking up, but he manages. Brynn walks behind him and grunts as she brings his chair upright again. I press a hand to my mouth as she breathes raggedly, facing the man who ruined her life.

Seconds tick by and she doesn't say a thing as she stares at him. I shift on my feet and glance out the window, knowing the police are on the way.

"Brynn?" Dominic murmurs and her eyes widen. Despite it being dark, I see the tears filling her eyes.

Then a shrill scream fills the cabin as Brynn brings her elbow back and slams a fist into Dominic's face. He cries out as she yells, "That's for hitting Shavonne!" She throws another punch—one strong enough to make his nose bleed harder—and shouts, "And that's for trying to *kill me*, you ignorant, evil piece of shit! I should kill you right now! You took *everything* from me and I have nothing to lose!"

Dominic whimpers as blood drips onto his shirt and over the cords around his body. When Brynn takes another step forward, he flinches, but she doesn't hit him again. Instead, she bends down so that her lips are close to his ear.

As sirens screech in the distance, she says, "I hope you rot in jail, Dom. And when you die, I hope the devil wraps his evil hands around your throat and dunks your head in the flames. I hope he burns your soul when he realizes that, even in hell, you're not worthy."

I walk up to her as she takes a step away from him.

"Brynn, come on," I whisper. "We have to get you back in place."

She blinks, then nods, turning her eyes to me. She doesn't need my help getting back to the room, but I follow her anyway. She sits in a corner and says, "I'll curl up here, pretend to be unconscious."

"Okay," I breathe, ready to leave the room.

"Jolene?"

I stop, peering over my shoulder at Brynn. "Yeah?"

"Why did you really help me?"

I turn fully to look at her, even as I hear the sirens growing louder. They'll be here any minute now.

"I'll go cut Dominic out the cords," Sam murmurs.

When he's gone, I draw in a breath and release it, eyeing Shavonne who is trembling with damp eyes before focusing on Brynn again.

"Because I see myself in you, Brynn. I see a girl who once loved her life but got knocked off her feet and found it hard to stand up straight again." I swallow to block the dryness in my throat as Brynn uses the back of her arm to swipe tears from her eyes. "You and me? We're just two people who've been swimming against a current. We get dragged by tidal waves, or bitten by sharks, but we keep going because we know there's a safe place for us somewhere. We don't give up because we want to find that safe place and live in peace, so that's why, Brynn. Because I *see* you."

Brynn sniffles, and a tear rolls down Shavonne's cheek as she drops her head.

"Let's stick to the plan and with the same confessions, okay?" I ask. "Nothing has changed."

Brynn lays on her side, getting into position as Shavonne bobs her head and I walk out of the room to meet Sam in the living area.

SIXTY-SIX

JOLENE

The sirens are even louder now. The police are getting close.

"All done?" I ask Samuel.

"Yep." Samuel picks Dominic's gun up with the end of his shirt, wipes it off, and places it closer to the living room.

I glance at Dominic who is sprawled on the floor with blood on his shirt. His face is already swelling, and blood is spilling from his nose to his cheeks. For a split second, I feel like a traitor. Aren't wives supposed to protect their spouses? To love them through thick and thin? To be there for them, through sickness and in health? Because I know for a fact Dominic is sick. He may not be officially diagnosed with a mental condition, but something is wrong with my husband. All his narcissistic ways, the abuse, the lies, and still going day to day as if he's a saint? That can't be the mind of a good person.

I do realize how this can play against us. Whoever represents Dominic could bring up his past, his mother's diagnoses, and claim insanity for him. If it proves to be true that Dominic is mentally unstable and has been for years, they'll slap him on the wrist when it comes to the charges. But, regardless, he'll be put away in a psych facility and no one will believe a word he says because it's ours against his, and that's all we want. To me, it's still a pretty fair punishment. A man who wanted to be nothing like his mother—to seem perfect and without a single flaw—will suffer in his own head because of his horrible actions. Not a day will pass where he doesn't think about what all his cruel decisions led him to.

Dominic's eyes flutter open as I'm staring at him, and I hold back a gasp. His eyelids twitch as he tries focusing on me. The sirens are wailing now, drowning out every creak and groan of the cabin. I drop to my knees next to him.

"W-why would you do this, Jo?" Dominic croaks.

I sigh, carrying my gaze across the cabin. This place . . . it's the reason he's the way that he is. He never felt safe here. Perhaps he keeps it as a form of his own strength—a symbol in his life to prove he can overcome anything. Maybe if his mother was different, or if she hadn't killed herself, he would be a different person. Someone with more empathy and kindness. The thought of what he's lost out on—a normal childhood, with a stronger parent—brings tears to my eyes. It wasn't his fault, but at the end of the day we're responsible for our own actions.

To be frank, I don't think Dominic ever really had a chance. How do you go about life after suffering such horrors? After being compelled to write your mother's suicide letter, knowing she was on the brink of death? I'm sure no one knows about that note but him and me. We're all a little messed up. Every single human on this earth has endured a trauma or a tragedy that they want to heal from, but what happens when you *don't* heal? I like to think people like Dominic are a product of that: *unhealing*.

"Because, Dominic," I finally whisper. "You've hurt so many people—people who only wanted the best parts of you." I work to swallow as blue and white flickering lights appear outside the cabin, along with the wailing of sirens. "But the truth—the *bitter* truth—is that I *hate* you. I hate you for stealing the last ten years of my life. I hate you for what you did to Brynn and Shavonne and for going so far as to try and murder them. And I hate you even more for always taking the coward's way out. There is no love within you. I see that now. You can only love *yourself*, and if you're not first, everyone else suffers. Someone like that doesn't deserve to have it all."

He looks like he wants to say something, but he whimpers and his head shakes as it weakly falls to the floor. He knows this is it. All the lies, the cheating, the deceiving . . . it's over. Even if he wanted to fight back, he wouldn't make it far. Truthfully, after all those punches to the face, I don't think he can.

A hand touches my shoulder and I look up at a blurry version of Samuel.

"You ready?" he asks, offering a hand to me. I nod, taking it so he can help me to my feet. He moves several steps away from Dominic, and I lay on the middle of the floor while Sam kneels down next to me.

"This is it," Sam says, smiling. "The police will walk through that door, take him away, and you'll be a free woman. No lying, abusive husband to hold you back anymore."

I cup one of Sam's cheeks with a sigh.

Then I close my eyes and do my best to fight a satisfied smile, just as the police pound on the cabin's door.

PART FOUR

A YEAR AND FOUR MONTHS LATER

SIXTY-SEVEN

BRYNN

There was a question Shavonne asked me the night I told her about my plan to get back at Dominic: *"What do you hope to gain from this?"*

At first, I couldn't figure out the answer. I once was too afraid to look back at the events that had transpired, or to think about how badly he'd hurt me. It was easier to pretend it'd never happened or that I'd just had a stroke of bad luck, than to face the truth.

I would have rather lied to myself. After all, we humans do it best. We lie to ourselves and fabricate these stories in our heads so we can believe them. But eventually the story will crack, and the lies will spill out, and you'll drown in the truth.

There was something about seeing Dominic as a state governor. Knowing he was this crooked man overseeing all those innocent lives and making decisions for others when his decisions were downright evil, did not sit right with me. Men like Dominic Baker and John Bolton are corrupt, and they hide behind their money to find loopholes in the law, so they don't go down. They make sure everyone else is burned and charred before the flames dare come their way.

It finally hit me a few hours later that what I wanted out of this was simple: *to win*. I wanted Dominic and John Bolton to see that even at their superior levels, they could not prevail and that a simple woman like me could take them down, no matter what.

It's been a year and four months since the events at the cabin and the verdict for the North Carolina v. Dominic Baker case will be read today. I wish it could've been Brynn Wallace v. Dominic Baker, but his wrong doings amount to much more with his status. After finding out what he'd done, everyone hated him. The state of North Carolina immediately impeached him after his arrest and didn't waste any time arranging a trial. This trial has been the talk of the country for a very long time.

I'm sitting on a park bench with my phone in hand, over-sized sunglasses on my face as my leg bounces relentlessly. John Bolton's verdict was given two weeks ago, and now it's Dominic's turn. Of course, John got off with a weak sentence. He threw Dominic under the bus when the news came out that I'd been preyed on and raped, but his role as a New Orleans judge was still revoked. The police had asked why Shavonne and I had come to North Carolina, and I admitted that I wanted to face Dominic. I wanted him to own up to what he'd done, and I had Shavonne do most of that for me. I also told them that when Shavonne confronted him, he panicked about his role as governor and kidnapped her, then came after me, and that's how the whole thing at the cabin transpired.

The proof about John was in the phone records between him and Dominic, as well as the unsigned nondisclosure that Dominic stupidly had left in a pile of old files. There were calls made several times between John and Dominic the night of my attempted murder, and witnesses who came forward to inform officials that John and Dominic had been eating at the same restaurant I was a waitress in. To my complete surprise, one of the neighbors in Marshview claimed to have been walking their dog when she saw Dominic pull up to the house with a woman of my description.

Dominic confessed that he'd spent a few nights in John Bolton's rental. There was no proof of rape, so John didn't get charged for that (some straight bullshit), but Dominic did confess to receiving drugs from John to make sure I couldn't fight back or deny his advances. Despite Dominic's confession, John still denied raping me. The only reason John confessed to the drugs is because they caught his dealer, who was willing to rat him out for a shorter sentence of his own.

John Bolton is now serving eight months of community service and is on house arrest for an additional six months. It's a crappy sentence, but I knew from the beginning it would be hard taking John down after so many years had passed.

Is it crazy to say that despite what John had done to me, it *still* didn't feel as bad as Dominic's betrayal? I suppose a part of it is because I couldn't remember much of what John had done, but what I do remember is the way Dominic *watched*, the way he negotiated with my body like I was nothing more than an object. Don't get me wrong, both of them deserve to burn in hell, but the person I wanted to see go down the hardest was Dominic.

My breath stalls as the camera from the news channel pans to Dominic standing and facing the judge. He's dressed in a decent suit and has clearly had his haircut, but he looks thinner and his face is hollow like he hasn't eaten properly or slept in months. I hope he hasn't and that if he does manage to catch a whisper of sleep that it's filled with nightmares. I have dreams where I take a gun and shoot him in the chest. He comes alive again, just for me to pin him down with another bullet. He feels every ounce of pain and bleeds everywhere. I love that dream.

One of the jurors reads off the criminal charges, and Dominic is found guilty for every single one. I feel a flutter of a relief when I see Dominic's shoulders sag with defeat. The camera zooms in and there are tears in his eyes. He's hand-cuffed and dragged away with a mixture of shock and sadness. I don't know why he's so surprised. He had this coming.

After the judge declares Dominic's prison sentence and the trial wraps up, the camera shifts to Jolene who is instantly swarmed by a flock of journalists. I should be there with her, but I couldn't bring myself to go. I had a feeling if he was not guilty of *any* of the charges brought against him, I would've thrown a fit of rage, or at least, fled the courtroom to vomit. Shavonne and I figured it was best to avoid the court today, but that didn't mean I couldn't watch from somewhere else. Jolene is wearing a white blouse with a black pencil skirt. I'm not sure if it's the belt with her outfit that makes her appear thinner. Samuel approaches Jolene with his security detail and pushes through the crowd with her until they disappear out of the courthouse and into a tinted SUV.

I haven't spoken much to Jolene in between the trials. When we were "rescued" by the police, we were taken to the police station in the back of cruisers. We all had our story about Dominic, and we stuck to it, just as we'd planned in the hotel the week we met. Dominic was now going to prison with no insanity plea, despite his shark of a lawyer fighting like hell for it. And sure, Dominic's lawyer was a good one, but mine and Jolene's was better.

The hardest part about the night when we set Dominic up was going back to the motel after spending hours at the police station. As soon as Shavonne and I were inside the room, I sat on the edge of the thin, lumpy mattress, dropped my face into my hands, and sobbed. It was finally over. We could've died, or Jolene could've killed us if she wanted to, just to cover for her husband, but she didn't. We'd risked *everything*, shoveled our money together just to get across the country and fulfill my crazy plan. I figured I'd end up in jail or worse, killed, but I was willing to go to jail if it meant Dominic was dead.

I admit, I was upset with Jolene for changing the plans at

the last minute, but after having time to think about it, it made sense. She didn't do it only to protect herself (because she'd have been fine either way) but she did it to protect me and Shavonne too. She must've seen how vengeful I was, and I admit that I wasn't thinking clearly. Shavonne even had moments where she wanted to back out and fly back to New Orleans because I simply wanted to go to Dominic's house, sneak in through a window, and shoot him point blank. I admit, I was a little unhinged. But Jolene spared me any heartache in the process, I suppose. I guess she figured I deserved better than going to jail and because she thought ahead, we've all come out on the winning side. It felt surreal to finally be able to confess it all to the police, in the courthouse during the trials, and to hear the confession Jolene milked out of Dominic through the recording on her phone. I also never felt more alive.

Prior to this plan, I was numb for months. I was lost and confused and afraid. But getting to this point, despite the hiccups, has given me a strength I never knew I had.

"And now we wait," Shavonne had said when I'd finished sobbing like a baby in the motel. We both laughed, then we went to Cook Out and bought ourselves burgers and shakes. It was the best burger and shake I'd ever had—a victory meal we both deserved.

I turn off the screen of my phone and stare ahead at the lake. It's early spring, butterflies flutter by, and the emerald water ripples beneath the sun. The sun feels good on my skin, giving me a sheer reminder that I'm here. That I made it.

No longer do I have to carry that massive weight on my shoulders.

No longer do I have to hide.

I won. I finally won.

SIXTY-EIGHT

JOLENE

It's been a month since Dominic's sentence, and I feel like an entirely different person. There is no fear inside me or worries over what I eat. In fact, I'm eating an oversized chocolate chip cookie right now as I sit in a café called Monet's and wait for the person I've agreed to meet.

It's astounding what comes from having a husband—well, *ex-husband*—like mine. You think your life will be worse without them but ever since Dominic was found in that cabin, I received way more attention for his horrible acts and my stress has dwindled. Publishers wanted me to write books for them for millions of dollars, talk show hosts wanted me to come on for interviews. Is it bad to say I took them all? I did, and it felt amazing getting so much of what Dominic had done off my chest, but I didn't do it without crediting Brynn and Shavonne. They should've been the people receiving all the praise, not me, but I will get to that as soon as the person I'm seeing arrives.

As I sip my chai, the door of the café opens and a lean woman in jeans and a lavender T-shirt walks into the shop with a young boy's hand in hers. Her hair is piled into a neat curly bun, and she wears small pearls in each ear. She stops when the door closes and scans the restaurant, and I wave a hand for her to see me. When she does, she presses her lips, then grips the boy's hand as she weaves through the tables with a slight limp.

As they approach, I can't help seeing the resemblance of Dominic in the boy. He has his eyes and nose. Even his ears are like Dominic's, but he has his mom's mouth and almond skin tone.

Michelle Dawson stops at my table and pulls one of the chairs back for the boy to sit on. When he does, he grins at me and rests his forearms on the tabletop.

"Hi," he says meekly.

My heart snags a beat and I can't help smiling at the sweet sound of his voice. "Hi."

Michelle claims the seat beside him and wedges her hands between her thighs. "Thank you for meeting me, and I'm so sorry we're late," she murmurs.

"It's no problem." I wave a hand. "You're a mom. You have your hands full."

She smiles, then glances at her son. "He loves this café."

"What's your name?" I ask the little boy.

"My name's Elijah," he says proudly. "What's yours?" He's six years old now and very well spoken. Pretty sure he gets that from his father. Michelle wasn't really much of a speaker.

"I'm Jo. Would you like a cookie, Elijah?" I ask.

"Yes, please!" he cheers.

I give him one of the two cookies I ordered. I ordered an extra one on purpose, just to have something to give him and something that proves I didn't come here fueled with animosity. He unwraps the cookie and digs right in and Michelle asks him, "What do you say, Lijah?"

"Oh—thank you, Jo," Elijah responds, grinning with chocolate bits in his teeth.

I can't help laughing at the sight of it. Adorable. He really is and though it pained me to know Dominic had a whole *child* with someone else, there was no way I could take anything out on this boy. He's so handsome and kind and besides, I'm not evil like my ex. For awful parents, they sure have done a good job raising him. Or perhaps that's all Michelle. Perhaps she's changed, and a little part of me believes that, and it's *that* part of me that's willing to sit right across from her all these years later.

I watch her dig into her purse and pull out her cellphone. She hands it to Elijah who grins and says, "Thank you, Mommy!" before unlocking it with ease and opening the YouTube app.

While Elijah is watching a video and nibbling on the cookie, I shift my gaze to Michelle. "You know, I almost didn't bother coming here."

She nods, lowering her gaze. "I would've understood if you hadn't." She collects a breath, eyeing me. "Listen, Jolene. Before we speak about *him*, I want you to know that I am so sorry for the way I treated you in college. I had no right to make your life that hard. The truth is I was a sad, miserable person and you always seemed so *happy*. Plus you were rich and I was jealous, so I found a weakness of yours and used it to my advantage. I think when I told *him* who your dad was, and how you came from money, he took that as his opportunity . . . I just didn't know it then."

I look away, pressing my lips to avoid any tears.

"Anyway, it was wrong of me to treat you that way and I never should've done that. I also never should've kept seeing him behind your back. We were a thing in college, but it was never really all that serious until later. Regardless, it was wrong and I'm really sorry. A-and that man who um . . . caused the injury to my leg. Well . . . I get why he came for me."

My heart drops when she mentions Boaz and I meet her eyes again. "Michelle, I—"

She raises a hand to stop me. "Call it even."

But it isn't even. She's literally *disabled* because of an emotional decision I made. I fidget in my chair, then pick up my tea to take a long sip.

"Secondly, I had no clue the money *he* was giving us was from your company. I did know you were married. I won't lie about that. For a while, I was doing it to be spiteful because I hated you. I—I was just willing to do anything to have one up on you. I don't know if you know this, but *he* was the only person who continued seeing me after the surgery while everyone else forgot about me. We were friends before but became a little more than friends during my recovery and even after."

All I can do is nod. I have to admit, even though I'm glad I'm done with Dominic, this stings to hear. When did Dominic have the time to do all this with her? We'd spent so much time together in college and even after. We were a unit—inseparable . . . or so I thought. It's like she's rubbing salt into a fresh wound, but not intentionally, of course. At least, I don't think she is. She seems sincere, like she means every word. I glance at Elijah, who is almost done with his cookie, his eyes focused on the small screen of the phone.

"We were an on and off thing, even when college was over. He, um, would always say he'd give me the life of my dreams, that he would leave you for me, but I never believed him. And I didn't know that he would be stealing from you in order to try and make that happen. I know it sounds stupid, considering where you came from, but I honestly thought the money he was sending me was his and that he'd worked for it. I figured he'd built himself *through* you, you know?"

"Sure." I peer out the window of the café before asking, "Do you still keep in touch with *him*?"

Her head shakes rapidly. "No. Absolutely not. The last thing I want Elijah around is that." She leans forward and says in a lower voice, "I can't have my son knowing what his father is and what he did to those girls and that man. If he asks one day when he's older, I'll tell him. But not right now."

I nod, and she relaxes in her chair again.

"It's best that I stay away and out of contact," she goes on. "He's tried calling me a few times, but I don't answer."

I nod. That was good to hear, at least. But how long will it last before she caves? Dominic has a way of making people lower their guard for him.

"Anyway," Michelle says, shifting forward and digging into her back pocket. She drops a folded sheet of paper on the table and slides it toward me. Elijah glances at it but returns his attention to the more interesting view on the phone screen. "I really wanted you to meet me here so I could give you this. It's a check that I hope covers some of what he took from you. My dad helped me with some of it, and I had some cash saved for emergencies."

I stare down at the paper. It's ten thousand dollars. I should take it all. I should put it back into my account and walk away, but I look at her son again and sigh, then slide the paper back to her.

Michelle's eyebrows incline.

"Keep your money, Michelle. Sure, *he* may have been giving it to you without my knowledge, but this helped you take care of your son. It helped you create what has clearly been a good life for you." I pause, studying her face. "How was he with Elijah, anyway?" I ask, gesturing to her son.

"Oh, he was really good, surprisingly. He didn't visit much, but when he did, he spoiled Elijah rotten. Elijah loves books so he bought him a lot of them, read with him, took him to the park. He always made it his mission to get Lijah out of my hands for a bit so I could relax." She huffs a sorrowful laugh and I hate that I feel guilty for obliterating her peace. "I know Domin—*he* did a lot of bad things, and sure our son was a surprise, but I think being a dad was the one thing he wanted to be good at. The one thing he hoped to keep pure."

"I see," I murmur.

Michelle sighs and shrugs and I can't be here anymore. Hearing how he was with them has lit a fire under me and the last thing I want is for Elijah to see me, this random woman, start bawling her eyes out in front of him, nor do I want to feel sympathy for Dominic.

I collect my purse and stand. "There will be a final deposit that you can withdraw from the bank account he opened within the next week. It should total to six hundred thousand dollars. I hope that's enough for you to invest in Elijah's future, in yourself, and to make sure he turns out to be *nothing* like his dad."

Michelle's eyes fill with tears as she gapes at me. "Jolene, that's—you *really* don't have to do that."

"I want to." And it's true. I do want to. All these years, I've felt awful about what Boaz did to her. In my head, I wanted him to rough her up and scare her a little bit, not disable her. At the end of the day, she was a human and I tried to do what Dominic did: play God. I know money won't make up for what I did but I hope it helps. We're all imperfect. We all make mistakes. You don't realize how badly your mistakes will rip you in half until you're facing them.

"And as long as you don't give any of that money to the man who shall not be named or ever speak to him again, we're good. I'll know if you contact him." I wink and Michelle forces a smile and averts her gaze to Elijah. I realize that's a bad joke to make right now, considering how she was once terrified to even *look* at me, but I go on with, "I appreciate your apology. That takes a lot from someone, to realize their own errors." I want to tell her I'm sorry for sending my mysterious goon after her, but then I'd be confessing to a crime, and she could use that against me. Regardless, she knows I was behind it deep down, and every time she looks at her leg, she'll know.

I bid her and Elijah farewell and leave the café. When I'm inside my car, I check my phone and there's a text from Sam: **Hotel room is ready.**

I start the vehicle so I can make the two-hour drive back to Raleigh, emotional but also hopeful.

SIXTY-NINE

BRYNN

Samuel pours champagne into my glass as I sit at the same table we all gathered around over a year and a half ago. I'm in the hotel room with Shavonne, only I'm not here with anxiety or trepidation. I'm here anchored in peace. Samuel fills Shavonne's glass too and she guzzles some down, just as a knock comes to the door.

Samuel heads over to open it, and in walks Jolene. She's wearing a white business suit with a satin peach shirt beneath, her hair in Fulani braids and her gold jewelry adding a luxurious pop. Sunglasses cover her eyes, but she pulls them off, revealing beautifully set eye makeup with lengthy lashes. She's always been an impressive dresser, but she took it up a notch after Dominic was arrested. I suppose that was what she needed to thrive.

Her lashes flutter as she peers up at Samuel, and he places a kiss on her lips after shutting the door.

"Hi baby," he croons.

"Hey my love," she whispers.

I sip my wine, still unsure how they've gotten so deep into a relationship. Oddly enough, no one has questioned why Jolene and Samuel are together. No one has even leaned toward the idea of them conspiring to take Dominic down so Samuel could become the new state governor. Jolene and Samuel were smart. In public, they were very open without being too touchy. When Dominic had campaigns, Samuel would appear for her, he'd have conversations, and he often bragged about how he supported her tea shop to their colleagues.

When Jolene finalized her divorce in between the trials, it only took two weeks for Samuel and Jolene to be seen together in public. To everyone looking in from the outside, they were simply friends supporting one another from the beginning, and that relationship blossomed to more the night of the cabin. It only makes sense that they grew closer after everything. Many people bond through trauma. Shavonne and I did and look at us now, closer than ever.

The public takes one look at Jolene and Samuel, and they have stars in their eyes. They're survivors. Samuel is strong and wonderful for taking initiative and trusting his gut (as a governor should do) and Jolene is a powerhouse for facing her husband, despite possibly being hurt or even killed in the process. Sure, the story makes us look like saplings, but Dominic is in jail, and everyone hates him and that's all I ever wanted. Well, that and to shoot him. Yes, I know it's over with but still. Just one little bullet would've satisfied me.

"You must have another interview lined up," I say as Jolene approaches the table. "You look really nice."

She sets her purse down in front of one of the chairs, then rests a hand on her hip. "Actually, no. I had one this morning but haven't gotten the chance to change. I had things to do before coming here." She and Samuel pass a knowing glance.

I sit up straighter in my chair.

"Anyway," Jolene says, "There's a reason I wanted all of us to gather in this room again. The last time we were here, we were all a bit down, right? We felt hopeless or useless, but I promised that was going to change."

Shavonne sips her drink, eyeing Jolene who digs into her purse and pulls out two white envelopes. She slides them across the table, to me and Shavonne. Both are labeled in her cursive handwriting with our names on them.

"What is this?" Shavonne asks, hesitant to pick it up.

I swallow, setting my champagne glass down and grabbing the envelope with my name on it.

"Open it," Jolene says with a warm smile.

I blink at her before sighing and opening the top flap. Then I gasp when I pull out the check inside. It's made out to me, Brynn Wallace, and it's twenty thousand dollars. Shavonne sees hers and squeals so loudly it hurts my ears.

"*WHAT?* Jolene, what is this?" Shavonne shrieks. She places the check down on the table in front of her, smoothing it out despite there being no creases on it. I'm almost positive Shavonne has never seen a number this big made out to her.

I shift my eyes to Jolene who clasps her hands together while Samuel drapes an arm over her shoulder with a proud smile. "I know you girls didn't want to take on all that publicity during Dominic's criminal trial. I totally understand why you didn't. The people never would've left you alone and you two like your private lives. I promised myself I would do them so that any money I made from them, I could give to you." Samuel clears his throat and Jolene glances up at him. "And, of course, I can't forget that Sam agreed with me that it was the right thing to do."

My heart races as I study the check. Jolene shifts on her feet when I look up, her eyes wide as she eagerly waits for my response. Shavonne is over the moon, I know it. There's so much she can do with twenty grand. But to me this is just . . . *wow*.

Jolene gives Samuel a wary glance before saying, "Also, um, this is only one of many checks to come. The total amount of money you'll receive from me is one million dollars."

"Each?" Shavonne gasps.

Jolene smiles and nods. "Each. I can only give so much before the IRS comes to bite me in the butt," she laughs.

All I can do is stare at her because I can't figure out if this is real. I'll be honest, after the cabin thing, I still didn't fully trust Jolene. And when she did all those interviews and took that publishing deal, she seemed so selfish for doing it. Yes, she gave us credit and mentioned us, but all of it felt wrong. But now I see . . . she did it for us. Just like she'd had our backs at the cabin. All this time, I thought she was some selfish rich lady with daddy issues. I was wrong, and I feel horrible for judging her. She never asked me for anything.

That night in the cabin, I was afraid of her, but only because I was unaware of her plan. I realize now that my lack of trust in her and my wariness was because of my lack of trust in the world and within myself. I still don't know who I am. Dominic ripped my former self away and I loved that younger version of Brynn. But a new one has developed, and I don't know her all that well. But with this check in front of me, perhaps I can figure her out. Give her a shot.

So, I don't say anything. I just *cry*.

Right there at the table.

I drop my face into my hands and weep.

"Aw, Brynn. No, please don't cry," Jolene coos.

"Yeah, girl. We're good! We did it! We made it out the other side," Shavonne says. "We won!" A hand rubs my back and I get a whiff of Jolene's vanilla-spice perfume. A pair of hands take mine away from my face and through my blurry gaze, I look into Jolene's glistening eyes. She's bent down beside my chair, peering up at me.

"You can live your life now, Brynn. No more hiding. No more holding your breath. It's time to free yourself, do you hear me? Let this all go and become the best possible version of yourself."

"I just . . ." I sniffle and tilt my head to wipe my damp

cheek on my shoulder. I look at Samuel, whose eyes are moist too. "I've been stuck in survival mode. Constantly feeling like someone is out to get me. And I guess all of this just solidifies it, you know? Makes it feel like all I did wasn't for nothing." I gesture to the check on the table. "Jolene, you didn't have to do this. Seriously."

"I wanted to," she says with a smile. "And you better be glad because some of the questions those interviewers asked made me want to blow my damn brains out. Now I see why Beyoncé doesn't do interviews anymore!"

I bubble a laugh as she does, then she leans in to hug me. I hug her back, finding comfort in this moment. Even if Jolene and I never speak again after I leave this hotel, I'm forever grateful. I wouldn't have been able to do any of what I did without her. This is how it should be in the world: women helping women. People supporting each other.

We spend the rest of the night drinking champagne and Samuel orders Indian food for us before he has to take off to visit Cabarrus County for an event.

"So, what will you two do with all that money coming in?" Jolene asks. She's stripped out of her work suit to just the silk camisole beneath. Shavonne sits next to me on the bed, her hands planted and locked behind her head as she stares up at the ceiling.

"Well, first I'm going to get a new car. I'm thinking a Lexus or something snazzy," Shavonne says, grinning. "Then I'll probably go back to New Orleans, help Krystal out a bit more with her shop. Might even take over it so she can relax. Believe it or not, she makes pretty good money there. I can expand things for her. Add another shop in the mall or something."

"She'd love that," I say.

"What about you, Brynn?" Jolene asks.

"I've always liked cooking," I say, shrugging. "I used to make Pinterest boards of how I'd design my beachfront bed and breakfast if I ever owned one. I'd move to Cape Cod and start one up, have in-house breakfast, lunch, and dinner. Make it a true escape, or a hidden gem, you know?" I look between Jolene and Shavonne. "I might do that. Something calm and quiet after all the chaos."

"That's beautiful," Jolene murmurs.

"And if my idea in Nola doesn't pan out, I'll join you at the bed and breakfast," Shavonne declares, bumping my shoulder. I wrap my arm around her, resting my head on her shoulder.

I'm not sure what it is about this moment, but what I do know is that I've never felt safer than I do now. Tucked between two powerful women, all of us ready to tackle our dreams and blossom into the women we're truly meant to be. Even Jolene. Though she has it all, her growth was stunted by Dominic. Now she can bloom.

I was wrong about myself before. I'm not worthless. I *am* someone with a soul and a divine right to be here. I have a purpose just like every other human on this earth and if that isn't enough to live for, I don't know what is.

ACKNOWLEDGMENTS

I'll be the first to say that writing about someone in politics was not on my writer bucket list! However, when it came to *The Bitter Truth*, I wanted the stakes to be high and for people to question just how far someone in power will go to bury the truth.

I thought of this story because I kept asking myself, "What would happen if someone powerful ruined someone else's life? What would happen if that *someone* sought revenge?" It sucks to be betrayed, but I admit writing about betrayal and revenge is one of my favorite things to do.

As always, I want to thank my husband for being my rock and holding down the fort while I finished up my chapters. Thank you to my agent, Georgana Grinstead, for everything you do for me and for championing my books. Thanks to Dafina and Kensington for allowing me creative freedom and for supporting me endlessly.

To every single person who has picked up a copy of this book, or any of my books in the past, I'm forever grateful. Thank you to the readers who look forward to more of my over-the-top thrillers. It's so nice knowing there are people out there who understand my madness.

And, lastly, if you're reading this sentence right now, thank *you* for taking the time to pick up and read my book. My gratitude for you is endless.

The Bitter Truth Discussion Questions

1. How did you feel reading the prologue from the younger version of Dominic?

2. What are your overall thoughts about Dominic? It's clear he's dealing with some serious trauma and has never properly processed his grief. Do you understand why he grew up the way he did?

3. Though this book isn't heavy on the political standpoint, do you think situations like what Brynn went through with Dominic and John happen in real life? Do you think there are people out there willing to do *anything* for power and money, even if it tarnishes their morals?

4. What's your first impression of Eden? Why do you think Dominic was so disturbed by her appearances?

5. Jolene's story is interesting. She grew up as a rich kid who didn't have many worries, however she developed a binge eating disorder. Do you think this had more to do with her upbringing and having everything at her disposal, or more to do with her mom and the harsh criticism she dished out about Jolene's appearance/food choices?

6. In chapter 48 Brynn says:

> *"I truly felt like I'd died that night. And perhaps a part of me did—that bright-eyed, kind, and generous version of myself."*

Do you believe this to be true? Do you think Brynn lost herself completely after what was done to her? By the end, do you think she's healed from it?

7. Why do you think Dominic held onto his mom's cabin all those years later? Why didn't he sell or abandon it if he hated living there?

8. Considering the risks and the fact that they gave up *everything* to take Dominic down, do you think you'd have joined Brynn on her hunt for revenge like Shavonne did? Explain why or why not?

9. What did you think of the ominous notes when you first read them? Who did you originally think was leaving them for Dominic to find?

10. Which character's side of the story would you say you trusted the most? Why?

Visit our website at
KensingtonBooks.com
to sign up for our newsletters, read
more from your favorite authors, see
books by series, view reading group
guides, and more!

Become a Part of Our
Between the Chapters Book Club
Community and Join the Conversation

Submit your book review for a chance to win exclusive
Between the Chapters swag you can't get anywhere else!
https://www.kensingtonbooks.com/pages/review/